To Nellie,

Enjoy the journey!

God bless
"Cotton" Ketchie
2009

Little Did They Know

Published by Lorimer Press
Davidson, North Carolina.

Printed in United States

Book Design - Leslie Rindoks
Cover Photo - Jonathan Kendrick
Author Photo - Vickie Ketchie

Library of Congress Control Number: 2009938127

ISBN 978-0-9789342-9-3

Little Did They Know

a novel by

"Cotton" Ketchie

LORIMER PRESS
Davidson, NC
2009

ALSO BY "COTTON" KETCHIE

Memories of a Country Boy

A Country Boy's Education

For Vickie, without whom I would be nothing.

CHAPTER 1

JAKE MCLEOD hadn't slept through an entire night since the day he lost his beloved wife, Kitt, to cancer. It had been more than two years since her death, but he still dreamed of her. Last night was no different. There she was…her silky hair falling about her shoulders as she leaned over him. "Jake," she said and gently kissed his cheek.

"Kitt," Jake called reaching for her only to realize it was another cruel dream.

The warm air whispering through the vent overhead was the only sound he heard as he rolled over amid the tangled sheets and comforter. Through bleary eyes, Jake looked at the digital clock, its bright green numbers illuminated the room. 4:16 A.M.

The telephone on the nightstand rang, startling him. Jake heard the voice of his closest friend, James Caldwell, even before he got the receiver to his ear.

"Jake, Gail hasn't come home yet!"

"Wait a minute, James! What are you talking about?" Jake asked.

"Gail left before five yesterday to meet with her Wednesday Night Club," James continued, "and I haven't heard a word from her since."

Kitt had also been a member of the club, so Jake was familiar with their normal routine. "I thought they met at seven o'clock for dinner."

"They usually do," James said, "but last night Carmen had arranged for them to meet in Statesville and have dinner in the country somewhere north of there."

"Isn't Carmen the attractive brunette who works at the bank?" Jake asked.

"Yes, that's Carmen."

"Where were they meeting in Statesville?" Jake asked.

"I don't think Gail knew. The last I heard was that Carmen was going to call them individually and give them directions. She told Gail and the others that their final destination was to be a surprise. That's all I know."

Why Statesville? Jake thought to himself and had to admit that sounded a little strange! They had always met in Mooresville. "What time did you say she left?" he asked James.

"Before five o'clock yesterday afternoon."

"That's early for a seven o'clock meeting, don't you think?" Jake asked.

"Well from what I understand, they were going further north than Statesville."

"Maybe that's the reason," Jake agreed.

"Gail's never done anything like this before. She's always the one who has to know all the details. Where could she be? I can't imagine her not calling."

"I know," Jake agreed, "Gail is the dependable one."

"She's always home by 10:00 at the latest," James said. "You've got to help me, Jake. I don't know what to do."

It's too early to file a missing persons report with the Sheriff's

Department—it's only been about twelve hours, so Gail won't be considered a missing person at this point. But, this is so out of character for Gail, something must be wrong. Not wanting to alarm James any further, Jake kept his thoughts to himself.

"Let me slip on some clothes. I'll be there as soon as I can," Jake assured James.

Jake slipped into the wrinkled, faded jeans that were still beside the bed where he'd left them a few hours before. He pulled yesterday's shirt over his head, laced up his running shoes, and was out the door in five minutes.

CHAPTER 2

J AKE'S BATTERED Jeep Cherokee was waiting for him and, thankfully, it started on the first try. He pulled out of his driveway on Ferncliff Drive onto Iredell Avenue and then headed across town to James Caldwell's home on the shores of Lake Norman.

Jake's thoughts raced as he approached Main Street. Jake had a sinking feeling that something had gone wrong concerning last night's meeting of the Wednesday Night Club.

Mooresville is barely recognizable as the place I grew up, thought Jake as he turned onto Main Street. The Jeep's headlights penetrated the predawn mist as he passed Bob's Grill, The Aisle Pawn Shop, and then McLeod's Fine Arts.

He gave a cursory glance toward his gallery's large plate-glass window in passing. The window lights enhanced the brilliant colors of his paintings. Jake realized he hadn't painted a single watercolor since Kitt's death.

It was all he could do to drag himself to work and face his customers day after day. "How are you doing?" they would ask. Considering that he had lost the love of his life, his response was always the same, "Fine, thank you for asking." He just didn't want to discuss it. What good would it do—she was gone.

Jake had been forty-seven when he'd met the beautiful Kitt Kendall on the windswept plains of Kansas. Kitt, an artist in her own right, eventually agreed to move to Mooresville and work alongside Jake in his gallery. She quickly became friends with James' wife, Gail, and the rest of The Wednesday Night Club that included: Carmen Romano, Debbie Seacrest, and Joanie Mitchell. Gail and the other women welcomed Kitt into their fold.

Tragically, Kitt discovered she had pancreatic cancer while having a pre-wedding physical. Jake persuaded her to marry him sooner than they had planned, but sadly, they were only married a few short months before her untimely death. Those few months Jake spent with Kitt were the happiest months of his life.

Since Kitt's death, Jake had not been able to focus on his career as an artist. He'd lost interest in most things, including his painting. James and Gail Caldwell were the only people with whom he had much contact these days.

Memories of Kitt flooded Jake's mind as he drove through the sleeping streets of Mooresville in the cold, October morning. *Why her, and not me? I was fifteen years older! I should have been the one who was taken first!* He didn't think it was fair and felt that God had cheated them out of many years of happiness. They'd had such grand plans. They were looking forward to an extended trip to Yosemite National Park and the coasts of California and Oregon the following year. There were so many things they had planned together, but now, those plans were just unfulfilled dreams.

As Jake passed The Crimson Cape, a Mooresville institution for over forty years, he thought about how little it had changed since its opening in 1963. Banquettes covered in black leatherette ran along the side walls where sconces hung above each one, dimly lighting the quaint restaurant. The only change in the original décor was a few of Jake's framed limited edition prints that adorned the back wall of the main dining area. Jake smiled as he thought about his prints being the only new addition to the entire establishment.

The Wednesday Night Club had been meeting at The Crimson Cape regularly since the club's conception, almost five years ago. Most weeks they enjoyed a nice dinner and a glass of wine. Much of their evenings were spent talking about the men in their lives or their work.

Kitt had looked forward to going to The Crimson Cape with her new-found friends on those Wednesday nights, but Jake and Kitt also spent many romantic evenings at the "Cape" as well. She particularly loved going on Saturday nights when songs from the Big Band Era were played softly on an old Hammond organ by the distinguished J. R. Blythe. He played the familiar tunes made popular by Frank Sinatra, Nat King Cole, Glenn Miller, Benny Goodman, and the Dorsey Brothers—the easy-listening, soulful songs of the past. Sometimes, Jake requested *Moonlight in Vermont* and *September Song* especially for Kitt.

Those wonderful memories of Kitt and the times they had spent together at The Crimson Cape helped the drive to the Caldwell's house pass quickly. Jake hadn't given much thought to The Wednesday Night Club since Kitt passed away. James' phone call assured him that the group was still carrying on their tradition. He wondered what could have happened to Gail and what he could do to help.

CHAPTER 3

JAKE MADE a right turn onto West Wilson Avenue and noticed a light in the kitchen window of the Victorian house on the corner of West Wilson Avenue and South Academy Street. Someone else in the world was awake at this time of morning, too. He wished he had a hot cup of coffee about now. As Jake rounded the curve alongside the fifth hole of the municipal golf course, he noticed the traffic signal was green just ahead on Highway 21. Jake pressed down on the accelerator and sped through the light just before it turned red. West Wilson Avenue became Brawley School Road after crossing Highway 21 and lead down the long peninsula to the Caldwell's house.

This once sparsely populated area had experienced tremendous growth due to the advent of Lake Norman, the largest man-made lake in North Carolina. Everything from cottages to multi-million dollar homes dotted the shoreline from one end of the lake to the other, making it a popular retirement destination as well as a bedroom community for the city of Charlotte, thirty miles south.

Gail Caldwell had moved to the Mooresville area from Akron, Ohio nearly fifteen years before. Not long afterward, she met James at an art auction that was held to benefit Hospice of Iredell County.

In fact, that's where Jake met both of them. You might say he helped bring them together. He fondly remembered that evening as clearly as if it were yesterday.

Jake's contribution to the auction that evening was an original watercolor of a scene along North Carolina's most scenic highway, the Blue Ridge Parkway. A man Jake had seen around town, James Caldwell, was the winning bidder and had asked Jake to sign the back of the frame.

A strikingly beautiful, young woman approached the two of them as Jake was writing his signature. "Pardon me," she said timidly, "my name is Gail Daniels and I was also bidding on this beautiful painting. I just wanted to congratulate you on your taste in fine art and for your purchase of the painting," she remarked to James.

James was so tongue-tied he could barely speak to the auburn-haired, green-eyed beauty with the Midwestern accent. "I…well…I," James stammered and finally managed to say, "It is a beautiful painting, isn't it?"

"Yes, it truly is," Gail said as she flashed a warm smile at James, "and I hope you will give it a good home and appreciate it as much as I would."

"I certainly will. You are welcome to come visit it anytime you like," James offered with surprising bravado.

Gail said to the startled James Caldwell, "I just might do that."

"I'm sorry," James managed to say, "where are my manners? This is the artist, Jake McLeod."

"It's an honor to meet you Mr. McLeod," Gail said and extended her hand.

"Please, just call me Jake. It's a privilege to meet you Ms. Daniels and thank you for your kind words," he replied.

"It's really lovely and if the bidding had not gone quite so high, this gentleman would not be its new owner," she said.

"Forgive me for not introducing myself. I'm James Caldwell,"

James said with embarrassment.

"It's been a pleasure meeting both you gentlemen," Gail said as she turned to walk away, "and congratulations again," she reiterated to James.

"I think I'm in love," James said as he watched her move gracefully across the room.

Jake just looked at him and smiled.

Only seven months after the art auction, Mr. and Mrs. James Caldwell moved into their sumptuous new home in one of Lake Norman's most exclusive neighborhoods, English Downs Country Club.

The impressive stone entrance to English Downs soon appeared in his headlights and Jake made a right turn through the gate. The moon was bright and glistened on the calm waters of the lake as he neared the peninsula where the Caldwell's house stood among a grove of maple and pine trees.

CHAPTER 4

JAMES SWUNG open the hand-carved door and led Jake through the opulent foyer into the den. The spacious room had twenty-foot ceilings with tall windows facing the placid waters of Lake Norman.

"Thank you for coming, Jake," James said, tears welling in his eyes.

"Are you okay?" Jake asked.

"I feel better now that you are here. I'm sorry to call you so early, but I didn't know what else to do," James apologized.

Jake surveyed the room as he entered; the den itself looked almost as disheveled as James. Obviously, he had been up all night waiting for Gail to return. Magazines lay on the floor beside his chair. Water rings from his coffee cup covered the surface of the glass-topped table.

James motioned for Jake to have a seat on the leather sofa as he sat heavily in his recliner.

"Got any fresh coffee?" asked Jake.

"I'm sure the pot's empty by now, but I can brew another one," offered James as he started to get up.

"Just sit back and try to relax a little bit. I'll get the coffee," Jake said.

"You need some help?" James asked.

"I got it," Jake assured him as he headed out of the den, through the butler's pantry, and into the kitchen. He had stayed with James and Gail for a while after Kitt died until he could get back on his feet, so Jake was right at home in their kitchen.

There were only dregs stuck to the bottom of the coffeemaker's carafe. Jake rinsed it out, cleaned it thoroughly, and added fresh water. The aroma of fresh brewing coffee soon filled the kitchen.

Everything was neat and tidy, just like Gail. Jake agreed with James, this was so unlike her—there had to be a logical explanation, there just had to be. Jake poured two steaming cupfuls of freshly brewed, high-octane coffee and made his way back to the den.

James had laid his head back on his chair. His eyes were closed. It was unsettling for Jake to see his friend so upset.

James opened his eyes when Jake entered the den. "Thanks Jake," he said reaching for the cup. "I'm praying that nothing bad has happened to Gail. I'm trying to stay positive in all of this, but I feel so utterly helpless."

"I know you do," Jake said as he handed him his cup. "Did Gail seem anxious or upset when she left yesterday?"

"No, everything seemed normal. She came by the office and kissed me goodbye as always. She was on her way to Statesville where she was supposed to meet the other ladies."

"Have you called her cell phone?"

"Of course, but it goes straight to voicemail."

"Have you called anyone else?"

"No, I thought it was too early. Maybe we should call now, before we start out on a wild-goose-chase. I can't just sit around and wait for something to happen. I have to try to find her."

"Let's try calling Joanie Mitchell."

James went in search of the phone book and Jake found himself thinking about the unusual relationship of the Mitchells. He had never known anyone quite like Joanie. She and Ed were divorced, but Joanie lived in a comfortable townhouse on North Main Street not very far from Ed. The Mitchells were still friends and dined together at least once a week.

Joanie had done well out on her own and had become quite a successful businesswoman. She was currently the proud owner of *Joanie's Flowers and Gifts* on North Main Street. Joanie was what one might call a "high maintenance woman." Her hair was the color of Miss Clairol 100 and she didn't care who knew it. Joanie had a reputation for her colorful vernacular, but all of her customers and friends accepted and loved her just the way she was—foul language and all. You always knew where you stood with Joanie Mitchell. She was about as Southern and as country as anyone can get and that was just one of the things that made her so lovable.

James dialed Joanie's number only to have an answering machine pick up. He left a message for Joanie to call him. "No answer at Joanie's house," James said as he hung up the phone.

"Maybe you'd better call Ed and see if he has heard from her," Jake said.

James dialed Ed Mitchell's number and found that he was also up and worried about Joanie. Ed hadn't heard a thing from Joanie since the previous afternoon. James asked, "Do you know where they were planning to meet?"

"Somewhere in Statesville is all I know," said Ed. "Joanie's never done anything like this before. She's never stayed out all night. Even though we're divorced, she still calls me every night when she gets home and checks on me. To tell you the truth, I don't know what to make of it. I wish I did. This just ain't like Joanie. Let me know if you hear anything at all and I'll call you if I hear anything."

James looked at Jake as he hung up the phone. "Do you really think Joanie would call Ed if she needed help?"

"I sure do. They still love each other. Joanie's just a little mixed up right now," Jake said.

Some folks thought Ed was crazy to wait for his wayward ex-wife to return, but he still loved her and wasn't willing to give up on her even though she liked other men and dated often. That was just Joanie, and Ed couldn't quit loving her, even if he tried.

James was definitely feeling more uneasy after talking with Ed.

"Let's see if Debbie Seacrest is at home," Jake said.

James looked up the number for the Seacrest's residence and dialed.

CHAPTER 5

KEVIN SEACREST was sleeping soundly when the phone rang. He was dreaming he was on a sandy beach in Cancun, Mexico. A raven-haired beauty sat straddling him. Her bronzed skin glistened with tanning oil in the tropical sun as she leaned over him and kissed him with her open, eager mouth…he could feel the fullness of her breasts against him as he reached around her body and unhooked her bikini bra…

The phone rang again chasing away Kevin's dream. "Dammit," he growled as he picked up the receiver. "This had better be good. Who in the hell is calling at this time of day?"

"I'm really sorry if I woke you," James apologized.

"Well, you did. Who is this?"

"This is James Caldwell, Gail's husband, and I was wondering if I could speak to Debbie?"

"Why would you want to speak to my wife at this time of morning?" Kevin demanded.

James was startled at the terse response from Kevin, but pressed on. "I just hung up from talking to Ed Mitchell and neither Gail nor Joanie came home last night. Frankly, we're worried that something may have happened to them. Could I please speak to Debbie?"

"Hang on dammit. I'll go get her."

James covered the mouthpiece of the phone and said to Jake, "This is not a nice man."

"So I've heard," Jake said.

Kevin came back on the line. "Debbie ain't here."

"She didn't come home last night, either?" James asked.

"I assumed she was at the Crimson Cape last night, just like she is most every Wednesday."

"She didn't tell you they were meeting in Statesville?" James asked.

"No, she didn't! She never tells me anything. Anyway I didn't even see her yesterday. I left early before she got up and worked in Charlotte all day. I just came home after work, had some supper, watched TV, and fell asleep in my recliner. I've been asleep ever since."

"Aren't you worried about your wife?"

"She's old enough to take care of herself."

"Do you want me to call if we find out anything?" asked James, hardly believing Kevin's lack of concern.

"You can call if you want to, but don't ever call again at this time of morning," Kevin said as he slammed the receiver back into its cradle.

James hung up the phone and looked at Jake with disbelief. "Can you believe that son-of-a-bitch? Please excuse my language, but that really upsets me. He doesn't seem to give a damn if she comes home or not. What's the matter with that man? I feel sorry for Debbie being married to that jerk."

"I do, too," Jake said.

Maybe we ought to see if Carmen's home." James checked the phone book for Carmen's number only to find it was not listed.

"Well, that takes care of that," Jake said.

"Now what?" James asked.

"Ed verified that they were to meet in Statesville, so that sounds like the place to start," Jake said. "Let's stop and see who's on duty at the sheriff's annex this morning. It's on our way out of town."

"Wouldn't hurt. I'll leave a message for Gail. In case she comes home, she can call my cell." James scribbled a note and stuck it on the refrigerator door. "Let's take my car," he said as they went out the door.

CHAPTER 6

WEDNESDAY, LATE AFTERNOON

GAIL CALDWELL, one of the most successful realtors in the Mooresville/Lake Norman area, was busy trying to add a property on Langtree Road to her website when Carmen Romano called. "We're meeting at the Walmart parking lot in Statesville at five-thirty," Carmen said without the usual hello and how are you pleasantries, "Don't be late, okay?"

"Hi Carmen...how are you?" asked Gail, taken aback by the curtness of Carmen's voice.

"I'm fine. We can talk tonight at dinner. It's getting late and I still have to call Debbie and Joanie," Carmen said.

"Why are we meeting at Walmart?" asked Gail.

"It's a surprise," Carmen said, "but I will tell you this; we're going somewhere I'm sure you've never been before, a place nestled in the country just north of Statesville. See you at five-thirty." And she hung up.

Before leaving for Statesville, Gail stopped by James' downtown office. He was meeting with a client, but motioned for her to come in. Gail apologized for interrupting them. "I'm heading to Statesville to meet the girls at five-thirty, so I've got to hurry."

"Where are you going to dinner?" asked James.

"Somewhere in the country, north of Statesville. Carmen wants it to be a surprise," Gail said. "Guess she's bored with The Crimson Cape. I just wanted to say bye before I left."

"I would have never gotten over it if you hadn't," James said chuckling.

On her way to Statesville, Gail's Maxima seemed to be on autopilot. It had been a busy day and she looked forward to getting her mind off work, at least for the evening.

Sometimes Gail wondered how well they really knew Carmen. They knew Carmen had a good job with the Metro Bank and Trust Company. They also knew that Carmen, a vivacious thirty-six year old with raven hair, dark flashing eyes, and a teasing smile, was accustomed to getting what she wanted from just about any man she met and never hesitated to use that ability to the fullest. Gail was surprised Carmen had volunteered to select tonight's location and wondered why she was being so secretive.

CHAPTER 7

CARMEN ROMANO watched with envy as Gail Caldwell circled the Walmart parking lot in her shiny new Maxima. *Now that I finally have a good job, a nice car, and fabulous clothes—I just bought a new townhouse, right on the lake—and the damn bank announces it's outsourcing 4,000 jobs to India. Well, I'll be damned if I'm gonna give up everything just because my job is being handed to somebody who can't even speak decent English.*

She wasn't at all surprised that Gail had arrived first. That was Gail, so punctual and dependable. Carmen greeted her with a dutiful "air-kiss" and said, "The others will be here soon."

Carmen and Gail looked up as Joanie sailed into the parking lot so fast in her new Jetta you would have thought she was going to a clearance sale at Belk Department Store. Almost before Joanie got out of her car, she asked, "Where's that Debbie? She's always late! Why in hell are we meetin' up here in Statesville, anyway?"

"I thought it was time we did something different," Carmen said.

"Well, we have been in a rut lately. Any men at this place you takin' us, Carmen?" Joanie asked.

"Oh Joanie," Gail chided her good-naturedly.

Joanie was always ready for a good time. She had retained her youthful good looks and as a result hid her age well. No one knew how old she really was, but everyone knew she liked men of all ages.

"There is one particular man that you might find very interesting, Joanie," Carmen said, a slight smile parting her lips.

Joanie thought that sounded good. But before she could ask more about the mysterious man, Debbie Seacrest, late as usual, pulled into the parking lot in her aging Honda Accord.

"Isn't it about time that husband of hers bought Debbie a new car?" Joanie said.

Debbie worked as secretary for Carson Wells, a respected Mooresville attorney. Joanie suspected that Debbie was happiest at work. The women knew things between Debbie and her husband were not good. They'd seen bruises on her arms and neck, but were hesitant to pry.

Kevin Seacrest had owned a contracting business up North that went bankrupt. The move south was supposed to have given them a fresh start. Business had been better for a while, but now it seemed things were slipping.

Before Debbie got out of her car, Gail said, "Debbie has seemed quieter lately, have you noticed?"

Joanie nodded her head yes and then greeted Debbie as she walked up, "How's it going girlfriend?"

"I don't want to talk about it!" Debbie replied with a tone in her voice that suggested the subject was closed.

Joanie backed off when she saw tears well up in Debbie's already reddened eyes. "Okey dokey then, where're we going, Carmen?"

"Well, if you must know, we're going to dinner and a wine tasting at a Yadkin Valley winery."

"Well, why didn't you just say so?" Joanie said. "Let's get goin'. I'm about to starve!"

"Come on," Carmen said, "we can all ride in my car."

Gail said she wanted to take her own car so she get home early. She usually had one glass of wine with dinner and went home to James.

"I'll ride with you, then" Joanie said as she climbed into the Maxima with Gail. "Debbie and I can ride back to Walmart with Carmen after dinner."

Debbie rode with Carmen in her Lexus in silence. Carmen had barely spoken to her since they began their ride north on I-77. *How can Carmen just sit there and act like nothing's wrong?*

"What's gotten into Carmen?" Gail asked as she followed Carmen's Lexus up the interstate.

"She's turned into a regular bitch, if you ask me," Joanie said. "I said something about it a couple weeks ago, but nobody paid any attention to me."

"I've been noticing it too, I just didn't want to say anything," Gail said. "I thought maybe it was the pressure of Corporate America."

Joanie said, "All I know is we're already in Yadkin County. Let's enjoy our evening out."

Carmen left the interstate at the Highway 421 exit and Gail followed her steadily as they drove west. Carmen soon turned down a secondary road and then onto an unpaved road. The countryside became less and less populated as they bounced along. Gail followed the Lexus as it made a hasty turn to the left onto a tiny, graveled drive.

Joanie looked at Gail and said, "What in the hell have we gotten ourselves into, girlfriend? I didn't see a sign about any winery down this pig path, did you?"

"No, I didn't," Gail answered, "and it's getting dark."

The farther the lane wound through the trees, the narrower it became. The graveled path rounded one last bend and ended abruptly in front of a rustic, abandoned barn. Carmen drove through an open metal gate and parked her car. A faded, hand-painted sign was nailed crookedly to the right side of a battered, wooden door. The words, LOST CREEK WINERY, were scrawled across its weathered surface.

Gail followed Carmen through the gate, but stopped before she got as far as the barn. She turned her Maxima around and parked near the gate. Joanie jumped out of Gail's car and took in the surroundings. "Where in the name of God have you brought us, Carmen? Is this your idea of a winery?"

"I think the sign's a nice touch, don't you?" Carmen laughed.

Gail and Debbie slowly climbed out of their respective vehicles and witnessed the exchange of words between Carmen and Joanie. *Is this Carmen's idea of a joke?* Gail wondered as a sense of foreboding swept over her.

When Gail turned to get back in her Maxima, Carmen said, "Where do you think you're going, Mrs. Caldwell?"

Gail was shaken to hear her name said with such animosity. She turned around to see Carmen closing and locking the metal gate across the only way in or out. A wooden fence ran from the gate to the rear of both sides of the building, making it impossible for Gail to drive her car out of the enclosure.

It was clear they weren't going anywhere for awhile.

Debbie began to cry.

"Oh shut up!" Carmen said in a hateful tone.

"Listen here, you don't have a right to talk to Debbie like that." Joanie said. "I don't know what you think you're planning here, but I'll tell you right now, it ain't gonna work."

Carmen laughed again and said, "I'll do whatever I want and you can't do a damn thing about it. So just shut up, Joanie Mitchell."

The change in Carmen's voice took the women by surprise. Joanie thought, *I wouldn't have believed it if I hadn't seen it with my own eyes. She's just like Jekyll and Hyde.*

CHAPTER 8

C ARMEN LOOKED pleased as she saw the fear in their eyes and
yelled, "Come out here, Yancey!"

Yancey was one of the biggest men that any of the women
had ever seen. He stood at least six-foot-seven and had muscles piled
on top of muscles. His massive frame filled the doorway and he stared
at each of the women. He was shirtless and bristly, black hairs covered his entire torso. Yancey's body resembled a hairy Sherman Tank.
He wore no shoes on his dusty, bare feet and was clad in a pair of
Pointer brand bibbed overalls.

Joanie stared at him. "I like men," she said under her breath,
"but this, by God, is where I draw the line." To Carmen she said,
"What in the hell's going on? I thought we were going to a nice little
wine tasting, eat some good food, and be on our merry way."

"You aren't going anywhere until I say so. You got that?"

"Don't you give me any of that crap; I'll leave when I damn well
please."

"I don't think so," said Carmen.

"We'll see about that," Joanie said. "How you've kept that fancy
job at the bank all these years is beyond me. I always thought there

was an odor about you, but I didn't recognize what it was until now! Why, you smell just like 'King Kong' here! I'm surprised that the bank hasn't fired your sorry ass before now!"

With that Carmen slapped Joanie across the mouth so fast that no one saw it coming. Joanie's head recoiled from the slap as she blinked back stinging tears. Bright red blood appeared at the right corner of Joanie's mouth and trickled slowly to her chin. "You do anything like that again girl and you're history. I'll beat your sorry, good-for-nothin' ass so far in the ground, you'll have to have a shovel to dig yourself back out. You got that?"

"We'll see," Carmen said.

Yancey looked each woman up and down. "You got some fire in you, girl—" he said to Joanie, "I like that." He licked his lips and laughed.

Gail and Debbie huddled together near Gail's car. They both were crying, the fear of uncertainty etched across their faces.

Carmen yelled, "Enough of that crying, for God's sake! " She had lapsed into her southern, country drawl. Gone were the years of refinement and professionalism. A sinister-looking sneer replaced her once attractive smile. She had changed before their eyes to an evil presence that frightened them all.

CHAPTER 9

C ARMEN AND YANCY herded the women into the barn and the women surveyed their surroundings. There was only one small window on the back wall, about ten feet above the dirt floor. Years of grime and cobwebs made it almost impossible to see through the once-transparent panes of glass. There were two closed doors to the right.

Joanie looked around the barn in the dim light and could make out what appeared to be large sacks of sugar stacked along one wall. The rest of the room was nearly bare. "What you got behind those doors, Yancey, an old still? I see all this sugar; you ain't foolin' this ol' country girl. I bet you ain't fixin' to put up preserves, are you?"

"It's none of your business what I do here," Yancey said.

"Moonshine! That's what this is all about? I'll be damned if I'd drink any of that nasty stuff!" Joanie was as defiant as she could be under the circumstances. "You said it was going to be a surprise, didn't you Carmen? Well, you sure as hell surprised us. What's the plan now? When do we get to taste this fine wine you been talking about?"

"Shut up!" Carmen yelled.

Joanie continued anyway. "I'd like to know what in the world this gorilla knows about wine. He looks like he ain't nothin', but a worthless moonshiner to me!"

Yancey scrunched his eyes until they were nothing but reptilian slits and snarled, "It'll be my pleasure to take the sass out of your smart mouth, Girlie."

"Don't you call me Girlie, you big, ugly ox! I ain't afraid of you or nobody like you. I ain't afraid of 'Miss Congeniality' here, either. Now, let us outta here."

"Nobody's goin' anywhere, just yet!" Carmen said. "Settle down and make yourselves comfortable. You're gonna be here for a while."

"What in the hell do you mean by that?" Joanie asked.

"Just try to keep your big mouth shut," Carmen replied, "or I'll turn Yancey loose on you."

Gail grabbed Joanie by the arm and dragged her back before she made matters worse.

"Come on Yancey, let's go," Carmen said.

He followed her outside and closed the barn door. He threaded a big Yale padlock through its hasp and snapped it closed with a determined click.

"Now get their purses, lock the cars, and meet me at your place," Carmen said.

"Okay girls, the sun's done set and I'm not staying here another second longer than I have to," Joanie said after Yancey and Carmen left. "But my purse is still in your car, Gail, and my dad-blamed cell phone's in it. By God, if I could just call Ed, he'd come up here and straighten Carmen's ass out."

"I left my cell phone charging on my desk," Gail said. "I knew that both of you had one, so I wasn't worried about not having mine."

"Mine's in my purse, too," Debbie said.

"Aw hell, the damn things probably wouldn't get a signal up here in the sticks anyway," Joanie said.

"I wish I knew what was going through Carmen's mind right

now," Gail said.

"What mind? I think she's lost what little she had."

"Well, she's mentioned several times that her job may be in jeopardy and you both know how she likes nice things. I think Carmen is worried about losing everything she's worked for. I think she's a little jealous of us."

"What?" Joanie interrupted, "I can't believe what I'm hearing. Jealous of who? Hell, I work my ass off every day of the week and I don't have benefits like she does! She gets off work for more damn holidays in one year than I get in vacation in ten years! I don't want to hear it!"

"I'm sure you've noticed how much Carmen has changed in just the past few weeks," Gail said.

"Hellfire and damnation, she's changed in the last few minutes. Maybe she's just going through 'the change'," Joanie said. "Hell, I get like that myself sometimes, but I ain't ever slapped any of my friends."

"Maybe we should try to find a way out of here while we have the chance. Frankly I'm scared of what they might do to us," Debbie said.

"Carmen's probably jumpin' old Yancey's bones somewhere right now. This would be a good a time as any to start lookin' for a way out."

"You're right," Gail said. "That might be the best thing to do. Get out of here and get some help."

Joanie and Gail began looking around for anything that could be used to help them escape.

Debbie lifted her head, and spoke up, "You know what? Kevin can have Carmen and her trashy ways and they can both go straight to hell."

"What are you talking about?" asked Gail.

Debbie Seacrest stood beside the sacks of sugar with both hands on her hips and looked at her astonished friends. "Carmen and Kevin must have been getting together every time he is working in Charlotte. I've always suspected it, but didn't want to believe it was really happening."

"I thought I was up on everything, but you've surprised me with this," Joanie said.

"The other day, Kevin asked me when we were going to visit the wineries up in the Yadkin Valley. I didn't think much about it at the time, but after all that's happened this evening, how would he have known about this trip if Carmen hadn't told him?"

"Why in hell haven't you told us about all this before now?" asked Joanie. "I would have taken the hussy somewhere and beat the snot out of her."

"I know you would have Joanie," Debbie said.

"I never did like that son-of-a-bitch husband of yours," Joanie said. "No offense. Now let's find a way out of this hellhole and get back to civilization so we all can get our lives back to normal."

"I don't want normal," Debbie said, "I want out. I want a life without Kevin Seacrest in it."

"I think that may be the best thing for you Debbie," Gail agreed.

The three women joined hands and made a pact. "We're going to get through this together, girls," Gail said.

"You got that right!" agreed Joanie.

"Let's do it!" said Debbie.

They got up, dusted themselves off, and checked the two doors on the right side of the room only to find them locked.

"That danged Yancey's probably got all kinds of stuff hidden behind these doors. We at least oughta find something in this place we could use to break that damn window," Joanie said as she rattled the first door in vain.

Gail said, "Let me try." She grabbed the doorknob with both hands and twisted, pushed, and pulled on it before finally beating on the door with her fists.

Debbie tried the other door. "This one is locked, too," she said, exasperated.

Joanie watched them for a minute until her patience gave out. "These sonsabitches ain't ever gonna open without a key or a pry-bar. We might as well give up on 'em and try to find somethin' else."

The women searched the floor around the big room for anything that could be used to break the window.

The sparse surroundings soon made it obvious that Carmen and Yancey had made sure nothing was left in the barn that the women could possibly use to escape.

Defeated, they sat down on the sacks of sugar and huddled together for warmth against the October chill.

"I guess we'll just have to wait until morning," Joanie admitted. "Where would we go in the dark, anyway? What really burns my butt is that the assholes didn't even feed us before they left! God, I'm hungry!"

"Me, too" said Debbie.

Gail wondered aloud, "What I don't understand is; what could Carmen possibly expect to gain by locking us in this barn?"

"Damned if I know," Joanie said.

"James doesn't even know where I am right now. He probably thinks I'm having a good time enjoying a nice dinner, but he'll be worried sick if I'm not home by eleven o'clock," Gail said.

"I usually call Ed before I go to bed and check on the old bugger," Joanie said. "He'll be worried, too, if I don't call by midnight."

"Kevin certainly won't be worried about me."

The realization that they were going to have to spend a cold night in the barn sank in. They grew quiet and tried to find a comfortable place to lay their weary heads. The sounds of mice scurrying in the dark and the wind rustling the half-naked limbs of the trees outside were all they heard.

CHAPTER 10

Y ANCY LIVED in a small, ramshackle house that sat in a clearing a few hundred yards through the woods from the barn. The house, more like a cabin, was as run down as the barn. Shingles from the sagging roof were strewn on the ground. Trash was piled on the front porch and the foundation crumbled beneath the weight of it. Carmen, leading the way as usual, climbed the rickety steps and threw open the door. Inside it looked as if a small war had taken place.

"Why in the hell don't you clean this place up? No wonder you smell! Look at this mess!" she said.

Yancey had never seen Carmen act this way. "I'm sorry, Carmen."

Carmen spun around and slapped Yancey across the mouth with the back of her hand. "Stop apologizing and clean this mess up."

More puzzled than ever, Yancey rubbed his mouth with the tips of his fingers. "Sure sure, Carmen, whatever you want." Yancey picked up empty Budweiser cans, potato chip bags, dirty dishes, and filthy clothes. "How's that?" Yancey asked.

"Yeah, yeah, that's better Yancey. I've got some good plans

and you can't mess them up!"

"Are we gonna feed them women somethin', Carmen? I know I'm hungry. I'll bet they are, too."

"Quit worrying about them Yancey; we have things to do. I want you to go the store and call their husbands for me first thing in the morning. I've got their numbers right here," Carmen said as she handed Yancey a piece of crumpled paper. "Here's all you have to say."

Yancey looked at the papers and then at Carmen. "What? I can't do this. You're gonna get me in trouble."

"You have to make the calls Yancey. They know my voice."

"And that's all I have to do?" Yancey asked.

"You can do it Yancey, I know you can."

"I don't know—"

"Sure you can."

"But Carmen, I ain't never done nothin' like this before. I just make moonshine and sell it. That ain't at all complicated. Not like this."

"You like me, don't you, Yancey?" Carmen put her hand on his chest. She waited until he nodded. "First thing in the morning, you have to make the calls."

"Okay."

CHAPTER 11

JAMES STEERED his Lincoln Navigator onto Brawley School Road and headed toward I-77 in the predawn quiet. Traffic was not a problem that early in the morning. A few hours later, it would take forty minutes just to reach the interstate.

The Brawley peninsula was several miles long with numerous roads branching out in several directions to the coveted lakeshore properties of Lake Norman. More than 27,000 people lived down Brawley School Road, which had only one way in, and one way out. Shopping centers, convenience stores, schools, doctors' offices, and every kind of business imaginable, lined the often traffic-choked artery.

Because of the rapid growth in this part of the county, Sheriff Nichols had opened an annex office on Brawley School Road.

Sid Bellman was on duty. The burly man sported a gray crew cut atop a cheerful, round face. He had a few chins too many, a result of his prodigious appetite. His cheeks were splotched red as if he had just come inside from the cold. Sid had in enough years to retire, but enjoyed what he was doing, so he came to work early every morning like he always had. Jake noticed Sid's gray stubble and remembered that neither he nor James had shaved this morning.

"Whatcha doin' out so early this mornin', Jake?" Sid asked as they walked through the door. Sid and Jake were good friends and enjoyed fishing together on the lake.

Jake introduced Sid to James. "We hope you can help us," he said.

"Well hell, sit down first, how about a fresh cup of Iredell County Sheriff's Department coffee, if you're up to it?" Sid said.

"My wife is missing!" James blurted out. "I don't want any coffee. I want to find my wife!"

Sid heard the desperation in James' voice and got down to business. "How long has she been missing?"

"She didn't come home last night after a meeting," James said.

"Where was the meeting?"

"The meetings are usually in Mooresville, but she was supposed to meet her friends somewhere in Statesville this time."

"Who are her friends?"

James gave Sid the names of the other women and explained to him that none of them had returned home last night. He also told the deputy about the phone calls he'd made to Ed Mitchell and Kevin Seacrest.

"I couldn't believe the way Kevin Seacrest acted when I called him," James said.

"How was that?" Sid asked, thinking that name sounded familiar.

"Well, it was like he didn't care if his wife came home or not. He was ugly about it."

"Huh," Sid said and made a mental note to check the name Kevin Seacrest; that name had come across his desk before.

"Is there anything you can do?" James asked.

"Well, the required twenty-four hours haven't passed since your wife went missing, so an official missing persons report cannot be filed. I'm sure there must be a logical explanation. There usually is."

"Is there anything you can do now?" James asked.

"I'll go ahead and put out an APB on your wife's car. Maybe one of the third-shift deputies will come across it and call it in. What kind of car does you wife drive?"

"A four-door, 2006 silver Nissan Maxima. Her license tag is a vanity plate. It just says GAIL#1."

"Okay, I'll make a few calls."

"I really appreciate it," said James.

Sid said, "Let me pour you and Jake a quick cup of coffee and I'll put things in motion."

Sid poured some of the blackest coffee Jake had ever seen. Adding three heaping spoonfuls of sugar and as much cream as the cup would hold, did little to alter its strength.

Sid set a box of Krispy Kreme doughnuts on his desk. "Help yourselves. I picked these up on the way in this morning," Sid said. As Jake took one, he couldn't help noticing there were four missing already.

Jake bit off a generous chunk while Sid was busy on the telephone. The sugary glaze helped Jake get a swallow of the awful coffee down. The first doughnut was so delicious, he had another one. Jake began to understand how Sid could have a problem laying off these Krispy Kremes.

James watched as Jake reached for his second doughnut and decided to have one himself.

Sid ended his phone conversation and said, "I've requested that our deputies in the north end of the county be on the lookout for her car. I'm gonna call the Statesville Police Department, too. You never know, we might get lucky. What're you fellows planning on doin'?"

Jake said, "We thought we'd ride to Statesville and see if we could spot one of their cars."

Sid said, "Better still, why don't you go home and let us handle it. It's our job."

"I've got to be doing something or I'll go crazy," James said.

"Okay. Suit yourself," Sid said with some reluctance, "but be careful and keep us informed."

The sound of crunching gravel announced the arrival of another vehicle. Jake turned to see an attractive, red-haired female dressed in a navy blazer and khaki slacks walk through the door.

"Good morning, Sid," the woman said. "I thought I'd stop by and see if you needed any more doughnuts."

"We might after we finish with these," he chuckled.

"Oh, I'm sorry I interrupted something."

"That's alright, we're just finishing up. Do you know Jake McLeod?" Sid asked her, pointing at Jake.

"Yes, I know him, but I'm not sure he remembers me."

She was right, Jake didn't remember her.

"This other gentleman is James Caldwell," Sid continued.

"You don't remember me do you, Mr. McLeod?" she asked with a friendly smile. Her voice was pleasant and soft.

Before Jake had a chance to answer, Sid chimed in, "Heck, I thought everybody knew Marci. She's the first female to be promoted to the Detective Division of the Iredell County Sheriff's Department."

Jake studied her features carefully. "Are you Marci Jackson?" he asked. "You went to South Iredell High School with my cousin, Amy Dexter, didn't you?"

"I *was* Marci Jackson. I'm surprised you remember."

It was then he noticed the ring on the third finger of her left hand. "I'm Marci Meredith now. I was married to Mark Meredith for ten years," she paused, "but he was killed by a drunk driver a little over two years ago."

"I'm truly sorry, I didn't know," Jake replied. "I've been out of touch for awhile."

"I heard you lost your wife to cancer. I'm sorry for your loss, too," she responded sincerely.

"Thanks. Do you work out of this office now?" Jake asked to

keep the conversation going.

"No, not really. I work the entire county. I just get up early and check on ol' Sid once in a while and help him eat his doughnuts. Why are you here so early, Mr. McLeod?"

"Call me Jake."

"Okay then, tell me Jake, why are you here so early? Is there a problem?"

Jake told Marci about the missing women. "Sid's made some calls and alerted the county deputies and the Statesville Police to be on the lookout for Gail Caldwell's Maxima."

"I hope we can help you Mr. Caldwell, "Marci said to James.

James said, "I don't know what I would do if anything happened to my wife."

"Since the ladies were going to Statesville last night, we're going to head up that way and see if we can spot any of their cars." Jake told Marci. "Sid, we'll call you if we find anything."

"That's it!" Sid said. "That's where I've heard the name Kevin Seacrest. His name's been across my desk a couple of times for domestic violence."

"Hmmm," Marci said. "Isn't that a coincidence? You know Sid, I've heard one of those missing women's names linked to Seacrest."

"Which one?" Sid asked.

"The Romano woman, Carmen."

"Tell me more."

"Well, another deputy said she'd answered a domestic violence call at the Seacrest home several months back and was talking about Mr. Seacrest being quite the womanizer. She also said she had heard that Mr. Seacrest was involved with another woman—Carmen Romano."

"What a coincidence."

"Yeah, but I'm not a big believer in coincidences," Marci said.

CHAPTER 12

JAMES WAS driving north, the rising sun glanced off the hood of his SUV. He could do little but think of Gail and worry that she might be stranded on the highway or lost. "Why hasn't she called, Jake?" He'd tried her cell again, but the call went straight to her voice-mail.

Jake glanced over at James and could see the tremendous worry etched on his friend's face. "I don't know, James. Maybe her phone battery's dead or maybe she's in an area where there's no service. We'll know soon. I'm sure of it. You know, since Gail told you they were meeting for dinner somewhere north of Statesville, there's a good chance they carpooled."

"So," James said, "what does that tell us?"

"Well, it may mean that one or more of the ladies left their car somewhere in Statesville so they could ride together. If that's the case, let's try some of the big parking lots that are well lit."

"Okay, let's try Signal Hill Mall first," James said.

It was still early in the morning when they reached the mall and no one was there except a middle-aged man who was using an industrial-strength leaf blower to clean the parking lot of detritus left over from the day before. The tail of his red plaid flannel shirt flapped in the morning breeze.

"There's not a single vehicle here except that old man's beat-up truck," James said as he drove around the parking lot.

"Let's try the big box stores, like Lowe's and Home Depot's lots while we're at it," Jake suggested. "They're not far."

A few minutes later, they were heading west on Highway 21. "Hey, there's the entrance to the Walmart shopping center," James said as they sped past it.

"We'll catch it on the way back," Jake assured him.

James wheeled into the Lowe's parking lot only to find employee's cars and trucks parked near the highway. A man in a blue plaid flannel shirt was blowing off the huge parking lot with a powerful leaf blower—the only difference being, his shirt was blue and the man's shirt at Signal Hill Mall was red. Gail's car was nowhere to be seen.

Home Depot was directly across the road from Lowe's, but they found the same scene being repeated there as they had encountered at the two previous lots.

James was becoming more despondent and Jake offered him some encouragement. "Well, we're narrowing it down anyway," he said as James sped out of the lot and turned left toward the service road that led to Walmart's huge parking lot. James swerved so quickly onto the road that Jake's head hit the passenger window.

Several automobiles were parked at the back of the lot beside Walmart and James sped toward them as if he was on an open road. "I don't see Gail's car anywhere, do you?" James asked. "I don't see Carmen's Lexus either," he added .

Suddenly James yelled as they got closer to another group of cars. "There's a Jetta! Maybe it's Joanie's."

"And that old Honda parked beside the Jetta could be Debbie's car," Jake noted. "I'll call Sid and ask him to run the plates on them."

Sid picked up on the first ring.

"Sid, this is Jake McLeod."

"What's up, Jake?"

"We haven't found Gail's car yet, but we found one we think may belong to Joanie Mitchell and possibly one that belongs to Debbie Seacrest. Can you run the plates for us?"

"Let me get Marci for you, she'll do it."

Jake waited until Marci came on the line. As soon as he heard her soft, but authoritative voice, he gave her the plate numbers. "The two cars are parked side by side at the back of the Walmart parking lot. We thought it was possible that the women carpooled and only took two cars to their final destination."

"Hold on then, I'll run them."

Jake could hear Marci's fingernails clicking away on the computer keyboard as she entered the information into the department's database. "It's the Mitchell lady's car alright and I couldn't believe it when I found out that the Honda belongs to Debbie Seacrest. How did you find them so quickly?"

"We just did a little process of elimination and it paid off," Jake said. "We figured the ladies might park their cars in a place that would be well lit and narrowed it down from there."

"Pretty good police work. Wait there and I'll join you as soon as I can."

"I don't think I can hold James here. He's itching to get going somewhere and he doesn't even know where that somewhere is. He just wants to be doing something. I'll call you if anything else turns up." He thought quickly and added, "What's your cell, so I can call you directly?"

Marci gave Jake her number and cautioned, "You guys be careful."

"We will. James says we're going to head north on I-77 and see if we can spot Gail's car along the roadside."

"Okay, stay in touch."

CHAPTER 13

MARCI TOOK a deep breath as she hung up the phone. She thought about meeting Jake McLeod earlier that morning and realized she was looking forward to seeing him again.

"Sid, I'm going to cruise north and see if I can spot Mrs. Caldwell's vehicle. They found two of the other ladies' cars. I'll call you if I hear or see anything. Keep me informed, will you?"

Marci drove her Crown Vic toward Troutman, checking the parking lot downtown, the Food Lion parking lot, and the vacant Galaxy Supermarket lot, too. She continued her journey north through Troutman, past the Iredell County Fair Grounds, and on to Barium Springs.

She turned into The Church of the Springs parking lot and drove around to the back just to make sure there were no cars parked there. Marci thought about all the women involved. She thought about Kevin Seacrest's reaction when James called him about the disappearance of his wife. "There's no way Kevin Seacrest could be involved in the women's disappearance, is there?" Marci said aloud in the empty car. Suddenly, the hairs on the back of her neck began to rise like they did when she got an ominous feeling that something was just not right.

Marci picked up the mike and radioed the annex. "Sid, I've got a hunch and I need a favor," she told him.

"Shoot!" Sid said. He listened as Marci explained her idea. "Uh-huh. I think you might have something there, kiddo. Let me get right on it!"

Marci hoped she was wrong, but had a sick feeling in the pit of her stomach.

Marci continued toward Statesville. She caught herself thinking about Jake McLeod again. *I don't know how old he is, but that slight graying around his temples gives him a distinguished air. I wonder where he got the scar over his left eyebrow. It's more visible when he smiles and what a nice smile he has.*

Sid came back on the radio after a few minutes, interrupting Marci's thoughts. "I've got something for you. You want the skinny on Kevin Seacrest?"

"Of course."

"You're not going to like it. I think we'd better pay Mr. Seacrest a visit."

"Go on," Marci said.

"Well, for starters, it looks like our boy has been married before. The first Mrs. Seacrest disappeared four years ago. Now get this, they found her decomposed body near an abandoned winery in upstate New York about a year later. It was less than five miles from the Seacrest's home. Mr. Seacrest was questioned several times, but one of his drinking buddies provided him with an alibi, so he was free to go."

"My God!" said Marci.

"That's what the boys up North tell me."

"What else did they tell you?"

"The victim had been strangled and then dumped in a ravine about a quarter of a mile from the winery. According to them, the new owners were checking the nearby property as a possible site for expansion when they discovered the corpse. Anything else?"

"Well, Mr. Seacrest married Debbie DeCunzo about a year after they found the body of his first wife, Angela Dawson. His construction company went under after he had some run-ins with the building inspectors. He was also arrested in New York for assault on a female."

"That's very interesting," Marci said. "I think you're right, Sid. You and I need to pay a little visit to our Mr. Seacrest."

"Sounds like a winner to me. I'll see you when you get here." Sid said as he signed off.

Marci pulled the cruiser into the parking lot of Hughes Supply, near Statesville, turned around and sped south toward Mooresville. The morning was slipping away and she wanted to catch Kevin Seacrest at home.

CHAPTER 14

EVERY BONE in Gail's body ached from sleeping on the sacks of sugar—if you could call the fitful state she endured, sleeping. She was famished. "They never even left us anything to drink. I'm so thirsty, I can hardly stand it."

"I am too!" Debbie said. "What time is it?"

"It's six-twenty-five," Joanie said yawning as she looked at her watch.

Gail said, "James is probably sick with worry by now."

Joanie said, "So let's get busy and find a way out of here. It's almost daylight and I'm madder'n hell."

Now that it was getting lighter outside, the three women searched again for anything they could use to break the window. After not finding a single thing that would work, Joanie said, "Let's pick up one of these heavy sacks of sugar and throw the damn thing through the window."

"Great idea," said Gail. "Why didn't we think of that last night?"

"I was too upset to think straight last night," Joanie said as she lifted one corner of a sack.

"Do you think we can lift one of these things? It says here each sack weighs fifty pounds," Debbie said.

"We'll never know until we try," Joanie said. "Get hold of the other end of this thing."

Debbie and Joanie grunted as they picked up one of the sugar sacks and carried it several feet before it slipped from their hands.

"Hell's bells, I thought I was in shape," panted Joanie. "Alright Debbie, let's try it again." Joanie reached for the sack with both hands and swore, "We'll get out of this mess yet. You just wait and see!"

"Wait!" Gail said. "Why don't we stack some of the sacks on top of each other under the window so we can climb out."

"Hell, that might work even better." With that, Joanie took charge. "Okay then, let's start totin'. We still gotta get up to that window and break the damn thing out before we can get through it."

The women took turns helping each other stack the sacks of sugar beneath the window. It took some great effort from all three of them, but they managed to get the stack high enough to just about reach the window.

"Okay," Joanie said, "now we have to make another stack just like that one."

"Another one?" whined Debbie.

"Yeah, another stack right in front of that one so we won't fall off and bust our asses when we try to break the window," Joanie answered.

"Okay, Joanie," said Gail.

The three women set about the strenuous task of lifting, carrying, stacking and, in Joanie's case, cussing the fifty pound sacks of sugar.

"Alright, that looks good enough," Joanie said. "Debbie, let's carry one more sack up there and see if we can throw the thing through the damn window."

Debbie and Joanie picked up the final sack and swung it onto the top of the stacks. "Gail, you go listen at the door and let us know if you hear 'em comin'." Joanie climbed onto the top of the sacks, looked down at Debbie and said, "Give me your hand and let me help you up."

The two women gave one last nod to Gail standing at the door and then faced each other. Joanie looked at Debbie, smiled and said, "Well, you ready, kid?"

Debbie breathed in a few gasps of air and then said, "I'm ready when you are."

They both planted one foot on each stack of sugar sacks. "On three," Joanie encouraged Debbie. They began swinging the sack of sugar on 'one'; increased the arc on 'two' and on 'three', they threw it into the window hard enough to send shards of glass and splinters of the frame flying to the outside of the barn. "Hot damn, did you see that?" Joanie said exuberantly.

"We did it," Debbie said almost crying with relief.

An eerie silence filled the room after the loud crashing of the window. "Shhh," Joanie said. "Be real quiet for a minute. Wait and see if Carmen and Yancey heard that. If they don't come—we're outta here!"

"They might not be up yet. What do you suppose they did all night?" Debbie asked—not really wanting to know the answer.

"I don't know. It looked like they were in the ruttin' season, if you ask me," answered Joanie.

"Right now, let's just get out of here," Gail said.

"Okay, Gail; you first," Joanie said. "Come on up here." Gail joined Debbie and Joanie at the top of the stack.

Gail looked up at the jagged pieces of glass protruding from the windowsill and warned, "Wait, we have to break the rest of the glass out of the window before we can climb through or we'll be cut to pieces."

"She's right," Debbie added, "but we have to hurry. They could come back any minute."

"Okay, help me up so I can get a better look," Gail said. Joanie and Debbie quickly wrapped their arms around Gail's legs and hoisted her up to the window so she could survey the damage.

"There's a lot of sharp glass sticking up from the bottom of the sill," Gail observed, "help me down for just a second."

Gail raced across the barn to the sacks of sugar that had been their bed the night before and retrieved a piece of an old, discarded tow sack she had found during their first search. "This will work," she said triumphantly holding up the remnant of cloth.

Gail climbed back up to the top of the stack of sugar sacks. Joanie and Debbie once again hoisted her up to the window where, with her hand wrapped with the piece of old sack, Gail began to break the remaining glass as carefully as she could. She then picked broken shards of glass out of the window's casing and dropped each one of them at Joanie's feet.

"I've got an idea," Joanie said, looking at the shards of glass spread around her. "Let's pile these pieces of glass right in front of the door. When ol' Yancey comes in all barefooted, he'll cut the hell out of them big gunboats he calls feet."

"Sounds good," the other two readily agreed.

After Gail picked the remaining pieces of sharp glass out of the window, Joanie and Debbie helped Gail down.

All three hurriedly picked up the pieces of glass and spread them out on the dirt floor. They even stood some really jagged pieces on their ends so that Yancey couldn't help but step on them.

"Now let's get outta here before the 'Wicked Witch of the West' comes back," Joanie said.

"You first Debbie," Gail offered. "We'll give you a boost."

"No, you first, Gail."

"Hell's bells girls, we ain't got time for manners. One of you get your ass outta that window. Ol' Yancey and crazy Carmen could be breathin' down our necks any minute."

The three women scampered back up to the top of the stack and grinned at each other. Joanie and Gail convinced Debbie that she was going to be first and gave her a hefty boost up to the window. When Debbie finally got herself situated, Joanie pushed on her butt and Debbie went out the window, tumbled and fell hard to the ground.

They heard her land with a big thud.

"Are you alright, Debbie?" asked Gail.

"Yeah, but there's glass everywhere."

"Are you hurt?" Joanie asked.

"No, I'm alright, nothing serious. I'm just glad to be out here. Wait just a minute and let me move some of this glass."

"You next Gail," ordered Joanie. Gail didn't argue and reached for the window ledge. Joanie got under her and put her shoulder beneath Gail's butt. "Are you ready?"

"I'm as ready as I will ever be. Get me out of here."

Joanie gave Gail a push with her shoulder and Gail joined Debbie on the ground beneath the window. "How are we going to get you out, Joanie?" Gail asked from outside the window.

"I can reach the windowsill. I'll climb outta the son-of-a-bitch," Joanie said.

The two women on the ground could hear Joanie swearing inside the barn. "We can't help you now," Gail said. Since neither Gail nor Debbie could reach the window from the ground it looked as if Joanie was on her own.

"Y'all don't worry about me!" Joanie said to the open window. "Go get help! I'll be alright. I'll get out of here if I have to break the damn door down. Now get going!"

"We're not about to leave you here!"

"Yes you are! Run before they come back."

With determination Joanie reached for the windowsill and began hoisting herself up slowly but surely. She dug the toes of her shoes into the wall and pulled as hard as she could with her hands as she struggled to get her arms on the window ledge. Her tenacity paid off. Joanie had her arms across the windowsill and was climbing the rest of the way up when the door to the barn flew open with a crash.

Carmen's sudden entrance frightened Joanie; she lost her grip, fell roughly on the sugar sacks, and bounced to the bare floor. Carmen was standing there open-mouthed glaring menacingly at Joanie. "Where are the other two?" she shouted.

"I don't know. I woke up and they were gone," Joanie answered.

"I don't believe a word of that. You had to help them get out of here."

"So what if I did?"

"It doesn't matter. Yancey knows every inch of these woods. We'll find them."

CHAPTER 15

DEBBIE AND GAIL heard the crash when Carmen entered the barn. They crouched under the window listening to Carmen's tirade. Gail and Debbie didn't want to leave Joanie alone, but knew they had to get help. The two women crossed over a barbed wire fence behind the barn and slipped into the woods.

Carmen was mad as a hornet and never even noticed the broken glass in front of the door. All she had on her mind was the stunned Joanie, still lying on the floor. She gave Joanie a quick kick to the ribs and started yelling at her again. "Get up, damn it!"

Joanie slowly rose to her feet, favoring her right arm and her ribs. "Why are you doing this Carmen? What have we ever done to you? We thought we were friends."

"Friends! Ha! Gail is rich as hell. Poor old Debbie is clueless and you have your little flower business while I may lose my job to some damn foreigner that can't even speak good English. I don't have a damn thing in common with any of you anymore. So I'm doing something to make everything a little more fair."

"Like what?"

"You'll see. I didn't get you all up here for nothing."

Joanie, beginning to recover from her fall and the kick to the ribs, inched closer to the door. Her subtle movements were hardly noticed.

Then Yancey came barging through the door, stepped into the pile of broken glass with his bare feet, and began bellowing like a wounded bear. He started hopping up and down, swearing like a sailor. Blood oozed from the bottoms of his feet, leaving dark red spots on the dusty, barn floor. Carmen turned to witness the commotion and Joanie suddenly pushed her from behind with all the strength she could muster. Carmen hit the floor in front of Yancey and, as he tried to stop her fall, Joanie made a dash for the door and was through it before either one of them had a chance to react.

"Get her, damn it! She's gettin' away!" shouted Carmen.

Fragments of glass dug into Yancey's feet as he tried to run after Joanie. He sank to the barn floor unable to walk another step until he picked some of the jagged chards out of the bottoms of his feet. It gave Joanie enough time to scramble over the locked gate and start running for her life.

CHAPTER 16

"GAIL TOLD me they were going north of Statesville, didn't she?" James asked. Jake nodded. "Okay then," James said leaving the Walmart parking lot, returning to I-77 north toward Yadkin County. The elation of finding Joanie and Debbie's cars was short-lived. They really didn't have much hope of finding Gail's car along the heavily traveled I-77, but they didn't know what else to do. Jake looked over at James and saw that his cheeks were wet, but said nothing. He prayed they would find the women and that all of them would be safe.

"Do you think she's been in an accident?" James asked.

"I don't know. If she had been, you would've already been notified, and besides, there are the other three women, too. What are the odds of all of them missing at the same time?"

"I guess you're right." James drove for a few miles and then said, "Hey, I just thought of something. Let's turn off at exit 65 and head toward Union Grove. Maybe they went to The Cook Shack. Gail and I often go there and listen to Bluegrass music."

"Could be Carmen's surprise was The Cook Shack," Jake said.

"It's a fun place to go, and I'm telling you right now, the music played there is as professional as you'll hear anywhere. People come from everywhere just to sit and listen on Saturday mornings. I go there every chance I can and do a little pickin' myself," James said.

"Do they play on Wednesday nights?"

"I don't know about Wednesday nights, but they sometimes have special concerts on Thursday nights."

"Do you think there's a chance the women might have gone there?"

"Heck, I don't know, Jake, I'm just grasping at straws."

"Well, let's stop there anyway and find out if your friends have seen them."

James drove on Highway 901 toward Union Grove like a man on a mission.

"Maybe we'd better call Sid and Marci and let them know where we're heading," Jake said.

"Go ahead."

Jake dialed Sid's cell phone and again Sid answered quickly.

"It's Jake. We're heading for the Cook Shack in Union Grove. James thinks there is a possibility that the ladies might have gone there since it's north of Statesville and Gail has often been there with him."

"That's a possibility." Sid said.

"Sid," Jake said quietly into the cell phone, "I've got a question for you."

"There must be a problem with our connection, I can barely hear you," Sid said.

"I'm trying not to disturb James while he's driving," Jake said in a whisper. "Just one more thing and I'll let you go."

"Okay. What else do you need to know?"

"How well do you know Marci Meredith?"

"Damn," Sid laughed, "don't that beat all!"

"What's so funny?"

"Marci asked me the same thing about you!"

"You've got to be kidding!" Jake replied.

"No, I'm not, scout's honor."

"You weren't even in the scouts, Sid."

"I know, but I've always wanted to say that." Sid laughed and then told Jake what he knew. "Marci graduated from South Iredell High School, and I might add, quite a few years after you did from Mooresville."

"How old do you think she is?"

"Well, I'd say she's much too young for you, Jake."

"Quit kidding, Sid. What else can you tell me?"

"She's a smart lady, Jake. She studied Criminal Justice Technology at Mitchell Community College and went on to get her degree in Criminal Justice from the University of North Carolina at Charlotte. Marci was Iredell County's first female detective."

"Has she been dating anyone?" Jake asked.

"That woman has been moping around Iredell County for the last two years. This morning was the first time I have seen light in her eyes since her husband got killed."

"Thanks Sid, I owe you."

CHAPTER 17

"ARE YOU ready to hit the road, Sid? It's getting late." Marci asked as Sid hung up the phone.

"Yeah, I'm ready," he said, brushing crumbs from the last doughnut off of his shirt. "I can't wait to hear what our boy has to say for himself." Sid grabbed his hat from the desk, locked the door to the Annex, and climbed into the passenger side of Marci's Crown Vic cruiser.

Marci sped out of the parking lot spraying gravel up to the small porch of the annex.

"I don't know what's going on with these women, but something's hinky; I can feel it," Sid said. He was talking more to himself than to Marci.

"I agree," said Marci. "Maybe Mr. Seacrest can shed a little light as to their whereabouts."

They wanted to catch Kevin Seacrest at home before he left for work. It took Marci and Sid about twenty minutes to arrive at the vinyl-sided, two-story house on the east side of Mooresville. Marci turned into the Seacrest's driveway and pulled to a stop in front of the house.

Kevin's Silverado truck was still parked outside the garage. "I don't guess the lazy sucker's goin' to work today," Sid allowed.

"It doesn't look like it, does it?" Marci agreed.

"I think I'll get his tag number just in case we need it later," Sid added as an afterthought.

"Good idea, you never know," Marci said as she unbuckled her seat belt.

Marci and Sid climbed the brick steps to the front porch and rang the doorbell.

"What in the hell do you want? I ain't buying anything, so go away before I come out there and throw your ass off the porch," came the greeting from inside the house.

"Well, it looks like Mr. Manners himself is home and awake," said Sid.

"Sure sounds like it. How do you want to handle this?"

"It's up to you; you're the lead dog here," Sid said.

"I'll be nice first and see what happens," Marci replied with a grin. "Open up Mr. Seacrest! Detective Marci Meredith and Deputy Sid Bellman with the Iredell County Sherriff's Department. We need to ask you a few questions. We won't keep you long," Marci said to the closed door.

Kevin Seacrest partially opened the door, stuck his head through the opening and said, "What do you want?"

"Just a couple of questions if you don't mind, sir," said Marci, trying her best to be nice. "We're trying to help locate some missing women who have not been seen since yesterday afternoon around five o'clock."

"What does that have to do with me?" Kevin asked.

"Mr. Seacrest, one of the missing women happens to be your wife!"

"So?" Kevin said.

"Well, we would like to know if you have heard anything from her since that time. There are other people who are very concerned about the whereabouts of all four of the missing women. We were hoping you would be willing to help."

Kevin didn't invite them in nor did he step out onto the porch. He just continued looking at them through the narrow opening and said, "I didn't even see Debbie yesterday. I left for Charlotte before she got up."

"I see," Marci said, giving Kevin time to think. "When's the last time you spoke with her?"

Kevin didn't like the way this line of questioning was heading. "James Caldwell called and woke me up already this morning asking me this same kind of crap. I don't see how I can help you, but let me know if you find out anything," Kevin said as he closed the door in their faces.

"Well," Marci said, "I've got a notion to go in there and knock some manners into his hard head."

"Be my guest," Sid said.

Marci took Sid's night-stick and rapped on the door frame. She knew the loud banging would make Seacrest angry and this might provoke him into giving them some reason to arrest him.

Kevin opened the door again and asked curtly, "What do you want now?"

"We need to know if you have any idea where the women in your wife's club were going to meet last night," Marci said with a stern voice. "And for the record, do you have any interest in knowing where your wife is?"

"No, I don't know where they were going and to answer you second question, I'm not all that interested in knowing where my wife is. She's old enough to take care of herself," Kevin said as he tried to close the door again, but this time Marci stuck her foot inside the jamb.

"Why is that? Are you two not getting along?"

"I don't think it's any of your damn business, woman!"

Marci reached through the small opening in the door and

grabbed Kevin by the front of his shirt and jerked him out onto the porch. She backed him up against the wall and said with conviction, "I think you need a few lessons in manners when it comes to respecting the badge of a law enforcement officer; and especially when it comes to the proper way to address a lady. I don't know how you treated a lady in New York, but you are in the South now buster. Show a little respect or I'll throw your sorry ass in jail."

"Listen, I don't need this kinda crap! Leave me alone or I'll have your badge for harassment."

"Why don't you try and take it right now?"

Kevin said nothing.

Marci continued, "We're interested in the whereabouts of these women, whether you are or not, and we'll find them. We'll also find out if you know more than you are letting on. We know about your murdered wife back in Depew, New York Mr. Seacrest."

"I don't know what you're talking about."

"I think you do, Mr. Seacrest. We'll be in touch. You can count on that," Marci said as she released her grip on the man's shirt.

"I'll remember this visit. You better not forget it either!"

"Don't threaten me, Mr. Seacrest. Have a nice day." Marci handed Sid his night-stick and they got into the cruiser and headed back toward Mooresville." Marci said with a smile on her face, "I thought that went rather well, don't you agree, Sid?"

Sid laughed, "Yeah, I do. I don't think it could have gone much better. I really liked the way you threw in that part about his murdered wife."

"Yeah, I thought that would rouse him a little bit and give him something to think about," Marci said.

"I'd bet my bottom dollar that he's mixed up in this somehow," Sid said.

"So would I."

"Well, what'll we do now?" Sid asked.

"We'll just drive up the road a little ways to wait and see what he does next."

Marci and Sid parked behind a subdivision's landscaped berm, so they could watch for Kevin's truck.

"Doggone, I wish I hadn't drunk those four cups of coffee this morning," Sid said. "I don't know how long I'm going to be able to sit here and wait on our Mr. Seacrest."

Marci laughed, "It won't be long if he's the kind of guy I think he is. Something is just not right with him and we're going to find out what it is."

CHAPTER 18

KEVIN SEACREST collected his Dale Earnhardt, Jr. racing cap from the arm of his recliner, pulled it down tightly over his head, and bolted out the door.

Less than ten minutes later, he sped past Sid and Marci. She told Sid, "Radio the Mooresville Police Department and see if they have an unmarked car nearby. Tell them we need one in a hurry."

Sid dialed the MPD. "We need help with a tail on a 2002 black Chevrolet Silverado pickup." Sid gave them the license plate number and said that the suspect should be crossing Main Street soon.

Officer Cliff Sewell was at Bob's Grill, near the corner of Main and Iredell Avenue, grabbing a late cup of coffee and an egg sandwich when the call came through.

Kevin Seacrest caught all the traffic lights on green and hardly slowed down as he crossed Statesville Avenue, Church Street, and Main Street. As he crossed the railroad tracks at Broad Street, Officer Sewell fell in behind him and followed the pickup, but Kevin never noticed.

What has Carmen done? Kevin wondered. *She promised me we'd have enough money to leave North Carolina and go anywhere we wanted.*

She didn't tell me how she planned to get it. All I'm supposed to do is to act like I know nothing about it.

Officer Sewell reported to Sid Bellman. "He just turned west on Plaza Drive and is speeding a little. I don't want to give up my position so I'm staying back with a couple of vehicles between us. He hasn't made me yet," Sewell said. "I'll have to drop off when he leaves the city limits," he continued, "Can you get another back-up?"

"I'll call in a favor from the state." Sid said

As luck would have it, Trooper Michael Dunlap had just finished breakfast at the Waffle House near the intersection of I-77 and River Road and was getting into his cruiser when he got the call. "No problem," he told Sid. "I'll be in position by the time he gets here. I was ready for a little action this morning anyway."

Trooper Dunlap didn't have to wait long before he saw Kevin's truck taking the northbound ramp onto I-77. He immediately radioed for an unmarked car to join in the surveillance if and when Kevin got as far as Statesville. Trooper Sam Williams was heading south when the call came through. He hurriedly took the off-ramp at exit 45, crossed the bridge, turned left, and pulled over onto the shoulder of the on-ramp heading north.

Kevin was still oblivious to the tail when he pulled onto the northbound ramp of I-77 at exit 36. He was going to the barn himself to find out what Carmen was up to. He had a sick feeling in the pit of his stomach as he sped north. At exit 42, he pulled into the Hess station, filled his truck's tank with gas, and then pulled into a parking place in front of the on-site restaurant. Maybe some food would settle his stomach. He ate his eggs, bacon, hash browns, and toast, and after finishing a third cup of truck-stop-coffee, paid his bill and went to the men's room.

Trooper Dunlap waited in his cruiser. He was parked on the side of the restaurant. Dunlap notified Trooper Williams in Statesville that the suspect should be passing his location shortly. They planned to alternate surveillance to avoid detection.

Kevin got back into his truck and tried again to call Carmen. He had tried to call her before leaving his house, but the call went straight to voicemail. No answer. Damn. Her phone never had a signal when she was at that barn.

Kevin slammed the heel of his right hand hard against the steering wheel, pulled out of the parking lot, and waited for the traffic light to change so he could head north. Dunlap dropped in line behind a Buick LeSabre that was following Kevin's truck. He put a little more distance between himself and Kevin as they went north on I-77, but never lost sight of the black Silverado.

CHAPTER 19

JAMES AND JAKE pulled into the parking area in front of The Cook Shack and saw only one car parked in the lot. "They're not here," Jake said. "Got any more ideas?"

"No," James said as he leaned his head on the steering wheel out of sheer frustration.

Jake didn't know what to do either. They were at a dead end. Jake finally broke the silence, "Do you think I should call Marci and see if she's heard anything?"

"Sure, might as well. We haven't done much good, have we?"

"I wouldn't say that. We've found Joanie's Jetta and Debbie's Honda, didn't we?" Jake said.

"I guess so. Go ahead and see if you can get in touch with Marci."

Jake dialed her number. "Hi Marci, have you found Gail's car yet?" he asked.

"Not yet. Where are you?"

"James thought there might be a chance the ladies had gone to The Cook Shack in Union Grove. He and Gail have been here many times, but it's a dead end. We're hoping you had some good news."

"Nothing definite, but I do have something interesting to tell you."

"What's that?"

"We think Kevin Seacrest has been mixed up in this thing from the get-go," Marci said. "Sid and I went to see Mr. Seacrest this morning and he wouldn't even let us through his door. He left his house within minutes of our visit and is now headed north on I-77. We have a tail on him as we speak."

"What made you suspicious of Kevin?"

"We learned from the Depew, New York Police Department that Kevin Seacrest had been married before. His first wife's body was found in some woods near an abandoned winery in upstate New York. She had been strangled. I don't know if this info means anything or not pertaining to the missing women, but he's our only lead at the moment."

"I know Kevin's a rough character, but it's still hard to believe he'd have any reason to harm the ladies in the Wednesday Night Club," Jake said.

"Right now, we don't know the extent of his involvement, so we just have him under surveillance. I just talked to the Highway Patrol. Two troopers in unmarked vehicles are watching his every move. He's not going anywhere without our knowing it."

"What should James and I do?"

"Just sit tight. Sid's back at the annex and I'm headed your way," Marci said.

"We'll wait right here then," Jake assured her.

"See you in about twenty minutes," Marci said.

"What did she say, Jake?"

"What?'

"What did Marci say on the phone, just now?"

"Oh. She said for us to wait here. She's on her way and will meet us ASAP."

"Did they find Gail's car?" James asked.

"No, they haven't found her car yet, but what would you say if I told you, they think Kevin has something to do with the women's disappearance?"

James sat up straighter in his seat as Jake continued, "He was married once before when he was in New York and his first wife was murdered."

"You've got to be kidding," James said. "He was incredibly rude when I called, but I never thought he was involved."

"They don't know anything yet for certain, except Kevin broke and ran after Marci and Sid questioned him. He's on I-77 right now, headed this way. There are two Highway Patrol officers watching his every move."

"Do you think we should go back to the interstate and watch for him?" James asked.

"Marci said to wait here and I think that's what we should do. She'll be here shortly. Let's just wait, okay?"

"Okay, but I don't have to like it. Do I?"

"No, I don't guess you do," Jake agreed.

Marci headed north on I-77 at seventy-five miles per hour. Marci was glad to see James' SUV still parked where Jake said they would be.

Jake was waiting beside the door of the Navigator when Marci rolled the cruiser to a stop. "Hi! Looks like you made good time," he said as she got out of the Crown Vic. *I don't ever remember seeing a Navy blazer and tan slacks looking so good*, he thought.

"I'm glad you waited for me," Marci said. "Maybe we can put our heads together and figure out something." She glanced toward the Navigator, "Is he okay?"

"He's having a hard time right now, but I think he'll be alright. He just wants to find his wife and get things back to normal."

"I don't blame him. I hope we can find them soon."

James opened the door of the Navigator and nodded at Marci. "Any more news?" he asked.

"We're working on it," she assured him. "We'll find them, James, we'll find them."

Trying to lighten the mood, Marci suggested, "Let's go in and see Myles and Pal and get a bite to eat. It's a little early for lunch, but I'm hungry."

Jake was hungry, too. The doughnuts he'd eaten at the Sheriff's Department were history as far as his stomach was concerned.

"What about Kevin Seacrest?" James asked.

Marci answered, "The NC Highway Patrol will call me as soon as he turns off the interstate. There's really nothing we can do right now, but wait."

"I thought I heard somebody out here," Myles Ireland said from the open door of The Cook Shack. "Good morning, Marci. Y'all come in and have some breakfast. Pal still has the coffee on and she can scramble some eggs in a jiffy."

"It's a little late for breakfast, but a couple of those hot dogs of yours would sure hit the spot," Marci said.

Myles, a retired Iredell County deputy sheriff, had known Marci for years. Marci had trained under him as a rookie and still picked his brain occasionally for sage advice. Since their retirement, Myles and his wife, Pal, performed their own brand of western music at concerts throughout the area. Every Saturday, they opened the doors of The Cook Shack for musicians who wanted to join them in a pickin' session.

"What are you doing up here this time of day, James?" Myles asked. "We're not picking this morning. This ain't Saturday."

"I know it isn't, Myles. Let them two tell you all about it. I don't think I have the energy."

Myles looked at Marci with a puzzled brow. "What's going on Marci?"

She proceeded to fill him in on everything they knew thus far.

"What can I do to help?" Myles asked. "I know every nook and cranny in this end of the county. I know the boys in Yadkin and Wilkes County, too. Just let me know what I can do."

"Thanks, I appreciate it," Marci said.

Myles turned to James and said, "I'm sure sorry about your wife and her friends who are missin'. Keep your chin up, Buddy! They haven't been gone long and from what I'm hearing from Marci, everything that can be done is being done."

"I know," James said, "and thanks, but it's just hard to sit by and do nothing."

"Well, right now, let's go inside and see what Pal can throw together for you folks to eat." Myles opened the door for them, "Pal, we've got company," he called loudly.

Pal entered the restaurant area from their private quarters and smiled at the sight of Marci and James. Jake was introduced as they made their way into the quaint interior of The Cook Shack. Jake was astounded at the impressive collection of album covers, photographs, calendars, and memorabilia that filled every square inch of the walls. The place was like a hall of fame for country music legends. The atmosphere was homey and comfortable. Jake felt welcomed immediately.

James and Myles slid into one side of a small booth and Marci took the other side leaving Jake the seat next to her. As Jake slid in beside Marci, he realized this was the closest he had been to a woman in two years. Jake felt Marci's thigh rubbing against his in the cramped booth. She never made an attempt to move her leg and Jake made no attempt to move his. He looked around the interior of The Cook Shack at all the memorabilia, trying to get his mind off Marci's thigh next to his—it didn't work.

"What would you like?" asked Pal, looking at Jake. His mind was racing, thinking of Kitt and Marci. What would Kitt think about him sitting next to this beautiful woman? Would she be upset with him or happy that he might be finally interested in someone else?

"Tell your friend here, I'm talking to him. I think he's in some other world," Pal said to James with a wide grin.

"Were you talking to me? I'm sorry! I was thinking of someone, I mean, something else!" Jake said, his face flushed.

"What would you like to eat?" Pal asked again.

"I don't know yet," Jake said, "go ahead and take Marci's order."

"Marci, what would you like?" Pal asked.

"How about two of your famous hot dogs with slaw, mustard, and chili, and a Diet Coke? I may have a piece of pie later."

"It's a little early for hot dogs, isn't it?" asked Pal.

"Not for me. I've been up since four o'clock this morning. I'm starved," Marci said with much enthusiasm.

I really like a woman with an appetite, Jake thought. *I like a lot about this woman! I hardly even know her, and yet, it seems like I do.*

After hearing Marci's order, Jake said, "I'll have the same."

The hot dogs tasted so good, Jake also ordered a hamburger. He hadn't had much of an appetite since Kitt died. What was it about Marci Meredith? He felt more alive than he had in years.

CHAPTER 20

A SMALL SHED with a tin roof came into sight as Debbie and Gail fled through the woods behind the barn. They were scared of their shadows and hurried past it hoping nothing sinister would jump out of it.

"I'm glad they didn't put us in that little shed; I have claustrophobia," Debbie said as they gave it a wide berth.

"I suppose we should be thankful for that," Gail agreed.

Both women thought Yancey would expect them to head toward the main road, so Gail and Debbie decided to flee the opposite direction, and eventually get back to the road and find help.

They wove their way through the tangles of honeysuckle vines, blackberry briars, and brush. For the moment, they concentrated on putting as much distance as possible between themselves and Carmen and Yancey. After slashing their way through the woods for over an hour, they finally saw a narrow lane ahead of them. It was no more than a graveled path and didn't look well traveled.

"Whew! Let's sit down for just a minute. I've got to catch my breath," Gail said as she sat down heavily on the trunk of a fallen tree.

"What'll we do now?" Debbie asked.

"I think we should follow this road and see where it takes us," Gail said. "Maybe we'll find some help."

"I don't think we have much of a choice, do we?" Debbie acknowledged.

"No, I don't guess so. Which way should we go?" Gail asked.

"I don't know," said Debbie. "We're lost and I'm worried about Joanie. I don't know what to do."

"We can't just leave Joanie with those two crazy people." Gail said. "Did you hear the way Carmen was yelling and cussing?"

"Yes, and that scared me," Debbie said while still trying to catch her breath. "I've never seen anybody change like that. I guess she and Kevin deserve each other. How do you think Yancey figures in to all of this?"

"I have no idea," Gail said.

Debbie looked at Gail. "I think Carmen's just using him to get what she wants. I really believe she's planning to extort money from your husband, Gail."

"Extort money from James?" Gail asked incredulously.

"Yes and possibly Ed Mitchell, too," Debbie added. "Why else would she bring us to this deserted place? I think she and Kevin are planning to run away together."

"What about you, Debbie?"

"I think she just wants rid of me."

"You can't be serious. Neither Carmen nor Kevin would do something like that. Would they?" Gail said.

"There's a lot you don't know about Kevin Seacrest."

"What do you mean?"

"Kevin was married before," Debbie blurted out.

"What?"

"He was married to a girl in New York before I knew him. Her body was discovered near a deserted winery about five miles from their house. The police questioned Kevin but never charged him because he had an alibi conveniently provided by one of his drinking buddies." Debbie looked down at her lap and said quietly, "I didn't want to believe he'd had something to do with his first wife's murder, but when I asked him about it, he got so angry."

"Why didn't you ever tell us about this?"

"I didn't want you to think less of me. I've tried to make my marriage work, but I've become more and more afraid of Kevin and his violent temper. I decided I was going to quit the Wednesday Night Club because I just can't stand to be around Carmen anymore."

"We had no idea," Gail said, completely bewildered.

"You don't have a clue what it was like having to ride with her last night."

"I'm so sorry, Debbie. If I had known, you could have ridden with me."

"I know, I just didn't want to say anything, but now, I don't care who knows."

"Joanie and I are your friends, Debbie. You know that, don't you?"

"I know, but to tell you the truth, I'm really scared. What if Kevin and Carmen are planning to kill me after they get the money from your husbands?"

"You're kidding me! Do you really think Kevin is capable of that?"

"You don't know him."

"Good God, Debbie."

"I thought of mentioning it, but—" A look of horror suddenly swept over Debbie's face. "Oh Lord." Debbie said. "I just thought of something else."

"What could be worse?" asked Gail.

"Kevin's wife's body was found near an abandoned winery. Do you think it's a coincidence that Carmen brought us to this abandoned winery?"

"We have to get help," Gail said. "Let's get moving."

They chose to head right on the narrow lane. After following it through the woods for what seemed like a mile or more, Debbie asked, "What's that awful smell?"

"I don't know! I've never smelled anything like it before. It's sickening!"

"It smells like something's dead," Debbie declared.

"Look!" Gail cried. "What is that?"

"Where?"

"Up there, beside the road?"

"I'm not quite sure," Debbie said.

As they got a little closer, Gail said, "It looks like it might be a deer carcass."

They neared the carcass with great apprehension while they pinched their noses shut with their thumbs and forefingers. Debbie exclaimed, "This is definitely where that awful smell is coming from!"

"You're right!" agreed Gail.

"Don't go any closer!" Debbie almost screamed. "It's human!"

"What?"

"It's human, I tell you. Look over there beside the road. That's a woman's head!"

Gail approached the decapitated head and saw strands of sand-colored hair mingled with dried leaves and twigs. Seeing two lifeless eyes staring at nothing suddenly made her sick to her stomach.

"Oh, my God!" Gail said, as she fell on her knees retching in the grass beside the road. She remained quiet after the first wave of nausea passed, then raised her head, looked at Debbie, and then retched again. Gail cried, "I wonder who she is. What could she have done to deserve a fate such as this?"

"I don't know," Debbie said. "What are we going to do now? We have to get help!"

Debbie helped Gail to her feet. "We've got to get out of here!"

"And go where?" Gail asked tearfully. "We don't even know

where we are. We're lost!"

"We'll just follow this road."

"What if the murderer lives up this road, Debbie? Then, what will we do?"

"I don't know," Debbie replied. "I just don't know."

"What if this is some of Yancey's doings? What if he murdered this woman?" Gail said.

"Oh God, and he's back there with Joanie," Debbie cried. "We've got to go back with or without help! We just have to. She's our best friend."

"We can't help this poor woman now. Let's try to find our way back to the barn," Gail suggested.

Debbie said worriedly, "It seems like we've been doing nothing but going around in circles. How will we find our way?"

Gail turned and looked down the lane from where they had just come. "I think if we cut back across to our left through the woods again, we won't have to back-track this winding road. That should save time and take us back toward the barn."

"I hope you're right," Debbie said. "Let's get going."

CHAPTER 21

THE POSTED speed limit on I-77 north of Statesville was seventy miles per hour. The last thing Kevin needed today was to be stopped by a highway patrolman, so he set his cruise control at seventy-three. "Damn!" Kevin muttered. He wished he had paid more attention when Carmen had taken him to the barn. *All I remember is that the place is somewhere off Highway 421. Damn! I wish I could remember.*

Kevin took the 421 exit and headed west. Everything looked so different in the daylight. He glanced in his rearview mirror and noticed a late-model Crown Victoria a couple of cars back. *Hell! That looks like the same car that's been back there since I got on the interstate at Troutman. I haven't been speeding. Why is he following me?*

A sobering realization hit Kevin. They know! The sons-of-bitches know! Kevin wracked his brain trying to figure out how they knew about what had happened in New York. *The cops must have pressured Ronnie into giving me up. There goes my alibi.* Kevin continued west on the new multi-lane highway. *That woman detective from the Iredell County Sheriff's Department mentioned something about my first wife. That must be it! Well, by God, they'll never catch me and pin Angela's murder on me. That detective was too smart for her own good.*

Kevin was sweating. His mind raced as he gripped the steering wheel so tightly that his knuckles turned white.

That bitch knew! She was jerking my chain! Damn! They won't take me back to New York. I didn't really mean to strangle her. She just went limp while my hands were around her throat. It was an accident! Kevin continued justifying his wife's death in his mind. His speed was up to ninety miles per hour and he could see the Crown Vic still behind him. *That bastard is following me! By God, I've got to lose him.*

Just ahead was the exit ramp for Red White and Blue Road. Kevin made a split-second decision to take it and try to outrun the trooper. He peeled off Highway 421 still doing over eighty miles an hour and slammed into the rear of a tractor-trailer truck that was stopped at the end of the ramp.

Kevin had no time to react.

His truck plowed under the rig's trailer, sheering the top off his Silverado.

Highway Patrol Officer, Sam Williams, who had been following Kevin since exit 45, reached the horrific scene almost immediately. After seeing what had happened, the shaken officer radioed for fire and rescue and sat in his cruiser stunned at the recent turn of events. He'd seen Kevin's truck take the exit ramp much too fast. There was nothing he could have done.

The trooper got out of his vehicle and approached the accident scene. The driver of the semi was visibly shaken and kept repeating over and over as he climbed down from the truck's cab, "What was wrong with that guy? He must have been doing seventy-five or eighty on the ramp."

"He was. He was running from the law," the trooper assured him. "When a suspect starts to run, the chase usually ends with tragic results. Cleaning up the accident site is going to take a while. Why don't you sit in the cruiser and I'll be with you as soon as I can."

"Thanks," the trucker said as he walked toward Trooper William's vehicle.

The trooper peered into the demolished Silverado underneath the trailer and shook his head in disbelief. The roof of the cab was torn jaggedly from the frame of the truck. Williams could see the partially severed head of Kevin Seacrest resting on the crumpled steering wheel. It all happened so fast. Williams then went back to the cruiser, popped the trunk, took out some flares, walked back to the intersection and began placing them around the scene. Help arrived almost immediately from the other troopers who had been involved in the surveillance.

Officer Dunlap was the first to arrive. "What on earth happened, Sam?"

"All of a sudden, he rabbited and I could barely keep him in sight. The next thing I knew, he went barreling down the ramp and slammed into the back of the semi."

"Man, I hate it when something like this happens. Better call Detective Meredith and let her know. She thought he was involved in the disappearance of those four women from Mooresville."

CHAPTER 22

MARCI'S RADIO squawked to life, disrupting the comfortable chatter that had accompanied their meal. "I'll get this outside, if you'll excuse me," she said apologetically. Jake slid out of the booth and couldn't help noticing the subtle hint of Dove Soap as she brushed past him.

The others carried on with desultory conversation while Marci took the call. She soon returned with an indiscernible look on her face.

"What's wrong?" James asked.

"What's happened, Marci?" Jake echoed. "Is everything alright?"

"That was Patrolman Williams. Kevin Seacrest is dead."

"What?" James asked. "What happened?"

"He was killed when he crashed his truck into the back of a semi waiting at a stop sign."

"Oh, my God!" Pal said as she sat down heavily. "That's terrible."

"What will we do now?" James wondered aloud.

"He was our only good lead. About all we can do now is concentrate on the surrounding area where the accident occurred. It's not good, but it's all we have," Marci said. "I feel partly responsible for his death," she added sadly.

"You can't feel responsible every time a suspect 'rabbits'," Myles said speaking from experience, but it did little to console her.

"I know that, but it still bothers me."

"Where exactly did it happen?" asked Myles.

"At the bottom of the Red White and Blue Road exit ramp on 421."

"I know that area! Maybe the women are near there," Myles said excitedly. "Do you want me to go with you? It's not Iredell County, but I know just about all the guys in the Wilkes County Sheriff's Department. Maybe I can help."

"Sure," Marci said. "Wilkes County is definitely out of my jurisdiction, but from this moment on, I'm officially 'off duty'. I can go anywhere I want to go when I'm not working."

Jake paid Pal for the meals and thanked her for opening her kitchen for them. The day had gone to hell quickly. One minute he was sitting beside a beautiful woman sharing a wonderful meal and the next minute he was at a loss for what to do or say.

"What are we going to do now?" Jake asked Marci.

"We're heading to Wilkes County. Follow me," she said to James as she boarded her cruiser.

Myles said quickly, "All right if I ride with James, Marci? We haven't seen each other in a while."

"Sure thing Myles," Marci agreed. "Jake, you can ride with me and we'll lead the way."

"Do you think it's okay for me to ride in an official sheriff's car?" Jake asked.

"It'll be fine, get in."

Jake couldn't believe his luck. *I'll have to remember to thank Myles*, he thought. Jake had never ridden in a law enforcement vehicle before. A twelve-gauge shotgun was fastened vertically in a rack between them.

"I didn't know detectives carried shotguns," Jake said as they fastened their seat belts.

"This one does," Marci replied as a grin spread across her face.

She adjusted the Glock-40 in its holster on her right side as they pulled onto 901 and headed back toward I-77.

They rode in silence for a few minutes until Jake asked, "Why do you feel Kevin's death is your fault?"

"Sid and I really rattled his cage this morning. If we hadn't gone over there and put a little pressure on him, he might still be alive."

"What Kevin did was his responsibility, not yours. Running was his decision," Jake reassured her.

"I know that, but it still bothers me. Mr. Seacrest must have killed his wife in New York. The case is still open and he's been a suspect from the get-go. One of his drinking buddies conveniently provided him an alibi."

"It's hard to believe he killed someone."

"After seeing what has taken place today, I think there's a good possibility he did," Marci said. "Excuse me while I radio Sid with the news." She picked up her mike and related the facts to Sid. Jake could hear him on the other end.

"Damn. I knew it! I knew it!" Sid said excitedly. "I just knew that SOB was in this thing up to his Yankee neck. I'll call the boys in Depew and let 'em know what's happened. I still think he killed his first wife."

"So do I," Marci agreed. "Call the folks in Depew and we'll keep you posted on what's happening up here."

Will do," Sid said.

"And Sid, write in today's report that I'm officially off duty for the rest of the day."

"Repeat that, Marci."

"I'm off duty! We're headed to Wilkes County and I have no jurisdiction there."

"I'll radio ahead and let them know you are on the way and tell them what's going on," Sid said.

Marci signed off and pondered aloud, "Since they found the body of Kevin's first wife near a winery, I wonder if he was heading to one of the Yadkin Valley wineries?"

"Wouldn't hurt to look," Jake said.

"There are some really good ones along the 421 corridor that offer tours and wine tastings," Marci added.

"Is that right?" Jake said.

"North Carolina's Yadkin Valley is being slated as the next Napa Valley. Shelton Vineyards, at exit 93 on I-77 near Dobson, is one of the finest in the south."

"Do you like wine?" Jake asked.

"On the right occasion, I think it's a necessity."

"What's the right occasion?"

"Oh, maybe a candlelit dinner for two..."

"You know, I was thinking the very same thing," Jake agreed.

Marci turned slightly toward him. "Is that an invitation?" she asked smiling.

"Well, I suppose it is," he said. "It's been a long time since I've been out on a date."

"Me too," Marci said. "I might take you up on that some day."

"Well, what about Saturday night," Jake asked as he studied her profile. Her nose was small and delicate and her full lips were accentuated only by a touch of lip gloss. Marci didn't wear much make-up—just a hint of color on her cheeks. The effect was stunning.

Marci kept her eyes on the road for a moment and then turned to face Jake with misty eyes. "I'd like that, Jake McLeod. You've got yourself a date."

CHAPTER 23

AFTER SCRAMBLING over the locked gate, Joanie ran down the road a few yards and then doubled back. She, too, thought hiding in the woods would be the only way she could avoid being caught by Yancey. Joanie knew she couldn't outrun him, but she was fairly sure she could out think him.

"You stupid son-of-a-bitch!" yelled Carmen. "You let her get away. If you'd worn your damn shoes, this wouldn't have happened."

"I'm sorry, Carmen, but shoes hurt my feet."

"Come on. There's no telling where she is by now. She's got a head start on us, so see if you can pick up her trail."

"She couldn't have gotten far. I'll find her tracks and we'll get her back."

"Can you track her down without screwing up, Yancey?"

"I'll try, but quit yellin' at me. I can't stand having a woman yellin' at me. It drives me crazy." Yancey climbed over the gate and limped down the gravel road searching for tracks that would tell him which direction Joanie had taken. "It looks like she left the road and is headin' toward the back of the barn. Don't worry, we'll find her," Yancey assured Carmen.

CHAPTER 24

GAIL AND DEBBIE made their way through dense woods filled with hickory, red oak, maple, loblolly pine, and a few native cedars. After trudging along for more than an hour, the woods finally thinned and they could see a small pasture, enclosed by a barbed wire fence not far ahead. They helped each other through the fence as contented cows grazed lazily nearby.

"It sure is easier walking across a pasture than it is trying to find our way through the woods," Debbie said.

But by the time they had crossed the pasture and crawled out through the fence, Debbie was lagging behind.

"Okay Debbie, here are some more woods. Please try to keep up," Gail said looking at her watch. "We've been gone a long time." Dodging the low-hanging limbs, spider webs, and briars made the ordeal even more arduous. Not only were they tired; they were hungry, too. Nonetheless, they kept going.

Meanwhile, Joanie had circled behind the barn hoping to throw Carmen and Yancey off her trail and had run as fast as she could through the deep woods. She was determined to put as much distance between the barn and herself as possible. She stumbled across a small stream, trudged up hill after hill, and finally rested for a while beneath the cover of a cedar tree. Hours had passed since her escape and she wondered if Gail and Debbie had found help.

"Shhh! I thought I heard somebody coming through the woods," Gail whispered to Debbie. And with the most authoritative voice she could muster, she demanded, "Who's there? Stop or I'll shoot! I mean it!"

"Who in the hell do think you're gonna shoot when you ain't even got a gun?"

"Joanie?"

"Yeah, it's me!" Joanie said as she emerged from a thicket where she had been hiding. "I thought I heard someone coming through the woods, so I hid as quick as I could. I thought, at first, you were Carmen and Yancey, but boy am I glad it was y'all."

"Thank God, you're safe Joanie! We were coming back for you. We didn't know what else to do. You told us to get help, but we got lost and couldn't find anybody," Gail said as she hugged Joanie.

"How did you get out?" asked Debbie.

"Y'all shoulda been there," Joanie said. "I was just getting ready to climb out of the window when Carmen came barging through the door. She scared me so bad I fell off the sacks. She was mad as hell 'cause y'all were gone. The hussy even kicked me...can you believe that? Well, then Yancey came barrelin' through the door and stepped right into that pile of broken glass. He started hollerin' and hopping up and down. Carmen was a cussin' him right and left and not paying any attention to me, so I pushed her sorry ass right smack-dab into him. They both ended up in a heap on the floor," Joanie continued. I then just put my ass in gear and flew right past them and out the door."

"How did you know where to go?" asked Debbie.

"I didn't. I just took off, climbed over the gate, and was heading for the road when I realized that's just what they'd expect me to do, so I circled around to the back of the barn looking for you two."

Gail said, "We stayed away from the road too, thinking that was where Yancey would look for us. When we couldn't find anyone to help us, we knew we had to come back for you—we were so afraid that Carmen would hurt you."

"Where have you been all this time?" Joanie asked. Y'all look terrible."

"I don't really know where we've been, but we found a road—" Gail began.

"We found a dead body, too!" Debbie interrupted.

"What?" Joanie asked and looked at Debbie with disbelief.

"We found a body alongside a wagon road. It looked like it hadn't been there too long. It was a woman, but her head was lying across the road from the rest of her body. It was awful!"

"Where was this?" asked Joanie.

"We don't know exactly, but when we found her body, we knew we had to come back and find you," Gail said.

"Well, we're together now. That's what counts. There's definitely strength in numbers and we outnumber them three to two. Let's try and make it back to the main highway before it gets any later and maybe we can find someone to help us. Agreed?"

"Agreed!"

"The surest bet is to go back toward the barn. We can find our way back to the highway from there. That is, if we can get back to it without running into King Kong or Devil Woman." Joanie said.

Slowly and quietly the three women headed back toward the barn, keeping an eye out for Carmen and Yancey.

"Maybe we'd better make a wide circle. Let's go this way," Joanie said as she led them through some thick underbrush, "maybe they'll miss us."

In the distance, the sound of breaking limbs and a woman's voice raised in anger reached the women.

"Be quiet! That sounds like Carmen. She sounds madder'n hell. Hide under these branches," Joanie said, pointing to a large white pine.

They crawled for cover beneath the low-hanging limbs of the lush pine.

"Let's just wait here a little bit and see if they come this way," Joanie whispered. "If they don't find us, we can get back to the barn and fix their little red wagons for good."

"What do you mean by that?" Gail asked in a hushed tone.

"We'll clean their clocks, or kick their asses," said Joanie.

"I'm all for that!" Debbie agreed, amused at Joanie's unique way of getting her point across.

"Me, too!" Gail said.

"Here they come. Be really quiet," Joanie warned. The three women, prostrate on the ground, never made a sound.

Carmen and Yancey tromped through the woods scattering dried leaves and stepping on fallen twigs. They came within fifteen yards of the women. Carmen continued to yell at Yancey until they were finally out of sight and could be heard no more.

"Did you hear Carmen? She was givin' Yancey up-and-down-the-country about letting us escape. What was she sayin' about a ransom?" Joanie asked.

"I told you Gail!" said Debbie.

"Told her what?" Joanie asked.

"I told Gail I thought Carmen was going to demand money from Ed and James to get you two back. That's why they're holding us here."

"Well, what about you?"

"I think Carmen and Kevin are in on this together. I was telling Gail that he is a suspect in the murder investigation of his former wife. She was found buried near a winery not far from where we lived in New York."

"When did all this happen?" asked Joanie.

"A few years ago; it was before I even knew Kevin."

"Damn! You know where that leaves you, don't you Debbie?"

asked Joanie.

"I do and that's why I'm so scared. I think they could be planning to kill me and leave my body here."

"Well, what about Yancey? How does he fit into all of this mess?"

"I think Carmen is just using him and his property to pull off this kidnapping so she and Kevin can run away with the ransom money. When Carmen gets the money in her greedy hands, I bet Yancey will be history."

"Somebody shoulda kicked Kevin's ass a long time ago for the way he's treated you," Joanie said.

"Right now, I'm just scared. They can have each other, if that's what they want, but I don't like what they're doing to us to make that happen."

"We don't either," Gail concurred.

"That's right and I don't think we're goin' to let them get away with it either, are we girls?" said Joanie.

"Well, what'll we do?" Debbie asked.

Joanie said, "While they're lookin' for us in the woods, let's head back toward the barn and find the road we came in on yesterday. Surely to God, we can find somebody to help us." The women crawled from under the pine branches, got to their feet, and silently followed Joanie through the thick woods.

"Shhhh!" Joanie said. "There's an old house up ahead. Come take a look!" Debbie and Gail crept up to peer through the branches of a white pine tree. Parting the branches for a better view, Joanie said, "Maybe that's where Carmen and Yancey get on with the program."

"We're not going near it, are we?" asked Gail.

"Why, hell yeah. Why not?" asked Joanie. "Let's get a little closer and see if there's anyone home. If it's ol' Yancey's place, let's have a look around since he and Carmen are still out looking for us."

"You're serious, aren't you?" asked Gail.

"Serious as a heart attack," Joanie replied.

Gail and Debbie looked at each other apprehensively, but followed anyway.

When they got to the clearing, Joanie said, "Stay back here and watch out for anything that moves. Whistle if you see or hear anything."

Joanie snuck up to the front porch of the cabin and saw the ramshackle look of neglect she would have expected from Yancey. I think it's 'ol Yancey's house alright," she whispered to Gail and Debbie. She went up the rickety steps and looked through the only window in the front of the house. "Y'all come on. I don't see anybody."

Gail and Debbie crossed the small open area, climbed the rickety steps onto the porch, and joined Joanie.

"It has to be his place, but I'll be damned if I can see Carmen ever settin' foot in there," Joanie said. "I guess if you're desperate enough, you'll do just about anything."

"The Carmen we're dealing with now is not the same Carmen we used to know," Gail said as she cautiously knocked on the door and then pushed it open.

"Go on in! Hell, he ain't home—he's out lookin' for us, remember," Joanie said.

Gail looked from one side of the room to the other before deciding to take another step into the unknown. Joanie and Debbie were right behind her as she stepped inside. "How do people live like this?" Gail asked.

"This place is filthy," Debbie said.

Overturned trash bags spilled old newspapers, beer cans, and fast-food wrappers on the floor. A worn-out brown sofa sat in the middle of the room, oozing stuffing from its cushions. A broken recliner sat in front of an old black-and-white television set with rabbit ears. Gail tentatively made her way to the small kitchen located in the rear of the house.

"You'll have to see this to believe it," she called out from the kitchen.

Dirty dishes filled the sink where water dripped methodically from a rusty faucet. A frying pan with dried egg stuck to the bottom sat on top of the range. Egg shells lay in a pile on the cabinet next to the stove. *At least someone had breakfast*, Gail thought. A small, square, wooden table sat in the middle of the kitchen with two straight-back chairs pushed against it. Two half-filled coffee cups remained on the table along with toasted bread crumbs and pieces of dried egg.

"I've seen enough of this kitchen to almost make me swear off eatin' for a while," Joanie declared. She walked across the creaky floor to a closed door and slowly opened it as if she were afraid she would disturb trace evidence in a crime scene. "Oh my Lord! Would you look at that," she said. A huge, king-size bed sat against the far wall completely devoid of linens. Its bare mattress was covered with stains.

The three women were speechless. They envisioned Carmen and Yancey lying entangled on the filthy bed. "Well! I guess that removes any doubts about ol' Carmen, don't it?" Joanie said.

"Yes, it does," Gail said sadly.

Debbie said, "I really need to use the bathroom, but after seeing the rest of the house, I think I'll pass and use the bushes again."

Joanie laughed and said, "Me, too! I kinda dread lookin' in the bathroom." Joanie stuck her head through the door and began to gag. "Believe me, you don't want to go in there."

The odor that emanated from the bedroom and adjoining bathroom was too much for Gail and Debbie, too. They all left the room holding their noses and reunited in the kitchen.

They decided to search the cabinets for some food that would be safe to eat. "I don't know if I can eat anything I found in this place," Gail said, "but I'm starved."

Debbie said, "Here're five cans of pork and beans that look pretty good and something called Vienna Sausage. I don't know if I want to try anything else from this place, but the canned stuff should be safe enough."

"I don't see any bottled water or anything else to drink and I'm about to perish," said Gail.

Joanie laughed. "You really don't think Yancey would have bottled water do you?"

"Well, Carmen might have had some. I can't believe she'd eat or drink anything from this filthy place."

"I'll be damned if I'll drink water from that rusty faucet," Joanie said.

"Here's a jar of something that looks like water," Debbie said, holding up a quart jar filled with a clear liquid. "Want a drink of this?" Debbie said as she handed the jar to Gail.

Joanie took the jar and said, "Wait a minute!" She unscrewed the lid, put her nose down to it, and took a good whiff. "Whew!" she said as she grimaced and drew her head back from the mouth of the jar, "That stuff's potent enough to kill a horse. One slug would be enough to make me swear off drinking for the rest of my life."

"What is it?" Debbie asked.

"Moonshine," Joanie said. "Don't light any matches around it or you'll blow this place up."

"Is it really dangerous or are you just making that up?" asked Gail.

"Not only is it highly flammable, but a lot of folks have been poisoned from drinking bad moonshine."

"Flammable, huh?" Gail said smiling.

"Are you thinking, what I'm thinking?" asked Joanie.

"I sure am!"

CHAPTER 25

THE WOMEN took the jar of moonshine, the cans of beans and Vienna sausages, and a box of kitchen matches they found in a drawer near the stove and returned to the safety of the dense woods to devour their meager meal.

"It's a good thing these cans have those new pop-open tops on 'em," Joanie said.

"I would have never thought a can of pork and beans could taste so good," Gail said.

Debbie added, "Even these canned sausages aren't too bad. Have either of you ever tried them before?"

"You mean to tell me you never ate Vienna sausages before?"

"I've never even heard of them."

"I just don't understand you Yankees at all. It's a damn wonder how y'all ever won the war," Joanie said.

Gail and Debbie laughed.

"Hell, I'm serious," Joanie said. "Us country folks ate Vienna sausages all the time. Them things, sardines, a couple packs of crackers, and pork and beans were staples when we went fishin' or were campin' out."

Each of the women felt much better after eating. Now, they could focus on their mission.

They made their way through the woods and circled around to the front of the barn. Joanie led the way as they each climbed over the locked gate and found the door standing open and the lock hanging loose on the hasp. The women entered the barn and saw the blood on the dirt floor.

"We got ol' Yancey, didn't we?" Gail said.

"We sure did! I wish you two coulda seen him hoppin' around like he was playing hopscotch. Poor ol' Yancey, dumb as an ox. The hussy's usin' him, just like she was usin' us," Joanie said.

"Her using days are over," vowed Debbie.

"That goes the same for me, too," Gail said.

"Well, I guess that makes it unanimous," said Joanie.

They went back outside the barn and Joanie said, "Let's look around here and see if we can find something to use that would let the pair of them crazies know we mean business."

"It was really thoughtful of Yancey to leave us some food and matches. You never know when you may want to build a little fire," Gail said.

"Yes it was thoughtful of him," agreed Joanie. "And a little fire would be nice, wouldn't it?"

"Did you see that old shed behind the barn?" Gail asked Joanie.

"What old shed?"

"There's an old shed near the back of the barn, but we have no idea what's in it."

Joanie exclaimed, "When I found out that both of you were gone, I started running as fast as I could and didn't pay attention to anything except gettin' my fat ass out of there."

Gail said, "The building is just a few yards into the woods. It's hard to see it through all the low-hanging limbs. We saw it when we fled from the barn."

"Well, let's go see if there is anything in there that'll help us," Joanie said.

The trio headed behind the barn in search of the shed. "There it is," Debbie whispered. "Do you see it?"

"Yeah, I see it now," Joanie said. "I wouldn't have even noticed it was there, with all those bushes around it if you hadn't shown it to me. Let's see if we can get inside."

"There's a lock on the door," Debbie said. "How are we going to get in?"

"Just stand back and watch this old country girl at work," Joanie teased as she picked up a stout limb. She pried the board loose that held the rusty padlock in just a couple attempts. "See, there ain't nothin' to it," Joanie said with pride. Slowly, she pulled the door open and peered inside. "Hot damn!" Joanie muttered as she entered the shed.

Gail and Debbie followed Joanie inside the small building. Joanie exclaimed, "Look at all of that danged moonshine the codger has stashed. It must be worth a small fortune."

The women counted forty-four cases, each containing twelve quart jars of moonshine. Gail said, "Why don't we take some of these jars back to the barn and pour it along the walls and on the sacks?"

"What on earth do you have in mind Gail?" Joanie teased.

"You know good and well what I have in mind, Joanie Mitchell."

The three determined women each carried a case of Yancey's "shine" to the barn.

"Setting a fire should not only bring someone out here to investigate, but it will also show Carmen and Yancey that they can't get away with kidnapping us," Gail said defiantly.

"Right on, sister," Joanie agreed.

They re-entered the barn where they were held captive the night before. Their makeshift beds were untouched and the sugar sacks were still stacked beneath the broken window.

"Alright, we got a job to do, ladies," Joanie said. "Let's get with it. Somebody needs to watch for Carmen and Yancey while we get this show on the road."

"I will," Gail volunteered.

Joanie and Debbie poured the moonshine on the cardboard boxes and sacks of sugar while Gail stood her post.

"Be sure to splash some on the walls," Gail said from the door.

When the last jar was emptied, Joanie threw it crashing against one of the unopened doors. "That oughta do it," she said with satisfaction. "Now hand me some of those matches, Debbie, and let me do the honors. No, on second thought, let's all share in the glory."

All three women grabbed some matches, lit them, and then flung them into the puddles of moonshine. A blazing inferno burst forth with a loud whooooosh!

"Look at that," Joanie said. "Hell, soon you'll be able to see the smoke for miles."

They gave each other high-fives as they admired their handiwork.

"Come on girls, we'd better get outta here. Carmen and Yancey'll come back when they see this fire," Joanie said.

They hurried out the door and saw Gail's Maxima still parked where she had left it the day before. The keys were gone. So were Gail's and Joanie's purses. They might still be without transportation, but they were alive and they were together.

CHAPTER 26

"COME ON," Carmen said. "They have to be near here somewhere. We've got to find them. By God, this time, we'll tie
them up. Dammit. I can't believe they escaped!"

Yancey followed Carmen through the woods. *I ain't seen a
woman so determined in all my life. Well, maybe that one I had in the
barn a few months back. She was awful determined and she wouldn't listen
to a word I said. I told her more than one time that I wadn't goin' to hurt
her, but she kept yellin' at me. I told her to stop, but she wouldn't listen.
Carmen's gonna' stop yellin' at me, too, one way or another.*

Carmen yelled at Yancey, "Bring your lazy ass here and keep
up! You're the reason they got away, you big ape."

*She better quit yellin' at me. I had a good life, making me some 'shine
to sell. Nobody ever bothered me. How did I ever get mixed up with her
anyway?*

"Come on, keep up!" Carmen yelled.

She'd better quit that damn yellin', Yancey repeated to himself.

"We can catch them if you'd quit dragging your ass."

Yancey caught up with Carmen and spun her around. "Quit
yellin' at me, dammit! I ain't your damn slave." Yancey looked at her

like he never had before.

Carmen had always had him wrapped around her finger. Now she saw him in a different light. But she still needed Yancey. "I'm sorry," she began, "it's just that everything is going wrong. I heard sirens out on the main road earlier this morning and that scared me. I don't know what they were about. As long as they weren't coming here, we'll be alright."

Yancey was quiet and listened.

"We haven't even gotten in touch with Gail's and Joanie's husbands yet," she said. "I don't want to keep them here forever. I just want their damn money. You can do whatever you want to do with Debbie after I get what I want. Ed Mitchell still loves Joanie enough to cough up some dough. When I get the cash, I'm leaving."

"Where're you goin'?"

"Somewhere they will never find me. I can't tell you Yancey. I know you've been a friend ever since I met you. We've made a good team, but I have to be on my own after this."

"You think the sheriff'll find me back here? I like my place and I don't want to lose it because of what we're doing."

"You're not going to lose anything, Yancey. I told you I would look out for you, didn't I? You'll get your share of the money, too."

"Yeah, you told me that."

She gave him a quick peck on the cheek to mollify him and said, "Now come on and let's go get them before it's too late."

Carmen and Yancey pushed their way haphazardly through the woods with little hope of finding the three women. Nothing had gone according to Carmen's plan and she was angry at herself and with Yancey. *I wish I knew how to get rid of Yancey, too. He's getting on my nerves and I don't like the way he's been lookin' at me.*

Yancey took the lead with Carmen following closely behind him as they plowed through the brush. She was cursing all the way. Yancey let a low-lying limb loose too quickly and it slashed across Carmen's right cheek, bringing stinging tears to her eyes. "Damn!"

yelled Carmen. "Look at what you did," she said as she brought her hand down from the side of her face. She showed Yancey the blood on her finger tips and added, "That hurt like hell!"

"I'm sorry. I thought you were back a ways."

"That's your problem, Yancey, you started thinking again. I told you that I would do the thinking."

She'd better quit talking to me like that. I'll leave her up there with that other woman that wouldn't shut up!

Carmen and Yancey continued their journey through the woods with her cursing and stomping all the way.

"What's that noise? Listen," Carmen ordered.

"Sounds like a siren out on the main road. Wait! It sounds like it turned off and is headed for the barn."

"Look!" Carmen shouted. "Is that smoke coming from the barn? You better go see what's happening. I'll keep looking for the girls."

Carmen had no intention of hunting the other women. Yancey's mood had changed in the last few hours and now that the barn was on fire she thought it would be wise to put as much distance between herself and Yancey as possible.

Carmen knew now there would be no ransom money. It was time to cut her losses.

CHAPTER 27

"WE'D BETTER get going or they'll catch us standing here watching Yancey's barn burn down," Gail said.

"Oh! My God! Here comes Yancey up the road right now. What're we going to do?" Debbie asked.

"Hurry, I don't think the bastard saw us," Joanie said. "Let's get behind the barn and take off through the woods again. I don't see how the devil got back on the road so fast. He must have seen the smoke from the fire."

The three tired women ran behind the burning building and crawled through the fence to put distance between them and Yancey. The last place they wanted to be was back in the woods, but they had no other choice.

CHAPTER 28

Y ANCEY WATCHED the flames engulf his barn. Tears welled up in his eyes as he saw his way of life going up in smoke. *How can this be happnin'? My still was hid in that barn. How am I goin' to make a livin' now?* He heard explosion after explosion as his still and the jars of moonshine he had locked in the storage room burst into flames.

Yancey felt an overwhelming hatred for Carmen; he hated the way she talked to him; he hated her greed; he hated the fact that because of her he was losing everything. His life would never be the same and it was all Carmen Romano's fault.

When I find Carmen, she's gonna' wish she'd never been born.

Yancey raced through the woods to his house, gathered a few of his meager belongings and stuffed them into an old fertilizer sack. He found a pair of brogans, put them on, and looked through the cabinet for some food to tide him over while he was on the run.

"Damn," Yancey said. "Somebody's done stole my beans, my Viennas, and my good jar of shine." He went to the bedroom, reached under the bed, and drew out a 30-30 Winchester rifle. He grabbed his hunting knife and a box of cartridges from the nightstand drawer and left without closing the door.

Yancey knew his way around this part of the county. He fig-ured he could find a place to hole up for a while. First he was going to find that Carmen.

CHAPTER 29

ARCI EXITED I-77 and headed the cruiser west on Highway 421. The beautiful rolling hills of Wilkes County rose before them. The gentle slopes and valleys took on the appearance of a patchwork quilt with swatches of scarlet and gold material sewn together with golden thread. "Beautiful, isn't it?" she asked.

Jake was caught off guard by the question. He'd been absorbing the beauty of the countryside and had not realized that Marci was watching him.

"Yes. Yes it is. I'd like to come back here when this is all over and take some photographs. It's only a matter of time before housing developments and shopping centers take over every inch of farmland. I feel an obligation to preserve the beauty of our world before it all disappears," Jake said. "That's why I became an artist."

Marci said, "I understand Jake." Marci waited for Jake to finish his story.

"You know what was so strange about my first encounter with Kitt?"

"No, please tell me."

"Kitt understood too. I met her while she was sketching an old grain elevator in Kansas. She was afraid it would be torn down and that nobody would care. The grain elevator had 'Pearl' written across the top of it. That's all, just 'Pearl' in big block letters."

"What's so strange about that?" asked Marci.

"Pearl, Kansas is where my father was born in 1913. The grain elevator was all that's left of the entire town and Kitt was saving it on paper," Jake said choking back tears.

"That's beautiful. Having something like that to remember her by must give you great comfort."

"I was a lucky man to have had Kitt for a wife. She felt the same way about preserving the beauty of the land as I do."

"I know you must have really loved her."

"I still do. Kitt was a special woman."

"I know how hard it is to lose someone you love. I've been struggling for over two years myself," Marci said. "Sometimes I'm barely conscious of what's going on around me."

"That sounds just like the way I have been."

"I've heard you're not painting very much these days."

"You're right, I'm not. Kitt had become my inspiration and when I lost her, I lost my desire to paint. For the past two years, I haven't been doing much of anything except existing. I've felt a tremendous amount of guilt. I was fifteen years older than Kitt—I should have died first. I just don't understand. It doesn't seem fair."

"What was she like?"

"She was talented, beautiful, and witty. Kitt was one of the most caring individuals I ever met."

"I would like to have known her. I'm sure we could have been good friends. It must have been very difficult for you."

"It was hard. I'd waited forty years to find her only to have her taken away just a few months after we married. We had talked about having children, but then she became so ill with cancer and we never had the opportunity. All of our time was spent keeping her alive."

"I can't imagine you, a father," Marci said smiling.

Jake laughed. "It was hard for me to imagine too, especially at my age, but we wanted at least two children. How about you and Mark? Do you have any children?"

"No, but like you and Kitt, we discussed it a lot. We just never had time. Mark was taken from me so suddenly. I've been in shock for two years," Marci said. "You know Jake, I haven't been alone with another man since Mark died, except for business, like with another detective or Sid, but that doesn't count. I've never really shared my feelings with anyone because I didn't think anyone could understand. But you've experienced a loss like mine and know what I've been feeling. I haven't even been interested in dating. I guess I wanted to be true to Mark's memory."

"How long do we have to be in mourning, Marci? How long do you think they would want us to be miserable? I know Kitt loved me very much. She loved me so much, she made me promise I'd get married again when the right woman came along, can you believe that?"

"She really must have been one special woman," Marci said. "And she was a lucky girl."

"Mark was a lucky man," Jake countered.

Marci and Jake continued to talk about their spouses and it seemed to be a release for each of them to be able to share their pent-up feelings with someone who understood.

Jake turned and faced Marci and said, "It's been tough the last two years. I haven't even looked at another woman since Kitt died, until—" He reached over and placed his hand on top of hers. "Until now. You're quite something to look at Marci."

"You know, you don't look too bad for an old man," Marci laughed.

"What! I'm only forty-nine. I have a lot of living left to do."

"I know. I'm just having a little fun. I'm thirty-six, no spring chicken myself."

"You're the prettiest spring chicken I've ever seen."

CHAPTER 30

BEFORE LONG, Red White and Blue Road loomed ahead and fire and rescue vehicles crowded the roadway. A semi was at the end of the ramp with Kevin's Silverado pinned underneath its trailer. Marci slowed as they neared the wreck site. All other traffic had been re-routed to the next exit. "I know he was an SOB, but no one should have to die like that," Marci said.

She maneuvered past the wreckage and the emergency vehicles on the ramp and parked on the shoulder. Marci and Jake got out of her Crown Vic and walked back to the wreck site to talk with Trooper Williams. Marci asked him a few questions while examining the mangled wreckage. She looked back toward Jake to say something, stopped in mid-sentence, and pointed over his shoulder toward thick, black smoke billowing on the horizon to the northwest.

"Maybe we should check that out," Marci said. "The Wilkes County Sheriff's Department and the Highway Patrol have this under control. That fire may not be related to the missing women, but at this stage of the game, I don't think we should leave any stone unturned."

The highway patrolman on duty had allowed Myles and James

to follow Marci's cruiser past the accident site. They had pulled in behind her cruiser to see what their next move would be.

Marci told the trooper they were going to check out the origin of the billowing smoke and then walked over to James' SUV. "See that smoke? I'm gonna call it in," she told them. "It looks more serious than a brush pile burning. It may be nothing, but I think we should check it out."

"What are the odds of that smoke having anything to do with the missing women?" asked James.

"It might not have anything at all to do with it, but this is where Kevin Seacrest turned off. I'm not a big believer in coincidences and seeing that much smoke piques my interest just enough to check it out. The fire truck will have to stay at this accident scene until the wreckage is cleared away, so I'm going to call Wilkes County and see if they have a truck en route to the fire."

"Okay," said James. "We'll wait and see what you find out."

Marci got through to the Wilkes County Sheriff's Department and spoke with the deputy in charge. She explained about the missing women and told him about the thick smoke. "I appreciate you allowing me to continue the case in your territory. These are friends of mine and I'd like to see it to the end if I could. Yes, thanks. Let us know if Iredell County can ever help you down our way. Okay, thanks again," she said as she hung up the phone.

She looked at Jake and said with a satisfied grin, "I don't even have to be off duty. Chief Deputy Phil West welcomed my help and knowledge of the case. He also knows and has great respect for Myles. West said a fire truck has already been dispatched to the fire and if we wait here, we can follow it to the scene. The chief deputy is coming, too."

A little later, a red fire truck, its siren wailing and emergency lights flashing, roared by them without slowing down. Marci pulled in behind it and turned her flashers on. James followed closely behind her. The fire engine twisted and turned down the country road with surprising speed.

Suddenly the truck came to an abrupt halt while the flashers continued their pulsing strobes. Without warning, the fire truck began backing up, emitting a high-pitched beep, beep, beep.

Marci and James backed up to let the fire truck turn around, but it just kept backing up and finally stopped in front of the Crown Vic. One of the volunteer firemen climbed down from the cab, ran to the cruiser, and motioned for Marci to lower her window.

The young fireman apologized, "Did y'all see a dirt road that went off to the left? I'm afraid I missed it. I just got off the radio with the dispatcher who told me the fire was on a tiny dirt road that went through some woods to the left. The dispatcher said it's real easy to miss. If y'all could just back up a little more and give me some room to turn this thing around, we'll be on our way again."

"Okay, you lead the way," Marci said.

Marci and James backed up their vehicles so the fireman could turn the fire truck around. They followed the truck once again as it headed up the curvy road into the sparsely populated hills. The fireman made a right turn onto the graveled road he'd missed earlier and drove for a while through beautiful countryside that was dotted with livestock grazing peacefully, totally unaware of any emergency.

Marci saw the brake lights blink on the truck. She slowed the cruiser and followed as the truck turned down a tiny graveled road that was almost hidden by trees. The lane was barely wide enough for the fire truck to maneuver, but the fireman doggedly kept pushing ahead.

"I hope this road doesn't get any smaller or that truck won't have enough room," Marci said.

The fireman drove the truck down the narrow lane through thick woods and brush until it finally stopped in front of a metal gate.

A barn, engulfed in flames, stood a few yards past the metal gate. Huge orange flames were shooting skyward intermingled with the thick black smoke.

Jake noticed the fire truck was no longer moving forward and asked Marci, "Why's that truck stopped?"

"I don't know, but I'll find out." Marci said as she jumped out of the cruiser. "What's the hold up?" she asked the fireman.

"There's a locked gate across the road. We can't go any farther."

"Push it down with your truck, for God's sake. The truck is a heck of a lot bigger than that gate."

"I guess you're right," said the volunteer fireman.

He revved the motor, put the truck in gear, and lunged forward through the gate with a crashing sound that could be heard over the roar of the fire.

Marci pulled through the gate behind the truck and parked out of the way. With the fire truck no longer obstructing their view, Jake and Marci immediately saw Gail's Maxima parked to left of the destroyed gate.

James pulled up behind Marci's cruiser, got out of his Navigator, and ran to Gail's Maxima. "What's going on? What's Gail's car doing here?"

"We don't know," Marci said, "but we're on the right track."

The Maxima was locked. Marci, James, Myles, and Jake circled the car and peered inside. The car was empty and James almost collapsed with relief after realizing Gail's body wasn't in the car. His relief was short-lived. "What if they're in that barn?"

"James, we have to hope they're not," Jake said. He watched the flames lick the sky. "We have to pray they're not."

Marci spoke to one of the firemen, "There are four missing women and that Maxima over there belongs to one of them. They might be inside that barn."

"Good gosh a'mighty," he said. "I sure hope not! But we can't get any closer until we get this blaze under control. Tell everyone to stay back."

Firemen began pulling hoses from the rack and connecting

them to the pump on the side of the truck. In a matter of minutes, they were spraying water on the fire.

"We're going to run out of water before we even get started," said one.

"I think it's past savin' anyway. It went up awful fast, I wonder what was in it?" asked another.

"There's a lot of moonshining still going on around this area. I'm guessing a little 'white lightin' accelerated the fire."

"Let's do what we can, but I think we might as well let 'er burn. It's as good as gone, anyway."

"I agree," said one of the older firemen. "Just let 'er burn. You know, I'd forgot about this old place. I didn't realize anyone lived here anymore."

"We'd better hose down the surrounding area to keep the fire from spreading."

"I'll radio for backup and ask 'em to bring another tanker truck, too."

The firemen worked to contain the fire while Marci considered the significance of finding Gail's car in such an unexpected place. They were getting closer.

Another fire truck arrived and firemen spilled from the vehicle and began unloading their hoses.

Wilkes County's Chief Deputy, Phil West, arrived right behind the second fire truck and parked behind Marci's cruiser. Jake watched him climb out of his vehicle. The creases in Deputy West's uniform pants were pressed to a knife-sharp edge. His jacket fit him like it was tailor-made. *This man has been around a while and has years of knowledge stored beneath that official hat,* Jake thought.

Myles ambled over to the deputy.

Marci said to Jake and James, "Let's just sit tight for a minute and see what the chief deputy has to say. He and Myles are good friends."

"Hey Phil," Myles greeted the deputy. "Those are some friends of mine over there behind the Maxima. The car belongs to a missing Iredell County woman and that's her husband," he said pointing to James.

"What the heck's going on, Myles?" asked the deputy.

"There are actually four missing women. We don't have much to go on, but we were really shocked to find one of their cars in this barn lot."

Chief Deputy Phil West, nearing retirement, told Myles wearily, "I talked to a Detective Meredith earlier over the phone. I'd like to talk to the husband of the woman who owns the Maxima. By the way, how are you enjoying your retirement?"

"I highly recommend it, Phil," Myles said as they were walking toward Marci. "I sleep a lot later now, that's for sure."

"Is that Detective Meredith over there?" Phil asked. "

"Sure is."

Deputy West tipped his hat and said, "Congratulations on your new job, Detective Meredith."

"Thanks," Marci said. "Let me introduce you to James Caldwell and Jake McLeod."

"I understand you folks have some loved ones missing. You want to fill me in with what you know?"

"Marci, why don't you give him the details?" James said. "I just don't think I can go through it again."

"Sure," Marci said. With that, she took the Chief Deputy aside and talked to him in a voice so low that James and Jake couldn't hear what was being said. Once in a while she looked Jake's way and gave him a hint of a smile when their eyes met but then quickly turned back to Deputy West and continued their conversation. Marci thanked West and returned to James and Jake.

"What did he say?" asked James.

"He promised his department wouldn't quit searching until all the women were found."

"They have to be around here somewhere or Gail's car wouldn't be here," James said with excessive frustration.

"We're gonna find them, just hang in there," Marci said with encouragement.

Marci and Jake walked past the first fire truck and looked around the corner of the burning barn. Marci exclaimed, "Jake, look!"

"My God, that's Carmen's Lexus. It looks like they were all here last night." Jake rushed back to his friend and yelled, "James, come here!"

When James saw Carmen's Lexus he gasped. "What's going on here? Why in the world would both their cars be at a place like this, out in the middle of nowhere?"

"We're getting closer," Marci said.

CHAPTER 31

CARMEN WAS not waiting for Yancey. She pushed her way through the woods, stumbling across small, winding streams, and lost a shoe in the process. *Dammit! Dammit! I hope to hell all three of them are lost in the woods. It'd serve them right. They should have stayed in the barn. Now, how am I going get away from this godforsaken place?* Carmen, disgusted and exasperated with herself and her situation, sat down on the trunk of a fallen white oak. She listened briefly for any sound of Yancey coming her way and then put her face in her hands and sobbed.

After a bit, Carmen wiped her face with the sleeve of her jacket, rose from the log with new determination, and once again plodded steadily through the woods. Having only one shoe slowed her down. Her plan now was getting as far as she could from Yancey.

Hell, with my looks I should be able to get a ride with some hick goin' down the road. I'll promise him anything just like I did Yancey, but I'll be damned if I'm gonna ever have sex again with another half-crazy, moonshining bastard.

Eventually Carmen reached a narrow, rutted lane. She took off her remaining shoe and limped along the lane's winding curves, following it up the mountainside.

A foul stench emanated from somewhere up ahead. She stopped walking for a moment and tried to identify the odor. She continued up the road, still holding her remaining shoe in her hand.

"Oh my God!" screamed Carmen when she saw the human head with bits of flesh and long, stringy, brown hair still attached. She stood frozen with fear for only a moment and then ran for the safety of the thick woods, fell to her knees, and vomited. *God, I've got to get back on that road. I've got to get out of here.*

Carmen skirted the decapitated head and saw the remainder of the body lying across the road. Tattered clothes clung to the torso. Parts of the corpse were exposed through random holes in the material. One of the arms seemed to be missing. Carmen made her way past the remains and quickened her steps.

I wonder what that poor person did to deserve such an end. I'm gonna get as far away from this place as I can.

A mile or so further, she rounded another bend in the road. A small house sat a hundred yards ahead.

Carmen threw her shoe to the side of the road and approached the house. The windows were closed, the blinds drawn. She saw no fresh tire tracks. She climbed the leaf-covered steps to the porch and tried to look through the glass on the front door. "Anybody home?" she asked as she knocked several times. Carmen walked around the house hoping to find a back door, but found none—only a rear window too high for her to reach. Satisfied the house was empty, she returned to the front, broke the glass on the door, reached in and unlocked it.

She entered the darkened house and looked to her right at the neat, but deserted kitchen. She saw no trash, no unwashed dishes, and no dirty countertops. To her left was a small sitting area with a couch and two comfortable chairs. An Early American hooked rug lay between them, giving the area a cozy, warm feeling. Everything in the house looked as if it had come from a yard sale or secondhand store. All the furniture was definitely old and worn, but clean and serviceable. There was no television, but an old radio sat on an end table next to the couch. A cold, empty fireplace was the focal point of the living room. The rustic, pine mantel that rested over the native-stone fireplace held two photos of young children. One framed photo showed a red-haired boy with ears that stuck out from his head. Freckles covered his grinning face. He looked to be about ten years old and very happy. A somewhat younger girl with pretty blond ringlets peered out from the other frame. Bright blue eyes, crooked teeth and a wide smile convinced Carmen that these children must be brother and sister—probably the owner's grandchildren.

Carmen stared at the pictures a little while longer. They reminded her of what her life could have been like if fate had been kinder. She fought back more tears as she made her way down a narrow hallway that led to a tiny bathroom and two small bedrooms. One of the bedrooms was furnished with a double bed, a night stand, and a worn dresser. The other bedroom featured twin beds, perhaps for the grandchildren when they visited. The beds in both rooms had colorful bedspreads. All in all, everything looked neat and well-kept. Carmen opened the dresser drawers hoping to find some clothes that would fit her. There were a few tops and several pairs of shorts, but not much else.

She had better luck in the first bedroom. There were two pairs of jeans that were close to her size. She held them up to herself. She rummaged through another drawer and found three long sleeve shirts, folded neatly. They were size medium and her spirits lifted considerably. Carmen rifled through the closet and found a jacket that matched the jeans and she took it off the hanger with smug satisfaction. She then removed her torn jacket and flung it across the neatly made bed. What made Carmen the happiest was finding a pair of shoes in the closet that fit her almost perfectly. She smiled as she slipped them on. She carried the clothes into the sitting room and draped them over the back of the sofa.

Carmen returned to the kitchen and searched for some food that she could take with her. She was pleased to find some canned beans, soup, corn, applesauce and crackers. Carmen found a can opener in a cabinet drawer and opened the beans and applesauce. It wasn't exactly what she had in mind for a meal, but it was better than nothing.

Carmen heard someone coming up the dirt lane and looked through the broken window of the front door. *Oh, my God! Oh no! It's Yancey. I gotta' get out of here.* She ran to the rear of the house only to remember there was no back door. That's when panic set in. *Oh God, what am I gonna do?*

She ran to the bathroom, locked the door and tried to lift the window, but the window frame had been painted over so many times, it was stuck. Fear like Carmen had never known in her life suddenly overcame her.

CHAPTER 32

Yancey knew about a small weekend cabin not too far from his place; he'd been there several times and no one had ever been there. He figured the owners kept necessities in the house to save them the trouble of having to pack everything each time they visited. If so, he'd get some more food there before heading to the high country.

Yancey thought he heard a woman scream. He stopped where he was, stood still, and listened intently for a moment. Hearing nothing more, he hurried on. Yancey continued thinking about how he had lost everything—*burned to the ground! Destroyed! All because of that damn woman. If I ever come across her again, she's gonna wish she'd never met me!*

The sickening, recognizable odor of death stopped Yancey in his tracks. *Damn, I thought I buried her deep enough. Them dad-gummed coyotes must have dug her up, sure as the world.*

Yancey saw the woman's head lying beside the road. He picked it up and tossed it as if it were a softball, to the other side of the road toward the remainder of the body. He stared at the body for a moment, trying to remember what the woman had looked like alive, and then lumbered down the road toward the vacant house.

The first thing Yancey noticed as he climbed onto the porch was the broken glass on the front door. He quietly and slowly opened the door a little at a time. Yancey peered inside, looked around the living room, and noticed that some clothes had been thrown haphazardly across the back of the sofa. He then turned his attention to his right and saw two open cans of food on the kitchen table. A spoon handle protruded from the top of a can of applesauce.

"Anybody home?" he called out, as he pushed the door open wider and edged inside. As Yancey entered the house, he paused briefly, taking in the surroundings. Then without making a sound, he stealthily moved about the house carefully checking each of the bedrooms only to find the bathroom door locked. Locks never slowed Yancey down very much.

"Anybody home?" he asked again, this time to the closed bathroom door. Carmen was too frightened to utter a sound. "I know somebody's in there, I can hear you breathin'. Why don't you open the door, I ain't gonna hurt you."

In desperation, Carmen took the heavy lid off the commode tank and crashed it through the bathroom window.

Yancey heard the breaking glass through the door and realized that whoever had been hiding in the bathroom was now escaping. Without pause, he kicked the door in with a splintering crash.

The bathroom door crashed against the tub and Yancey saw Carmen through the broken window as she fled into the woods behind the house. "Come back here!" yelled Yancey. Furious, he ran to the front door and raced around to the back of the house where Carmen was desperately trying to escape through the woods.

Carmen prayed, "Oh God, help me! Don't let him catch me! He'll kill me! He's crazy! He's gonna kill me! I know he is!"

Running through the underbrush, limbs slashing her tear-streaked face, Carmen had never felt such raw fear in her life. Her heart was about to explode. She was crying desperately, praying, pushing branches out of her way, and stumbling through the woods not even knowing or caring where she was going.

"Come back here!" Yancey yelled. "You stop runnin' now and maybe I won't make you suffer too much." Yancey was gaining on her with every step.

Carmen sped up and zigzagged through the trees as fast as she possibly could. Blinding tears caused her to trip on an exposed root of an ancient, white oak and she fell head-first to the ground. Yancey quickly fell on top of her sprawled form, knocking the breath from her lungs.

Carmen lay there unable to breathe. Yancey rolled her onto her back so that he could look into her eyes. He wanted to see the fear.

"It's pay back time, Carmen," he said in a calm voice that frightened her even more. "You've tried to make me think I was nothin' but a worthless, stupid fool."

She could smell his foul breath. "No!" shrieked Carmen. "You know I care about you Yancey."

"Hell, I know better'n that," Yancey said, peering into the depths of her eyes, "I saw you with that damn Kevin. I knew then that you was just usin' me, I wadn't no dummy!" he said as voice grew louder.

"Didn't you like makin' love to me, Yancey? Didn't you enjoy that?" Carmen asked desperately trying to diffuse his anger.

"Yeah, I liked that. You wuz pretty good, too, but you run your mouth too damn much. I kept tellin' you to shut up, but you wouldn't listen!"

"Please don't hurt me Yancey. I'll do anything," Carmen pled with him as she laced her arms around his neck. Yancey's body odor almost made Carmen retch, but she pressed on. "Let's you and me go away together, Yancey, okay?" Carmen coaxed with all the sweetness she could muster. "We can go right now."

"They burned my barn down and I lost all my moonshine because of you. I ain't got nothin' left and you ain't goin' nowhere, but straight to hell," Yancey said as he drove his knife deep beneath her ribcage. Carmen's eyes opened wide in disbelief as she stared at Yancey. Her voice left her open mouth as if she had forgotten what she was going to say. Her arms grew limp and dropped from around Yancey Darwood's neck for the last time.

Yancey continued talking to the almost lifeless body of Carmen Romano as if she were listening to every word he was saying. "That other woman wouldn't listen when I told her to shut up either. Did you see her body beside the road? You did, didn't you? Well, they'll never find yours, Carmen. I told you to shut up more'n one time. You just wouldn't listen. You just kept on naggin' and naggin' and puttin' me down."

Yancey gave the knife a sudden twist and shoved it in deeper. Carmen's breathing was ragged as blood ran like a river down her body and onto Yancey's overalls. A bright red froth gathered in the corner of her mouth and slowly trickled down the sides of her face and chin. Yancey was oblivious. His voice became louder and louder as if he wanted Carmen to hear what he had to say without her interrupting him. "I told you, didn't, I? I told you to shut up but you wouldn't listen! I told you, dammit, I told you!"

Carmen's eyes stared blankly, seeing nothing as she grew limp in Yancey's grasp.

He suddenly rolled off of her and looked at his blood-soaked overalls. "Damn," he said as if he had just realized what he had done. Yancey dragged Carmen's lifeless body through the leaves and dirt and rolled her into a small ditch where she landed on her back so that her lifeless eyes stared at the October sky. He hurriedly threw branches and dried leaves over her. He kicked some loose dirt over her still form with his big brogans and threw more leaves on top of her for good measure. Yancey ran back toward the deserted house to clean the blood from his clothes.

He raced through the house and into the bathroom where he ran some cold water into the small sink. Yancey found a cloth hanging on the nearby rack and scrubbed furiously, but the blood would not come out of his clothes. He rummaged through the closet looking for something to wear. He had to get rid of his blood-stained overalls. In one of the dressers, he found a pair of jeans about five sizes too small and swore to himself.

Yancey remembered the sack he had brought with him. From it, he retrieved his only other pair of overalls and laid them over the back of a kitchen chair. He then quickly stripped off the blood-stained ones, threw them on the kitchen floor and donned his other pair.

Yancey picked up his sack and his rifle and left without closing the door.

CHAPTER 33

WHILE JAMES, Myles, and Deputy West discussed the discovery of Carmen's Lexus, Marci said to Jake, "There had to be another way out of this building." She and Jake slowly made their way to the back of the barn and discovered a wooden fence blocking their way. Marci placed her left foot on the bottom board of the fence and deftly swung her right leg over the top one and dropped easily to the ground on the other side.

"Come on," Marci said. Jake quickly climbed over the fence and joined her. "I don't see a door, but there's a small window up there," she said, pointing to it several feet above their heads. Orange flames were shooting from the broken window. Examining the ground below, Marci said, "Someone climbed out of that window. Look here at these tracks!"

"Yeah, I see them!" Jake said. "It looks like they could have been made by women's shoes."

"The tracks lead to the woods. We'd better get Chief Deputy West and some of his boys to take a look. Stay here and don't let anybody walk through these tracks," Marci said with authority.

"Yes sir, ma'am," Jake said with a grin as she walked off in search of the Wilkes deputies.

Phil West and two deputies followed Marci to the back of the barn where Jake stood guard over the tracks. Scorching flames now shot from the window, so they edged toward the woods where the heat was not as intense. The tracks led to a barbed wire fence and beyond it toward the heart of the woods.

"What do you think?" Marci asked Phil West.

West said, "First, we have two vehicles that belong to two of the four missing women from Mooresville. Second, we have some footprints of women's shoes leading into the woods. And third, we have a barn on fire that could have been set intentionally. I would say this means something's gone down, alright."

"What do you suggest we do?" asked Marci.

"Well, let's start by taking a look at these tracks," he said as he knelt down to examine them. "It looks like more than one person has been through here." The deputy rose and pulled his hat down tighter on his forehead. "I'll get our man and his bloodhounds on it. We'll see where these tracks lead. It'll be late evening before long and I don't think old Bert works his dogs much after dark."

James and Myles had followed Chief Deputy West around the barn and caught the last of the conversation. "I heard you found some tracks," James said.

"Yeah, they did," Deputy West said. "We're getting some bloodhounds on the trail as soon as Bert gets here."

"Bert?"

"Yeah, Bert's the man with the dogs. He lives outside of North Wilkesboro on Highway 18. It'll take him a good thirty minutes to get here, but as soon as he does, we'll get started. We don't have much daylight left this time of year," the deputy observed, "but we'll do the best we can."

"Okay," James said.

About forty minutes later, a 1953 Ford pickup truck rattled into the barn lot. Some of its original red paint was visible through the rust in numerous places. A wizened, old man, in a pair of Pointer Brand overalls, unfolded himself from the cab and sauntered their way.

"Bert Conroy," he said, extending his wrinkled hand. "I hear you need a little trackin' done." The old man launched a stream of tobacco juice that hit the dusty ground with a splat.

"That's right," Deputy West said.

Bert chewed some more and spat another stream of juice that hit the left rear fender of his pickup as he walked to the rear of the truck. Jake wondered if the tobacco spit had anything to do with all the rust. He watched as the brown juice ran slowly down the fender and dripped harmlessly to the ground. Conroy opened the tailgate and three, long-eared, wrinkled dogs bounded out of their cages and began barking enthusiastically.

Bert snapped leashes onto the barking dogs, took their leashes in hand, and asked, "Ya'll got anything for my dogs to pick up a scent from?"

James said, "I have a jacket of Gail's in the Navigator." He brought the jacket to Bert.

"This'll do," said the dog handler.

The dogs sniffed the jacket and started barking even more eagerly and immediately headed to the woods behind the barn.

"They have her scent and they won't quit 'til they find her or it gets too dark for us to see where we're goin'. If ya'll are comin' with me, you'd better hurry, we don't have much light left. These dogs don't wait for nobody."

Everyone fell in behind Bert and followed him and the dogs through the fence and into the woods at a rapid pace. The man and his dogs plowed through the thick woods until they could no longer see well enough to continue the search. "We gotta quit for the night. I can't go on any more," Bert told Deputy West. "The dogs could keep on trailing, but I'm getting old and can't keep up in the dark. Besides that, somebody's likely to get hurt running through these woods in the dark."

James asked Bert, "Do you really have to quit? Can't we take your dogs and keep going?"

"I'm sorry, mister. They'll only track for me."

James quickly turned to the Chief Deputy, "What're we going to do now? We can't just go home."

Before Phil West could answer, Bert promised, "I'll come back at first light and we can pick it up again. I've got to feed the dogs and let 'em get some rest, too." Everyone began making their way through the dark woods and back down the hills to the site of the burning barn.

Conroy continued, "I'm really sorry we didn't have more time. It looks like them women have been running around in circles. We can find them alright, but it's gonna take a little time and some daylight."

"I understand," Chief Deputy West told Bert as he was loading the last dog in the truck. "Let's get an early start, okay?"

"Sure, I'll be here at dawn," Bert said as he laid down his final stream of brown juice across some fallen leaves.

"Good enough," replied Chief Deputy West.

"God, I hate to leave without finding them," James said. "What will happen to them out in the woods over night? Gail probably hasn't camped out since she was a girl scout back in Ohio."

"I'm sure she'll be fine. She's not alone. Remember, there was more than one set of tracks," Jake said.

"I know that," James said, "but Gail's my wife and I can't just go home and leave her out here."

"Mr. Caldwell," Deputy West began, "I can't imagine how you must feel, but you heard Bert; he said he'll be here at first light. We'll get a fresh start in the morning."

Myles hitched a ride with one of the Wilkes deputies who lived near Clingman's Crossroads. He said goodbye and wished them luck as he climbed into the Wilkes County cruiser.

James said, "Jake, I think I'll stay here just in case they come back."

"You've been up since yesterday morning. You've got to get some rest," Jake said.

Deputy West walked over, "Mr. Caldwell, go home and get some rest. We have deputies here on site and there will be firemen here all night, too. Give me your cell number and I'll call you if there's any news. Why don't you drive up to Wilkesboro and spend the night at one of the motels. You need to get some rest if you plan on goin' with us in the morning."

"Gail's gonna be fine, James," Jake said. "It's like I said before, she not by herself."

"Okay," James reluctantly agreed. "I'll take the deputy's advice and get a room in Wilkesboro. I need some time by myself. Do you mind giving Jake a ride back to Mooresville, Marci?"

"No, I don't mind at all. Will you be alright, James?"

"I'll be fine," James said wearily as climbed aboard his Navigator. "We ought to call Ed Mitchell. Jake, can you take care of that?"

"Sure, I'll bet he's worried sick. So much has happened today, I forgot all about calling him. You get some rest, James, and we'll see you in the morning. Call me if your hear anything."

James cranked up the Navigator and headed toward Wilkesboro leaving Marci and Jake staring at each other.

"Do you think he'll be alright by himself?" asked Marci.

"I've known James and Gail for years. They're both devout Christians and I think James needs some time alone to talk with God. He'll be fine. He just has to work it out in his head as well as his heart."

"If you say so."

"I do." Jake said.

"Where can I take you, Mr. McLeod?" she asked as the last glow of the burning barn reflected in her eyes.

"Let's head home and come back early in the morning. But first, I should call Ed," Jake said.

"Why don't you do that while I turn this car around and we'll be on our way?"

Ed answered on the first ring. "What's going on? Why haven't you guys called? I haven't heard a word from Joanie. "

Jake told him about the burning barn, finding the cars, and the bloodhounds.

"No wonder you didn't call. I'm sorry if I sounded a little testy, but I've just been sitting here by the phone all day and you can imagine how it's been," Ed said

"I sure can," Jake agreed. "Why don't you come up here in the morning and help us?"

"You think it'll be okay?"

"Like I've always said, it's easier to get forgiveness than it is permission. Just come on up."

Jake gave Ed directions and hung up the phone just as Marci pulled up in the cruiser.

Jake slid in and buckled up. Marci retraced their route back to Highway 421 and headed the cruiser east.

Darkness had overtaken Wilkes County with authority as they headed toward I-77. Suddenly, Marci slowed the cruiser, pulled into a deserted road, and turned off the engine.

"Get out!" Marci ordered. Jake obeyed, having no idea what he had done to provoke such an authoritative tone in her usually sweet voice. "Walk down the road away from the lights."

"What's going on?" Jake asked as he turned around to face her.

"Just close your eyes and be quiet," Marci ordered. He did as he was told. And then, he felt her lips tenderly touch his as her arms encircled his neck. Her warm body molded into his and he could feel the softness of her ample breasts as she pressed against him. She kissed Jake hard and then whispered, "Mmmm, that's good. Now I can concentrate on driving back to Mooresville." She turned and headed toward the cruiser as if nothing had happened.

Jake caught his breath and said, "What in the hell was that all about?"

"The shotgun rack was between us in the cruiser and I felt like I couldn't wait any longer," she said as Jake caught up with her.

"I wouldn't have minded a little bit of warning," Jake said trying to catch his breath.

"Didn't you like it?"

"I liked it a lot."

Marci faced Jake and said, "I want you to know that I have not kissed a man in over two years and I wanted to remember what it was like." She kissed him again with purpose and turned once more and headed for the cruiser.

"Well, you might be able to concentrate on your damn driving now, but I'm not sure I'll be able concentrate on anything," Jake said.

Chapter 34

JOANIE, GAIL, and Debbie continued to run through the woods, hoping to avoid Yancey and Carmen. They were determined not to be caught again.

"It's no tellin' what that Carmen would do if she ever found the three of us again. She's bound to be as mad as an old wet hen," Joanie said. "I still can't believe she'd kidnap us and hold us for ransom. She must really be desperate, or off her rocker."

"Or both," Debbie added.

"Or both," Joanie agreed.

"Let's make a large circle and head back toward the barn. Maybe that way we can avoid them," Joanie suggested.

Gail said, "Maybe a neighbor saw the smoke and came to investigate."

"Does anybody know how to get back to the barn from here? It seems like we've been going in circles all afternoon," Gail said.

I sure don't," Debbie said and added, "and nobody is ever going to believe what has happened to us, are they?"

"By God, I'll make 'em believe it!" Joanie said. "Hell, what those two turkeys did was a felony. They kidnapped us and held us for ransom, for God's sake. They're not gettin' away with a damn thing. I'll see to that!"

"I'm starving!" Gail said. "It's been a long time since we ate those beans. We've been out here for hours and I'm afraid we're lost!"

"No, we're not lost, maybe turned around a little bit, but definitely not lost," Joanie said. "We heard some sirens earlier. I wish we'd hear 'em again so we could go in their direction."

"That would help. I wonder if they went to the little barn warming we had for Yancey?"

"More than likely," Joanie said, "but right now, let's just keep walkin'."

"God, I'm hungry Joanie," Debbie said.

"We all are, Debbie. Just hang in there."

As the women doggedly trudged on, Gail said, "Wait up Joanie. We can't even find the barn and we've been walking for hours. We're lost, aren't we?"

Joanie finally had to agree. "You might have a point there, Gail. The loop we made to get around Yancey must have been too big. I don't recognize any of these woods. I thought I could get us back to the barn. I'm sorry girls! Gail's right. I hate to admit it, but I think we're really lost now."

"Do you see anything that looks familiar?" Gail asked.

"I sure don't," said Debbie.

"Damn, damn, double damn, triple damn, crap!" Joanie swore. "We're all tired and it's getting dark. We've gotta decide what we're gonna do and do it pretty quick!"

"What if we follow the sun as it sets? That's bound to lead us somewhere," Debbie said. "We can't just keep going around in circles."

Gail said, "Follow me; I was a girl scout back in Ohio."

Joanie and Debbie laughed, but followed their friend.

Darkness settled over the countryside as the women picked their way carefully through the woods. "Hey, it looks a little lighter up ahead," Gail said.

Joanie ran ahead and stumbled into a leaf-filled ditch. She explored where she had landed slowly with her hands and could barely speak as she told the other women, "I think I found another body!"

"Oh no!" Gail and Debbie said simultaneously.

Joanie climbed from the ditch trembling, "Y'all look in there, I just can't."

"Are you sure, Joanie?" Gail asked.

"Can't we just take your word for it?" pleaded Debbie.

"Please take a look. It really scared the hell outta me and y'all are the ones with the dead body experience."

"Come on Debbie" Gail said apprehensively. "We can do this."

Gail and Debbie knelt down beside the ditch trembling. "I really don't want to do this," Debbie said.

"Neither do I," Gail agreed, "but we'll all feel much better if we find out she's mistaken."

Joanie watched as the two other women leaned over the shallow grave and carefully began brushing away the dried, brittle leaves and twisted limbs. "It is a woman's body Joanie, you were right," Gail said. "Can't we just leave her alone?"

"We'll have to tell the sheriff's department about the two bodies after we get out of this godforsaken mess," Joanie said.

"I guess you're right, but I wish you were doing this instead of me," Gail said.

"I wish I could, but when I landed in the bottom of the ditch and felt that body underneath me…it scared the livin' bejesus outta me. The whole situation makes my skin crawl, but part of me wants to see who it is," Joanie begged.

Debbie said, "Why don't you get over here and help us?"

"Please, I can do a lot of things, but this is just one thing I can't do," Joanie said.

Gail and Debbie tentatively brushed away the debris until the pallid face of Carmen Romano slowly appeared.

"It's her! It's Carmen!" Gail exclaimed, visibly shaken.

"I was afraid it might be," said Joanie.

"I was upset with Carmen, but I never wished her dead," Gail cried. "Oh God, what's happening to us? What's next! What are we going to do now?"

"I don't think there's anything we can do for Carmen," Joanie said as she helped the trembling Gail and Debbie out of the ditch. All three women embraced one another and cried.

"Who could have done this?" Debbie asked.

"Yancey must have. They were arguing something terrible. You know how Carmen can get. I guess he just couldn't take her mouth anymore," Joanie said.

"Look at you, Joanie! You're covered with blood!" Debbie cried out when she saw Joanie's clothes. Debbie and Gail hung onto each other as Joanie took dried leaves and tried in vain to clean the blood from her jacket and slacks.

"Alright, let's talk about this, girls. What do y'all think is the best thing to do now? Keep walking or spend the night with Carmen?"

"Spend the night with Carmen?" Gail asked.

"It doesn't seem right, leaving her here all night. Could we take her with us?" Debbie suggested.

"We can't do that, it would be disturbing a crime scene and it wouldn't help anything," Joanie said quietly, "and besides, I don't think we could carry her."

"I can't leave Carmen here like that. I just can't," Gail said.

"Okay. Let's all stay here with Carmen and wait for daylight, agreed?" said Joanie, taking charge again.

Unanimously, the women agreed and began making a communal bed to share by piling leaves and pine needles on the ground. "I think we need to say a prayer over Carmen before we try to sleep," Gail offered. "I'll do it if you want."

"That's awful nice, Gail. Let's stand beside her and hold hands while you pray," Joanie agreed.

Gail led them in a brief prayer. She thanked God for Carmen's life and prayed that He would receive her spirit and give her peace. Tears were flowing freely from each woman's eyes as the prayer ended.

"That was sweet, Gail," Joanie said wiping her eyes. "I think Carmen would have appreciated the prayer."

"She never confided in us about her faith, but I pray that God will rest her soul," Gail said. "Wonder why Carmen didn't say anything about losing her job until after she kidnapped us? We might have been able to help her. Carmen was a good friend when we started The Wednesday Night Club. I can't believe it came to this," Gail added sadly.

"She was a tortured soul at the last," Debbie added.

"Yes, she was," agreed Gail.

"Alright y'all, we need to try to get some rest," Joanie said. "I'm tired all the way up through next week. I'd give a hundred dollars for a bath right now."

Debbie said, "It's getting cold, I wish we could build a fire."

"I'd like one too, but we'd better not," cautioned Joanie. "We don't want to do anything that could help Yancey find us."

The women settled on their makeshift bed and nestled together to try and stay warm for the night.

The total darkness unnerved the women. They were used to living in urban areas where there were street lights, lights from passing automobiles, and lights from neighborhood homes to illuminate the darkness. They huddled closer. The rising of the morning sun would be a welcome sight.

To multiply their misery, a numbing cold settled among the trees and fell to the ground where they lay. The sounds of animals moving about in the night, kept them all on alert. The three friends lay together quietly, each engrossed in her own thoughts.

Joanie lay awake staring at the winking stars through the dark canopy of leaves that were still on the trees. *I wonder what Ed's doin'*

*about now. Probably watchin' that blamed old television set or readin'
one of his dad-gummed books. Damn, I wish I was with the old cuss right
now. I would make love to him at least three times and then snuggle up
to him and hold on. Damn, what kind of woman have I been?* Tears
leaked from Joanie's tired eyes and ran shamelessly down her cheeks.
What have I done with my life? Oh, God help me. She lay silently in the
cold, thinking about the changes she needed to make in her life.

*Look out, Ed Mitchell, I'm comin' home, if you'll have me. You'd
better get ready. Your ass is gonna be so tired from makin' love to me, you
ain't gonna be worth a damn!* The tears flowed until finally Joanie
pleaded in silence, *Oh Ed, I'm so sorry. Please be there. Please take me
back! Please forgive me!*

Joanie was not the only woman thinking about her situation.
Debbie lay snuggled against Gail, sharing the warmth of her body.
*I know it's over between Kevin and me, but I feel the best I've felt in
years. I wish I would have made the decision to leave him a long time
ago. I know there has to be someone who will love me. Kevin and Carmen
must have been in this thing together. He must love her. It's almost a
shame that Carmen's dead now and they'll never have a chance to be
together. When I get home and back to work, I just may invite Carson
over for dinner one night and see what happens.*

The leaves overhead in the late October night rustled in the
breeze and stirred Gail from her state of near slumber to being wide
awake. She felt Debbie nestled against her on one side and Joanie on
the other and found comfort in knowing her friends were close. *I
wonder what James is doing right now. I love you, James. I feel your
despair, but don't give up hope. I'm coming home soon. I love you—* Gail
drifted off to sleep, confident in her faith.

CHAPTER 35

TIRED AND confused, Yancey heard the bloodhounds off in the distance. He had no way of knowing they were searching for the lost women and not him. He picked up his pace and headed deeper and deeper into the rolling foothills of Wilkes County. Darkness and exhaustion eventually overtook him. He could no longer hear the dogs when he spied an apple orchard a few hundred yards ahead through the half-moon light. Yancey set his course for the orchard in hopes he would find some apples left over from the fall picking. He gathered a few apples from the ground and stuck them in the sack that held his meager belongings.

Yancey collapsed beside a gnarled apple tree and leaned his head against the trunk, his rifle by his side. Just for a minute, he thought. Minutes turned into hours as Yancey fell into an exhausted sleep.

He woke with a start and sat up. Yancey wrinkled his brow and thought through the last hours of the day. Those images became clearer to Yancey the longer he was awake.

He rubbed the sleep from his eyes with his knuckles and looked up and down the rows and rows of apple trees, hoping to find something that would ease his hunger pains, something besides apples. Seeing nothing, Yancey retrieved one of the apples from his sack and started munching away. The first one was so good, he ate two more. The paucity of food in his sack forced him to look for more apples that had been left behind. He added several more to his stash and decided to wait out the rest of the night where he was. He propped the 30-30 rifle against the tree and slept once again.

CHAPTER 36

EXHAUSTED, JAMES checked into the Addison Motel in Wilkesboro. He was not in the mood to spend time eating in a nice restaurant, so he opted for a nearby McDonald's. All James wanted tonight was to be with Gail, but he'd have to settle for fast food and a decent bed. Seeing his reflection in the bathroom mirror shocked him.

James stared at the empty, red eyes and unshaven face in the haggard reflection. It was as if a stranger was standing there in his disheveled clothes looking back at him. He sighed, ran his fingers through his hair, washed his face with cold water, and dried with a hand towel. He glanced in the mirror for approval, but decided that no one knew him in Wilkesboro, so his appearance didn't matter very much. James just wanted to flop down on the inviting bed, but decided that certain things needed to be done—like eating and shopping for necessities. If they found Gail on the morrow, he wanted to look decent.

He locked his door, walked the short distance across the parking lot to McDonald's, and ordered a Big Mac meal complete with fries and a Diet Coke. Gail wasn't there to chastise him for his selection of such a high-fat feast. He ate his meal in silence, but found no enjoyment in deviating from his restricted diet. He watched a teenage couple sitting directly across from him devouring their Quarter Pounders with relish. He envied them. They were able to share their meal with the person they loved, even if it was at McDonald's. He marveled at their ability to eat without getting food caught in their lip rings. *Why in God's name would anybody pierce their body in all those strange places?*

James only ate half of his Big Mac and hardly any of the forbidden fries. He got up from his booth, took one last look at the young couple, and deposited the leftovers into the trash receptacle as he left the restaurant. He sipped on the remainder of his Diet Coke as he walked across the parking lot to Walmart located directly behind McDonald's.

James watched a couple enter the store holding hands and thought of Gail and the times they had gone shopping together. He drained the rest of his drink, tossed the cup in the large waste can, and entered the brightly lit store. James walked up and down the aisles noticing pairs of happy shoppers laughing with each other as they piled their already heavily-laden shopping carts to overflowing. The entire atmosphere made him even sadder. He finally found the toiletry items he needed and grabbed a package of disposable razors. He then wandered the aisles until he found men's clothing, where he picked out some inexpensive underwear, two pairs of socks, and a decent looking shirt from the sale rack. The shirt wasn't much to look at, but at least it was clean.

James paid for the merchandise and took his purchases to his room. He undressed and took a much needed hot shower where he attempted to wash away the traumatic memories of the day, but was only able to cleanse himself of the odor of the fire's wood smoke. While drying off, still standing in the tub, James was overcome with anguish and began crying uncontrollably. After some time, he regained his composure, finished drying, and stepped from the tub. He then slipped into his newly purchased underwear and climbed wearily into bed. He felt much better after the steaming shower and the release of the stinging tears that had been building up all day long.

James was grateful to be alone in the privacy of his room to battle his fears and to pray. He reached into the drawer of the night-stand beside his bed, retrieved the Gideon Bible, and began reading from Psalms. A comforting peace eventually overcame him as he continued reading until he drifted off into a blessed, dreamless sleep.

CHAPTER 37

JAKE HAD all but forgotten how arousing a woman's attention could be. He'd missed the feeling of being loved, needed, and appreciated. His emotions had been put on the back burner for so long, he was afraid he had lost them completely. Jake had been numb for two years, but thankfully he felt as if he was alive again and some of those feelings were returning.

"Thanks, I needed that," he said, looking at Marci as the lights from the dashboard danced in her eyes.

"My pleasure," she answered.

They buckled in and rode silently, all the way to I-77, lost in their thoughts. She turned the cruiser up the ramp, leaving Highway 421 behind, and headed south, toward Mooresville and home.

"We can stop in Statesville and get a bite to eat," Jake offered. "Or we could go on to Mooresville."

"Mooresville sounds fine to me. There's a couple of chain restaurants near I-77."

It didn't matter to him where they went to eat; he just didn't want the evening to end. "Wait," Jake said, "I just thought of someplace. Let's get my car from James' house and head into town, if that's okay with you?"

"Where are you taking me?" Marci asked.

"To The Crimson Cape. It's just a couple of blocks down the street from my gallery. You'll like it, I promise," Jake said.

"Am I dressed appropriately for this place or do I need to change?"

"Don't worry your pretty head about how you look. You'd look beautiful in a tow sack."

"You're just saying that to get me to go there with you. I smell like smoke and so do you. You still think it's a good idea?"

"I surely do. I'd be very proud if you would accompany me to The Crimson Cape, Ms. Meredith," Jake offered gallantly.

"I accept your invitation, Mr. McLeod, smoky clothes and all," Marci said with a smile.

She increased the speed of the Crown Victoria as they sailed down I-77, to what Jake hoped would be a nice ending, to a thus far stressful, event-filled day.

Jake picked up his car at James' house and Marci followed him to The Crimson Cape's parking lot. "Are you sure, I look alright," she said as they each got out of their respective vehicles.

"Come here," Jake said, as Marci approached him under the mercury-vapor light that flooded most of the parking area. Jake took her hand in his and led her out from under the harsh glare of the light to a darkened corner of the lot. This time, he embraced her and kissed her passionately with the most feeling he'd had for a woman in over two years. She responded to his kiss and they lingered there in each other's arms before she stepped back to catch her breath.

"Wow!" Marci said. "Mr. McLeod! It's a crying shame that you have let something like that go to waste all this time; furthermore, I'm really amazed that you would take advantage of a young officer of the law in a weak moment."

"Turn about is fair play," Jake said playfully. "Now, maybe we both can concentrate on enjoying a candlelit dinner accompanied by a bottle of fine wine."

"Works for me," Marci said as she placed her arm in his. "Lead on, 'O' Great One', I'll do my best to concentrate on eating my dinner."

The Thursday night crowd was small and they were led to a dimly lit booth in the back of the restaurant. As they were being seated , Marci nodded toward the framed picture hanging above the booth. "Is that one of your prints, Jake?" she asked.

"Yes, that's *Lake Norman Afternoon*, an early one that's sold out now. The folks here have been good customers of mine for many years," Jake explained.

Marci examined the print again. "Not only do you take advantage of young women—you're a darn good artist, too. Let's order, I'm starved!" Marci said as she slid comfortably into the booth.

Jake had long been a regular customer at The Crimson Cape and all the waitresses who worked there knew him well. The petite brunette, Nicole, came to take their order. She was surprised to see him in the company of a vivacious, young woman. Jake ordered a bottle of Cabernet Sauvignon to be shared while they perused the menu. Nicole returned with the wine and gave Marci the once-over as she was taking their order of ribeye steaks and baked sweet potatoes. The waitress turned to go and winked at Jake as she headed to the kitchen. When she got to the door, she caught his eye again, gave him a thumbs-up, and mouthed the words, "Way to go, Jake."

Marci caught this from the corner of her eye and just smiled. Without a word, she and Jake went to the salad bar and loaded their bowls as if they had not eaten in days. The steaks came and they ate their meals while making small talk between bites.

"That was marvelous!" Marci said with appreciation, as she wiped her mouth with her napkin and leaned back in the booth. "That's the best meal I've had in a long time. The food, the candlelight, and the wine were really nice."

"It has been my genuine pleasure," Jake said, meaning every word of it.

Marci said smiling, "Even the company was right pleasant."

"Thanks," Jake replied, not sure whether she was joking or not. The look on his face prompted her to say, "I'm just kidding."

"Good, you had me scared."

Marci laughed and added, "Seriously, it's nice to get away from all the problems we ran into today. You don't know what this evening has meant to me. Thank you, Jake."

Jake reached over the table, placed both of Marci's hands in his, and said sincerely, "Please don't let this be the last evening we spend together."

"It won't be, I promise," Marci said with tears in her eyes.

Marci and Jake walked through the parking lot of The Crimson Cape, holding hands. They had both come a long way today. The shell of heartbreak and loneliness that had imprisoned them for two years was beginning to crumble. Jake was opening the car door for Marci when she turned and looped her arms around his neck and pulled him to her. She kissed him eagerly and Jake responded likewise. They were standing beneath the mercury-vapor security light and reluctantly pulled away from each other's embrace.

Marci said, "We can't have you getting caught making out in a public parking lot with an officer of the law, now can we?"

"That'd be something, wouldn't it?"

"This has really been some kinda day, Jake. Little did I know when I saw you this morning; how much you would change my life."

"Is that a bad thing?" Jake asked.

"No, it's not bad. It's just that it's been such an all-of-a-sudden thing that I'm totally overwhelmed."

"Let's just take things one day at a time and see what happens," Jake said.

"Sounds like a good plan, but can I kiss you again before we say goodnight?" Marci asked.

"Be my guest," Jake said as he led her down to the darkened corner of the lot. "Make it a good one."

Marci complied with enthusiasm. Both of them were trembling as they walked back to their cars.

"I'll call you first thing in the morning and you can ride back to Wilkes County with me, Mr. McLeod," Marci offered.

"I would be more than happy to accompany you, Detective Meredith," Jake answered happily. "Goodnight and have sweet dreams," he added.

"Oh, you don't have to worry about that," Marci said.

They climbed into their respective vehicles and left simultaneously.

Marci drove to her home in Troutman in a daze. She didn't even remember the route she took. She let herself into her modest home and went straight to her bedroom. She decided to take a quick shower to wash away the smoke and dirt from her body before going to bed.

Marci's body pressing tightly against his and her warm, soft lips covering his mouth was all Jake could think about as he drove to his home on Ferncliff Drive. He let himself in and found his way to the bedroom. It was just as he had left it hours before. The unmade bed waited for him as he took off his New Balance shoes, the two-day-old jeans and yesterday's shirt. He looked at the same green numbers on the digital clock that now read 11:45 P.M. Jake took a hot shower and fell into bed. "What a day!" he said as he lay down and for the first time in two years, fell into a dreamless sleep.

CHAPTER 38

THE OCTOBER sun broke begrudgingly through the few remaining clouds that had settled over the foothills during the night. Smoky shafts of sunlight filtered through the leaves that clung to the branches over the women's makeshift bed. Gail had always been an early riser and was the first one to rouse this morning. She got up from her damp bed of leaves and said, "Good morning," with as much cheer as she could muster. "I ache all over," she said as she stretched her arms and legs.

Debbie, curled in the fetal position, but without the warmth of Gail's body next to hers, stirred and began to yawn. "Man, I'm cold."

"Well, by God, we made it through another night," Joanie declared as she tried to stand. "What's for breakfast girls?"

"We don't have anything to eat and you know it Joanie," Debbie said.

"Hell, I know that, but do you know what I'd like to have for breakfast?"

"I couldn't imagine," said Gail.

"I'd like to have six slices of bacon, four or five scrambled eggs, a couple slices of tomatoes, and big bowl of hot grits with about a gallon of coffee."

"Grits!" Debbie and Gail exclaimed simultaneously. "You've got to be kidding."

"Hell, I forget you girls ain't from the South. Grits stick to your ribs. That's exactly what we need."

"What I need right now is a good hot shower and some clean clothes. However, any kind of food would be greatly appreciated," Gail replied, "even grits."

"Amen to that," Debbie joined in.

Joanie said, "What we really need to do is figure out which direction is gonna lead us back to your car, Gail."

"That sounds good in principle, but I don't have a clue which direction we should take. When we were running from the burning barn, I wasn't paying attention to anything. All I wanted to do was get away from Yancey and Carmen," Gail said.

"Looks like we did that alright, but we did such a good job of gettin' away from 'em; we're a damn long way from everybody else."

"Well, what'll we do now?" Debbie asked. "Stay here with Carmen or try to find our way back to civilization?"

Gail said, "I think we should try to protect her body as best we can. Everyone should know that we are missing by now and are probably searching for us. After they find us, we can bring the authorities back here to the grave."

"How will we find it again?" asked Debbie.

"We'll mark the trail we take from here," Gail explained, "and after we're rescued, find it again and lead the authorities to her grave."

"Hey, I like that idea," Joanie said. "Let's cover Carmen up so she'll be alright until somebody can get back to her."

With no other words spoken, the women set about the task of gathering more limbs and leaves to cover Carmen's cold body. They scrounged the woods and brought back rocks of different sizes and placed them around the makeshift grave.

"This took a lot longer than I thought it would," Joanie said

looking up at the sun. "The day's awasting and we've gotta get goin'."
There was no argument from either the subdued Gail or Debbie.
"We'd better make the most of the daylight we have left. Let's get
crackin'."

During the day, the morning sun disappeared and ominous clouds
drifted over the slopes of the Blue Ridge Mountains. Without the aid
of the sun, the three women lost all sense of direction in the thick
forest of hardwoods. Any trail that would have normally been visible
was covered with fallen leaves.

"We're so turned around now; I don't know what to do," Joanie
said, exasperated.

They twisted and snapped limbs on bushes and piled rocks
along their route as they attempted to find their way back to the barn.

Later in the afternoon, they came across a small stream and
Joanie exclaimed, "Water. Oh God, I'm so thirsty, my lips are splittin' in two." She sprawled face down on the bank beside the rippling
stream and, with her hands, began dipping water into her mouth as
fast as she could.

"You're not drinking straight out of that stream are you?"
Debbie asked.

"Why hell yeah, I'm gonna drink this water; do you see some
anywhere else?"

Debbie and Gail looked briefly at each other before falling on
the ground beside Joanie and lifting the refreshing water, handful by
handful, to their parched lips, too.

"I can't believe water out of a little stream could taste so good,"
Debbie said.

"It's probably the cows upstream that give it its flavor," Joanie
teased.

Debbie picked up a pine cone and threw it at Joanie.

"I don't know about y'all, but I feel a whole lot better," Joanie said. "Now, we gotta find us somethin' to eat."

Joanie surveyed their surroundings and said optimistically, "Squirrels eat nuts and we used to fatten our hogs on 'em, why don't we try some? The woods are full of 'em." She picked up some acorns from the forest floor and tried biting into one. "These things are about as hard as rocks."

Debbie suggested, "If they're that hard, why don't you take two rocks and try to crack one open?"

Joanie found two rocks nearby to her liking and sat down. She placed one rock on the ground in front of her and positioned an acorn in the center of it. "Well, here goes," Joanie said as she took the other rock and struck the acorn with a loud smack. The acorn was splayed open on the rock's surface, so she picked up some of the meat and put it into her mouth.

"Well, how is it?" Debbie asked.

Joanie made a funny face and said, "Ugggh, not very good. Try some, it won't kill you, and it's better than nothin'. At least it's something to chew on."

Tentatively, Gail and Debbie scoured the ground, picking up acorns, smashing them, and eating the bitter meat. "I don't understand what squirrels see in these things," Debbie said jokingly.

"I don't either," Gail offered, "but like Joanie said, it's something to chew on."

"My mouth's puckerin' from eating these things," Joanie said.

"Mine, too," Gail agreed.

"Maybe we'd better stop eating acorns," Debbie said, "I don't want to get sick on top of everything else."

The overcast day brought a damp chill to the air and Joanie said as she looked skyward, "By the looks of those clouds, I think tonight's gonna be whole lot colder that last night."

Gail looked at the clouds and shivered. "You could be right," she agreed.

"Should we keep walking or use what daylight we have left to make a camp for tonight?" Debbie asked.

"Let's just keep walkin' for a while longer," Joanie suggested.

Even though weary to the bone, the trio of exhausted women continued trudging through the rough terrain of the Wilkes County woods.

Finally, Joanie said, "I don't know about y'all, but I've had enough for today. Let's clear out a space on the ground and make a fire. We still have a few of Yancey's matches. Let's make use of 'em. At least we can be a little warmer."

"I just hope Yancey doesn't see the fire and come after us again," Debbie said anxiously.

"I don't think Yancey's anywhere around or he would've caught up with us by now," Joanie said with some confidence.

"I hope you're right," Debbie said as she began picking up fallen limbs and dried leaves that were strewn about the forest floor. A good-sized pile was quickly amassed before darkness overtook them completely.

Gail took some of the dried leaves and placed them in the area Debbie and Joanie had cleared. She then carefully arranged small twigs and limbs on top of the dried leaves.

"Hand me some of those matches, Debbie," Gail said. She carefully struck one of Yancey's kitchen matches on the side of a rock and held it against the dried leaves until a small blaze sprang to life. Gail began adding larger limbs to the flickering flames and soon a comforting fire filled the oppressive darkness, lighting up the distraught faces of the three lost women.

With the aid of the firelight, they began gathering more leaves and limbs that would, hopefully, be enough to fuel the blaze through the night. They prepared a makeshift bed of pine branches and warm dry leaves and huddled together for another night in the woods of Wilkes County.

Everyone was quiet, waiting for sleep that was slow coming, when a sad voice broke the silence. "I promised myself last night, that I'm goin' home to Ed, if he'll have me," Joanie said. "I know that old goat still loves me and I don't know why in the world I've been actin' like a fool all this time. If nothin' else, I may have come to my senses because of this damned mess."

"Good for you, I think that's wonderful. I have been praying for you a long time, Joanie," Gail said, as she leaned on one elbow and looked at her. "You know it says in the Bible, God works in mysterious ways, his wonders to perform. It also says that all things work together for good, for those who love God and are working according to his purposes. My faith in God has helped me get through the trials of these last few days. I think God put us all here for a reason and I think we all are going to be stronger women when we get back home," Gail said.

"Well, I don't know about all that stuff, but I do know that I'm goin' back to Ed as soon as I get my sorry ass home," Joanie said. "You can depend on that."

"I agree with you, Gail," said Debbie. "We've all learned something about ourselves. Look at me; I was a mouse of a woman when we left home on Wednesday. I wasn't a very strong person at all, but I feel that I have pulled my weight pretty well. I also have a peace in my life that I haven't had in years and I now have the strength and determination to divorce Kevin. I'll be out from under his abuse, once and for all. I also have hope for a happier future. I've never had that before."

"I think you're doing the right thing. It won't be easy, but we're here for you, girlfriend," Joanie said, wiping away tears.

"You know what else?" asked Debbie. "I was thinking last night, before I went to sleep, about Carson Wells. He's always been so nice to me. He treats me like I am somebody. Wouldn't it be nice if I could find someone like him?"

"Why not Carson?" Gail said. "When you are legally separated from Kevin, you could have Carson over for dinner."

"I'd really like that," Debbie said.

"Well, now that we have the problems of the world solved, maybe we can get some sleep tonight," Joanie said.

CHAPTER 39

Y ANCEY WOKE to the sound of barking dogs. They didn't sound like the same dogs that had frightened him the day before. He thought they were probably just somebody's pets. A cold, gray light was overtaking the eastern horizon. Mist hung heavily among the gnarled trunks and twisted limbs of the orchard trees. The morning sun would be slow in burning away the foggy shroud that was providing him a degree of protection. Yancey quickly surveyed his surroundings and grabbed his 30-30 rifle from against the apple tree and his sack of meager belongings.

Nobody will ever find me. Not where I'm goin', Yancey thought. He was determined to put miles and miles behind him before night fell again. He left the lonely orchard, picking up a few more apples on his way out, and headed northwest toward the Blue Ridge Parkway.

Yancey would have to cross many roads and open pastures on the way to the sanctuary of the deep woods of western Wilkes County. He had decided to return to the place of his birth beside little Bowlin Creek and he was determined to make it at all costs.

After heading northwest for a mile or two, he remembered that only a couple of bridges crossed the Yadkin River. If he was not careful, he'd be stuck on the south side of that broad expanse of water, so Yancey changed directions and headed back northeast. He finally saw the bridge ahead that crossed the river to the tiny community of Roaring River. Yancey made his way across the bridge when there was no car in sight and then stealthily hurried past the Hometown Café located on the very edge of Highway 268. The tiny restaurant had not opened for breakfast yet, but he could smell the bacon frying in the kitchen. Yancey fought down the urge to steal something to eat because he could not afford to be seen by anyone lest he be caught. Instead, he ducked down beside the restaurant and followed the curvy, Cotton Mill Road as it ran alongside the cascading waters of the Roaring River.

Each time he heard an approaching vehicle; Yancey hid at the edge of the rippling water. After following the stream for a while, he hid in a ditch waiting for a slow moving truck to pass so he could cross Arbor Grove Baptist Church Road.

Yancey set a fast pace for himself, but would have to spend another night or two outdoors before he reached his final destination. It was taking much longer than he had anticipated because he had to hide every time he heard an approaching vehicle on the road or a farmer on his tractor, taking hay to the cows in a nearby pasture.

Yancey decided to take a shortcut across Brinegar Hill Road to Rock Creek Church Road and then cut through some woods to stay out of sight. He found a secluded spot in the woods on the other side of Walter Brewer Road and thought it best to stay there and rest for the night.

The clouds came sweeping down the slopes, bringing with them, colder, damper air. Yancey wanted to start a fire, but he had no matches. He would have to make another cold camp tonight and fill his stomach with more pilfered apples.

Yancey found a stand of white pine trees clustered together that would provide shelter from the wind. He took his hunting knife and cut soft, green branches from a few trees and made himself a comfortable bed. He was set for another night on the lam. He lay down on the soft pine needles, with his rifle by his side, and quickly fell asleep. Hiking for miles through rough terrain was much harder on him physically than just making a little moonshine. He was thoroughly exhausted and slept soundly for a few hours. He woke sometime during the night, cold and hungry. Yancey pulled some of the needle-laden, pine branches over himself for warmth and went back to sleep.

CHAPTER 40

THE PHONE startled Jake from his sound sleep. "Hello," he said into the receiver.

"Good morning," a cheerful voice greeted him from the phone.

"Marci," he asked. "Is that you?"

"How many women do you have calling you at four-thirty in the morning?"

"Uh, none, I guess," Jake said sleepily.

"Meet me at the Galaxy parking lot in Troutman about five-thirty and you may have the privilege of riding with me again to the beautiful countryside of Wilkes County," Marci said.

"You've got a rider, detective," Jake answered wide awake now. "Wait on me, okay?"

"I think I have been waiting on you for a year or more and just didn't know it. Now get your butt up here, McLeod."

"Yes sir, ma'am, I'll be there ASAP and I'll bring us some biscuits from Hardee's, if that's alright? You've given me an appetite," Jake said laughing.

"That sounds great. See you soon," Marci said as she hung up the phone.

Jake showered, shaved, and put on clean, chino slacks and a blue oxford shirt. With some fresh socks from the drawer, his New Balance shoes were hastily donned before he grabbed his jacket and headed out of the door.

Hardee's at exit 36 opened early and Jake didn't want to be late meeting Marci. He went through the drive-thru and ordered four bacon and egg biscuits and two large coffees to go. He headed north on I-77 to exit 42. There was practically no traffic and Jake made good time. He left the interstate and headed north on 115 to Troutman and the Galaxy parking lot. Jake felt the best he had felt in two years. He even heard himself say aloud, "God, it's good to be alive."

Marci was already waiting in the parking lot when he arrived at 5:20. Jake climbed into the cruiser with the bag of biscuits and two steaming cups of coffee and was welcomed with a warm smile. "Good morning, Handsome," Marci said with a little mischief in her voice.

"Good morning Detective," he answered.

"Detective? Is that the best you can do?" Marci chided.

"You look beautiful, by the way. You hungry?"

"I could eat a bear!" Marci replied. "I slept like a rock last night—the first time since I don't know when. Let's see what you have in this bag," she said as she pulled out a biscuit. "Four biscuits? Do you think I'm a pig or something?"

"I thought I might eat three of them if you didn't want your two," Jake said.

"Fat chance," she said laughing.

They were eating their breakfast as Marci pulled out of the lot, crossed Highway 115 onto Murdock Road, and headed for the interstate at exit 45. She eased into the traffic and continued eating as they sped north. Time passed quickly and it wasn't long before they were pulling onto the narrow, graveled lane that led to the barn.

A fire truck was still there when they arrived. The young volunteer fireman was spraying water on the charred embers to prevent a flare-up. "Howdy," he said cheerfully. "Any news on the missing womenfolk?"

"No, but we're hoping the man with the bloodhounds will help us find them," Marci said.

"I hope y'all have good luck today," the firemen replied. "I've been here all night and there ain't much been going on."

"Thanks, we're going to poke around the back of the barn and see if there's anything we might have missed yesterday."

Marci led the way around what was left of the barn to the edge of the woods. "You know, I really think there were just two women who escaped through the woods," she said with conviction. "I've been thinking about it and I believe there were only two sets of lady's shoe tracks beneath that rear window yesterday."

"You might be right," Jake agreed, "but what does that tell us?"

"It means that only two women are accounted for and right now, we don't know which two they are."

"Gail must be one of them because the dogs are following her trail, right?" Jake asked.

"That's right, but we don't know who the other one is yet. It could be either Joanie Mitchell or Debbie Seacrest. I sure wish Bert would get here. It's light enough to start tracking."

They heard a vehicle on the graveled road and turned to see James driving up in his Navigator and right behind him was Ed Mitchell in his Chevy S-10 pickup.

"Y'all got here early," James said to Jake as he was climbing out of his SUV.

"Did you get some rest, James?" Jake asked him.

"I did in fact. I slept very well."

Ed Mitchell, who had been standing with his hands in the pockets of his jacket, said, "This place is in the middle of nowhere. How'd they end up here?"

"Believe me, we've been asking the same question," Jake said.

"Good, here's Bert and the dogs now and Chief Deputy West. We can get this show on the road," Marci said as the two vehicles pulled up and parked side by side.

Bert nodded to the assembled crowd as he lumbered out of his battered truck. He shot a stream of brown tobacco juice on the rear bumper of his truck.

As he was unlatching the tailgate, Bert turned his head and aimed another shot of juice; this one splashed on a rock not far from Jake's foot.

Chief Deputy West was in charge of the investigation since it was in his jurisdiction. Not wanting to alarm Ed, Marci shared with Phil West privately her theory about the footprints behind the barn.

He took a few minutes to check out the prints for himself before briefing the assembled search team. "It appears we will be tracking only two of the missing women. We know that one set belongs to Gail Caldwell because the dogs followed her scent yesterday. The other woman's identity is unknown at this time."

"What about the other two women? Jake asked.

"The two sets of prints are all we have to go on at the present time. Let's get moving and see where they lead us." The Chief Deputy asked that everyone stay behind Bert as his dogs tracked the scent.

The bloodhounds were excited and raring to go. Bert let the dogs get Gail's scent from her jacket and without preamble, he led the way with the dogs barking enthusiastically.

The search team followed Bert through the woods for several hours as the dogs relentlessly kept their noses to the ground. "Them women must be really lost," Bert said, looking at Deputy West, "they just keep goin' round and round in circles." No sooner than the words were out of his mouth, the dogs started barking wildly as they came upon a lane leading through an opening in the woods. "Somethin's really set them dogs off," Bert observed worriedly. "I got an idea and it ain't good. I've seen them dogs act like that before."

"What is it?" asked Marci.

"I think it'd be best if you fellers just stayed here," Bert suggested to Jake, James, and Ed. "Sheriff, you and the detective better come with me and see what them dogs've found." Sheriff West, Marci, and Bert followed the frenetic dogs a few yards up the lane and then stopped abruptly when they found what had sent the dogs into a state of agitation.

The trio peered down at a decaying, headless body. Sheriff West said a few words to Bert, who then pulled the dogs away from the corpse; calmed them down, and then headed back to where James, Jake, and Ed were waiting anxiously.

"What's wrong?" James and Ed asked simultaneously.

"Don't get upset. It ain't your folks or nothin', but it looks like they've been here."

"What do you mean, they've been here? Why don't we keep on going?" asked James.

"We can't," Bert said. "There's a body up there that looks like it's been dug up. Don't worry, it ain't your folks. This body has been there for a while by the looks of it."

"How do you know that our women have been there?" James asked Bert.

"The dogs followed the scent right onto that little road and right up to where the body is."

Knowing they would be upset by the discovery of the body Marci followed closely behind Bert to reiterate what he had told them.

"There is a decapitated female corpse, but it has been there for some time. By the tracks on site, it looks like two of the missing women discovered the body," Marci said. "Deputy West is radioing for the coroner, homicide, and forensics. He'll go back to the barn and wait for them to arrive. We're to continue with Bert."

Bert had the dogs trailing around the perimeter of the scene when the hounds started their barking once again. "Well, I'll be damned! It looks like they're headin' back toward the barn," Bert said unbelievingly.

"Back toward the barn? I don't think I can take much more of this," James said.

Everyone obediently trailed behind Bert as the dogs, following the scent, traversed through pastures and woods and eventually brought them back toward the barn. "Don't that beat all?" Bert said. "It looks like another woman has joined the two we've been followin'. Look here! The tracks lead off through the woods over that way," Bert said pointing to the footprints.

They followed the tracks a short distance when Bert asked in wonder, "What's goin' on here? Now there're two more sets of tracks that skirt a little to the right. One set of prints is huge. They must belong to a man and he's barefooted. The other set of tracks look like they belong to a different woman. What in tarnation's goin' on?" Bert said puzzled. "I ain't never seen anything like this before. At the beginnin' we were only trackin' two women. Then we found a dead woman that couldn't be either one of them. Now we're trackin' three women and all of a sudden a fourth woman shows up with a huge man and it looks like them two are trying to follow the three women. It's just about too much for this old man to sort out."

Marci looked at Jake and said, "I told you I thought there were only two women who escaped through that barn window and I was right."

"I never disagreed with you, did I?" Jake acknowledged.

Marci turned to Bert and encouraged him by saying, "Look Bert, you and your dogs are doing a great job. I know it's getting a little complicated, but hang in there."

"Hell, I'm not goin' to quit, but you've got to admit, this is one hell of a mess, ain't it?"

"I won't argue with you on that, Bert," Marci replied.

Bert turned his attention to his dogs once again. The sniffing hounds led them through a section of the woods they hadn't been in before. They followed the dogs through the thickly forested hills and up to a ramshackle cabin.

"Look!" Everyone said almost simultaneously.

"It looks like they went inside that cabin, yonder," Bert said, finally enthused. "I told you them dogs would find 'em, didn't I?"

"You sure did, Bert," Marci said. "I never doubted you one bit, but aren't we back near the barn, where we started?"

"We could be. Them women just keep goin' in circles," Bert avowed.

"Well, I guess I had better see what we have here," Marci said. She drew her Glock-40 from its holster and asked everyone else to stay behind. Marci stealthily walked toward the cabin holding the pistol with both hands. With her foot, she pushed open the door of the cabin and followed her pistol inside.

"What do you think she'll find?" Ed asked apprehensively.

"I don't know, but I think it's wise for us to wait here like she said," Jake said nervously.

"Why's that?" James asked.

"Well, we don't know what may be in there. Marci's just playing it safe. She knows what she's doing," Jake answered.

Before James could reply, Marci stepped out onto the rickety porch and said, "Whoever lives here is a pig. It's the filthiest place I've ever seen in my life."

"Did you see any sign of Gail or the other women?" asked James worriedly.

"No, I didn't, but it looks like they might have been here and left and that's a good sign."

Jake silently agreed with Marci. Their absence was a good sign. *I don't know what James would have done if Gail had been found inside that filthy house, injured or dead.*

Bert said, "I'm gonna take the dogs all around this place and see if they can pick up the trail again." The dogs began barking enthusiastically at the back of the cabin. "Here we go!" yelled Bert.

"Y'all better hurry around here if you're goin' with us."

The entire group followed the dogs expectantly as they wound through the woods once again. James asked Jake as they hurried along, "Why in the world would Gail even go to a filthy place like that?"

"You know as much as I do," Jake said, "but we're getting closer."

The dogs had the scent once again with Bert hanging on to their leashes. The trail led back to the barn and Bert said as he saw where they were. "Well, I'll be damned! Them women ain't just lost, it looks like they came back here on purpose!"

The firemen were leaving in the truck as they emerged from woods. The volunteer driving the fire engine stopped and rolled down his window. "I hope you folks find your missing women," he said sincerely.

"Thanks," Marci said as she tried to catch up with Bert and his tracking dogs.

Phil West stopped Marci before she could join the others and asked, "How's it goin'? Found anything yet?"

Marci filled him in about tracking the women to the cabin and back to the barn. The Chief Deputy just shook his head and said, "This case gets screwier by the minute. I'll see you later. I gotta wait here for the coroner and forensics team. They should be here any minute."

CHAPTER 41

MARCI WATCHED Bert lead his dogs around the perimeter of the property where the barn once stood.

"The dogs are confused a little bit right now," Bert said. "They'll get straightened out again, just wait a minute." The dogs suddenly set into barking wildly once more. "Here they go; it looks like the same three tracks that were at the cabin."

The dogs led them to a little shed with its door hanging askew like a loose tooth that needed pulling. Bert said hopefully, "I told you them dogs are gonna find them women yet, you just wait."

Marci said, "Wait here," and they did. She looked inside the shed. "They've been here, too. The shed is stacked with cases of moonshine. All the other stacks are even except the one near the door looks to be about three short. You know what I think, gentlemen? I think your womenfolk were held against their will in the barn but escaped. They broke into that cabin and this shed. And I believe they're the ones who set the fire in the barn to draw attention to their predicament."

"You gotta be kidding," James said.

"I'm serious," Marci said. "I've been thinking about the tracks and the way they have been going and coming, around in circles. I think they were kidnapped, but somehow got away and are running from their captors."

"Kidnapped!" the men all said at the same time.

"Yes, kidnapped. Personally, I think now they're just lost and confused, running round and round in circles."

"But there are only three sets of tracks. Whose do you think they are?' James asked.

"I would venture to say that your wife, Gail, Joanie Mitchell, and Debbie Seacrest are the ones we're following," Marci said .

"Why?" James asked.

"Because," Marci explained, "Kevin Seacrest was our only lead yesterday and he undoubtedly was headed to the barn when he was killed. He has also been associated with Carmen Romano according to a reliable source at the office. I didn't want to say anything without definite proof, but it would be my assumption that the two of them may have been the main perpetrators behind this fiasco. But I don't know who the other individual is or how he figures into this whole thing. I assume he owns the cabin, the barn, and this shed filled with moonshine."

"You said other individual. Are you referring to the huge set of footprints we found?" Ed asked.

"That's correct," Marci said, "and I, at this time, believe that the other woman's tracks belong to Carmen Romano. It looks as if she and the barefoot man are chasing the lost women. I feel it's imperative that we find the women before 'Bigfoot' and Ms. Romano do."

"Bigfoot?" James asked incredulously.

"At this time, that's what I'm calling him, for the lack of a better name."

"Why didn't the women just get in Gail's car and drive away when they came back to the barn?" Jake asked.

"Remember, the only way out was blocked by the locked gate."

Bert said, "What I don't understand is why they keep runnin' around in circles. It ain't that far from here to civilization. They're either hiding, or they're just plain, damned lost."

"Personally, I think it might be both," Marci said. "At first I thought they were trying to escape and stay hidden from whoever was pursuing them. Now I believe they're just lost and confused. Well, Bert, we'd better get started again."

"We can find 'em alright, but it'd be better if my dogs had somethin' else to go on—that'd sure help," Bert said.

James said, "We've been following Gail's scent so far. Do you have anything of Joanie's that he could use, Ed?"

Ed said, "I have an old sweater of Joanie's in my truck."

"Great! Bring it here Ed and we can see if Joanie's footprints are the third set of tracks, or one of the first two," Marci said.

Ed retrieved the sweater from his pickup and handed it to Bert. Immediately the dogs began barking and pulling Bert along as he held tightly to their leashes.

"Hot dog!" Bert said, "Now we're gettin' somewhere. Let's go find them women."

The dogs now followed Joanie's scent through the woods and it was all the band of trackers could do to keep up with their frenzied pace. They traveled in widening circles most of the afternoon and doggedly continued the pursuit. Evening once again was fast approaching and they still had not found the women.

A gravel lane appeared through the woods ahead of them. "Isn't this near the road we were on this morning?" James asked Marci, "the one where we found the body?"

"I think it is, but we're a lot farther north than we were this morning."

"Are you sure that body is unrelated to the missing women?" Jake asked.

"They're more than likely unrelated, but finding a body in this area makes me think there might be others. We may have stumbled onto a dumping ground."

"God, I hope not," James said.

"Me, too, James, me too," Marci agreed.

Bert's bloodhounds sped up when they crossed the graveled road and headed farther north. "How far do you think we are from the barn?" Ed asked.

"I'd say about three or four miles at least, maybe more," replied Bert as the dogs began barking wildly again. "Y'all better stay back a ways. Detective, you'd better come on with me."

Marci ordered the men to remain where they were until she could check out what had sent the dogs into such a state of frenzy. She and Bert approached a leaf-covered ditch piled high with rocks. Marci bent down and removed some of the leaves and rocks to get a closer look. She stood and motioned for Jake to join her. Marci asked Bert to take the dogs away to a place deeper in the woods.

"What's going on?" James asked Ed.

"I wish I knew. God, I hope they haven't found Joanie," Ed cried.

James laid his arm around Ed's shoulder to comfort him. "Whatever will be, will be, my friend. We just have to think positively and pray." And that is exactly what the two men did.

Jake approached Marci, "What's wrong?" he asked.

"That's why I wanted you to come instead of one of the husbands. We have another body. This one is fresh— possibly yesterday. Take a look. I've got to warn you, it's not pretty. She's been stabbed."

Jake's trembling legs finally obeyed and he knelt in front of the makeshift grave. He peered into the ditch at the partially covered body, and even though Marci had warned him, he was still not prepared to see the horrific pale face of Carmen Romano. Jake began to tremble. He was relieved that it was not Gail, Joanie, or Debbie, but Carmen had been a longtime friend and he was saddened to see that her life had ended this way. He could only imagine the horror Carmen had endured before her last breath.

"Are you okay?" Marci asked, as she helped Jake to his feet.

"Yeah, I'll be alright in a minute. I just wasn't prepared for that."

"Who is it, Jake?"

"It's Carmen Romano."

"I thought it might be," Marci said. "You know, somebody went to an awful lot of trouble to gather rocks and place them carefully over her to keep predators away."

"The murderer wouldn't have taken time to do that, would he?" Jake asked.

"No, he wouldn't have, but that same someone also marked the spot with rocks so we could find her. That tells me it was someone who cared, like her friends."

"I see what you mean."

James yelled to them from down the road, "What did you find?"

"Just wait, I'll be right there," Jake called back.

Jake hurried back to James and Ed. "We found Carmen Romano's body," he informed them.

James collapsed to his knees, hardly able to breathe. Ed yelled up to Marci, "Can we come up there now?"

"Yes," Marci called back, but be careful where you walk, this is a crime scene. Stay over to your right, out of the way."

"Thanks," Ed said as he helped James to his feet. They approached Marci as she was radioing the latest news to Phil West.

"Thank God it wasn't Gail," James said.

Jake said, "I know you're relieved. I'm thankful that it wasn't Joanie or Debbie either."

"I am too," James said embarrassed, "it's just that I was so relieved that it wasn't Gail. That's all I was thinking about."

"I know, you don't have to apologize," Jake assured him.

"Look over here," Ed Mitchell called. "There's a makeshift bed made out of dried leaves."

"Do you think it could have been made by our missing women?" James asked.

"It's a good possibility," Marci said.

"I wonder if they have had anything to eat since Wednesday?" Ed asked.

"I'm sure they're okay," Marci said.

"I hope so," Ed said.

"It's going to get dark again before long. We have to make some difficult decisions," Marci said with authority. "Bert, can you find your way back to the barn?"

"Sure, I can. I'd like to get started back if I could, while I still got some light left. I got my dogs to feed and water, too."

"You go ahead Bert and, if you don't mind, find that road back down the hill and see where it comes out. Then please let Phil West know. I'll radio him and let him know you're on your way out. More deputies and the homicide boys are on their way here."

"What do you want us to do?" James asked.

"You and Ed are welcome to stay with me until the deputies get here or you can go back with Bert. I have to wait here and protect the crime scene."

"We'd really rather stay if we could," James said. "I hate to leave tonight without finding Gail and I know Ed feels the same way."

"It's getting too dark to go any farther and like Bert said, he has to feed and water his dogs and let them get some rest."

"But, what about the women?" Ed asked. "What will they do tonight?"

"They've already spent at least one night in the woods and it looks like they did just fine. They'll probably huddle up together in another warm bed of leaves. We'll find them tomorrow, I promise. Go get some rest and be here first thing in the morning," Marci said.

"I just can't leave knowing that Joanie is out here somewhere in the cold," Ed argued.

"Remember, Joanie's not alone and they all seem to be very resourceful."

"Come on Ed," James said. "I've already had this same conversation with the detective and you're going to lose. You just might as well come with me."

Marci asked, "Do either one of you have any matches? It'll get pretty cold up here when the sun starts setting."

Ed said, "You can have mine. Joanie wants me to give up smoking, anyway. This is a good time to start."

"Thanks," Marci said as Ed fumbled through his jacket for his matches.

"Are you going to be alright up here by yourself?" James asked.

"Jake will stay with me, won't you Jake?"

"I'll be glad to stay," he said.

"Okay," James said. "We'll get our vehicles and go to Wilkesboro for the night. You'll call us if there are any new developments, won't you?"

"Most certainly. Now you gentlemen get some rest."

CHAPTER 42

WALKING ALONG the road was much easier than following the women's erratic ramblings through the dense woods of Wilkes County. The good thing about their return trip was that it was mostly downhill.

The October sun was disappearing behind the tops of the trees as the men reached the end of the road. "Well, I'll be damned," Bert said. "If them women would have just turned in the right direction they would've come out right here on Staley Road. I know where we are now, but we gotta hike back a little ways to get to the barn."

The men followed Bert and the dogs back to the barn to pick up their vehicles. "I guess I'll see y'all in the mornin'," Bert said as he loaded the dogs in the bed of his truck. "I gotta let Deputy West know where that road came out."

"What time do you think we'll start?" asked Ed.

Bert closed the tailgate of the truck and aimed a stream of tobacco juice at a random rock lying in the road—he missed it by two feet. "This late in the year, we won't have enough daylight until six-thirty or maybe seven, so get a good night's sleep," Bert added as he was climbing into the cab of his ancient truck.

James said to Ed, "Why don't you just leave your truck here and ride with me to Wilkesboro? There's no sense in wasting gas."

"Ain't that the truth? I've never seen the price of gas so high in my life. I appreciate the offer. Let me buy your supper," Ed said.

"We can share the cost of a room, if you want to." James offered.

"That sounds like a good idea."

The drive to the motel was mostly in silence, but interspersed occasionally with desultory comments as to what the next day would bring.

"I wonder what the ladies are doing now?" asked James. "I hope they're warm. It's supposed to get colder tonight."

"They're a smart group of women, James. I'm sure they'll find a way to stay warm. They' ain't like us men. They'll snuggle together for warmth and not be embarrassed about it."

"I guess you're right," laughed James, "but, I can't help but worry. I'll be glad when this ordeal is over."

"Me, too. I'm gonna do my level best to get Joanie to come back home. I'm even gonna quit smokin' for her."

"Good luck on both accounts," James said encouragingly.

"You know? Maybe we'd better call Carson Wells, Debbie's boss, and let him know what's been going on. I'm sure he's wondered where Debbie's been. I guess we should tell him about Kevin's accident, too," James said.

"Good idea. Will you call him?" asked Ed.

"Yeah, I'll call him," James said.

Ed went to the motel office and secured a room with two queen-sized beds while James called Carson Wells. Carson seemed very concerned and offered to meet them in the morning.

"We're supposed to meet at sunrise," James said and gave him directions to the search site.

After James talked to Carson Wells, he and Ed went to their

room to wash up. "I saw an Outback Steakhouse on the way in," Ed said.

"That'll be great," James agreed. "You know, Ed, I think we're going to find them tomorrow and I really believe they're going to be alright."

"I think so, too. I hope Jake and Marci don't have to spend the entire night in the woods."

"Oh, I wouldn't worry about Jake and Marci. Did you notice the looks going on between those two?"

"You gotta be kidding! Jake McLeod and the detective? Well, what do you know? Ain't that somethin'?" Ed said. "Let's get us a big steak. I can't wait 'til daylight."

"Me either."

CHAPTER 43

THE LATE autumn sun set early in the foothills of Wilkes County. Marci and Jake watched through the dwindling light as the men began their trip down the hill. She turned to Jake and said, "Maybe we should fluff up some of these leaves the women used for a bed last night and get some rest. We've been standing up all day and I'm tired."

"Let me get a fire started," Jake offered. "That'll knock off some of the cold and help the deputies find us quicker, too."

"A fire would be nice, then you can come over here and keep me warm?" Marci said standing by the bed the women had made of leaves.

"Why, Marci Meredith. If I didn't know better, I'd swear you were trying to seduce me," Jake teased.

"I am. Now get that fire started and get over here."

"I've got to find some wood first, be patient."

"I've been patient for two years," Marci said while she gathered more leaves.

Jake was trying to find enough wood to get a fire going when Marci hastily threw an armful of leaves on the bed and said, "Oh hell.

Let me help you or we'll never get warm."

Jake took Ed's matches, lit a small blaze, and then kept adding more wood until he finally had a romantic, flickering fire. Marci took Jake's hand and led him to the bed of leaves.

"Now, isn't this better?" Marci asked, as she snuggled next to him.

"Soitenly," Jake said in his best Curly impersonation. He'd been a fan of The Three Stooges for years and couldn't resist mimicking the comical icon of slapstick. "Most soitenly," he whispered as he closed his eyes and held Marci close to him before the flickering fire-light. The fire provided warmth, but not the same kind that Marci Meredith was providing. The moon continued its path toward the western horizon, but its journey went completely unnoticed by Jake and Marci. The couple was deep into a long kiss when they heard a noise in the distance.

"What was that?" Marci said, breaking away. "I thought I heard a truck."

"I did, too," Jake agreed.

"Damn!" Marci said out loud as she brushed leaves from her tousled hair. "Bert must have found the beginning of the road. I wasn't expecting the coroner up here this soon."

"That's obvious," Jake said.

Marci picked up an acorn from their bed of leaves and threw it at him, bouncing it off the side of his head. "Ouch!" he said as he rubbed the spot where the acorn hit him.

"Oh, Jake, I'm sorry; I didn't mean to throw it so hard. I didn't hurt you, did I?"

"I may live. I'm not sure, though," Jake kidded. "Maybe you should kiss it and make it feel better."

"Here," she said as she kissed him one more time for good measure. "Does that help, you poor thing?"

"Yes, indeed it does, but I think I'm hurting in several more places too," Jake said.

"That's going to have to do for right now. Here they come," she said. Jake and Marci could see the beams from the county investigator's flashlights as they made their way through the woods. Marci looked at Jake one more time and added, "You behave yourself now; I have work to do."

Marci greeted the team from the crime scene unit as they walked up.

"Thanks for waiting for us Detective Meredith. Your camp fire really helped direct us to your location."

"No problem, glad to help," Marci replied.

The coroner said with a degree of amusement, "That looks like a leaf in your hair, Detective."

"It could be," Marci said as she brushed her fingers through her hair. "We've been scrounging the woods all day looking for the missing women."

It was all Jake could do to keep from laughing at her feeble attempt at lying. He thought the coroner noticed, too.

"Yeah, there are a lot of leaves this time of year, that's for sure," the coroner said grinning. "Now, show us where the body is, Detective."

Marci then led them to the spot where Carmen's body lay.

"Any ideas?" asked the lead homicide detective who was now in charge. One of the deputies began photographing the corpse of Carmen Romano.

"I have a few, but they are just speculation," Marci said.

"Let's hear 'em anyway," said Homicide Detective George Chamberlain. "This is the second body you folks found today. What's with you people? Finding bodies a hobby or something?"

Marci let the remark slide. She wasn't sure whether he was kidding or not. "The victim is Carmen Romano who resided in Mooresville. She was a friend of the three women who were reported missing early yesterday morning. We have been tracking them for the last thirty-six hours. Ms. Romano may have been holding the three women against their will. We strongly believe the three victims escaped and are currently lost. The search for them will resume in the morning at first light. It appears that Ms. Romano was in the company of a rather large man who may also be involved in the disappearance of these women."

"Any names?" Chamberlain asked succinctly.

"Gail Caldwell, Joanie Mitchell, and Debbie Seacrest are the missing women. The Seacrest woman's husband was killed in an automobile accident yesterday morning. He rabbited when we questioned him at his home in Mooresville and we think he was on his way here to meet the Romano woman when he had the accident. He may have been Ms. Romano's accomplice."

"That's it?" asked Chamberlain.

"That's it."

"Why don't you folks call it a day and go get some rest too? It looks like you're going to need it. Deputy West will keep us informed if anything else happens tonight."

Marci and Jake hitched a ride back to the barn with one of the deputies. The ride was short considering the distance they had walked during the day. They thanked the deputy for the ride and got into Marci's cruiser.

Jake wondered if he'd ever get to take Marci somewhere in his own car and not ride shotgun in her Iredell County Sheriff's Department Crown Victoria with a twelve-gauge shotgun between them.

Marci maneuvered the cruiser through the gate and drove onto the graveled lane without saying anything. She turned and looked at Jake intensely as she pulled onto Red White and Blue Road and asked, "What do you think?"

"About what?" he responded.

"About us."

"Oh."

"Yes, about us. About how things have escalated so fast."

"I think meeting you and spending these last couple of days together is the best thing that's happened to me in two years. That's what I think!" Jake said. "I want to see a lot more of you, Marci. I realize now I can't go on just existing like I have been since Kitt's death. I need someone in my life that enjoys the things I do, someone to hold at night, and someone who believes in me."

Marci pulled the Crown Vic to the side of the road. She looked up at him with glistening eyes and said, "Oh, Jake. What's happened? Is it just because we've been thrown together in this crazy search for these women; or is it something more than that? I haven't kissed another man since Mark passed away. I was afraid I had forgotten how. With you, it just feels natural—like it's the thing to do."

"Let's get one thing straight right now," Jake said. "You definitely have not forgotten how to kiss."

Marci laughed. Wiping away a tear, she looked at him and said, "Thanks."

Jake reached across the ever-present twelve–gauge shotgun and grabbed her hand. "Let's go. There's plenty of time to sort things out."

She pulled back onto the road and wiped more tears from her eyes as she set the cruise control on sixty-three miles an hour. They were in no hurry. They treasured every minute together and the ride through the pastoral scenery, lit only by the moonlight, was intoxicating. The two rode for a while, lost in their thoughts, until Marci broke the silence. "I feel so guilty—like I am betraying Mark's memory. How do I ever get over that?" she asked.

"One day at a time, Marci. One day at a time. I have exactly the same problem, but I honestly can't help but think Kitt and Mark would both want us to be happy," Jake said confidently.

"Mark often told me how much he loved me and made me promise; that if anything ever happened to him, I'd not sit at home and mourn my life away. He said I should go on with my life—that's what would make him happy. Maybe that's the way I have to look at our situation."

"Kitt made me promise, right before she died, that I would find someone else. I never thought I could love anyone else. My world was literally turned upside down when I lost her, but for the first time in two years, I feel like living again, and it's all because of you, Marci."

"Dammit, Jake!"

Marci yanked the cruiser off the road again. "Alright buster," she said seriously, "out of the car. You know the routine."

Jake got out of the car and walked to an unlit area where the cruiser's lights didn't shine on them. He turned and said, "Okay, have your way with me. Arrest me. Do whatever you want. I'm yours."

"Shut up and kiss me," she ordered. "I'm officially announcing that my mourning period is ending, but is it okay if I think about Mark once in a while?"

"Sure, as long as it's not when we're doing something like this," Jake said. He took her in his arms and they kissed each other passionately, as if their very lives depended on it.

"Thank you, Jake," Marci said as they walked back to the cruiser. "Thanks for understanding. I apologize for being the aggressive one. I hope you don't mind."

"You haven't heard me complain, have you?" Jake responded.

"I know, but it's just that everything is moving so fast."

Jake looked at Marci and declared, "Life seems so unfair sometimes—like when I lost Kitt and you lost Mark. I don't know about you, but I was angry at God and almost gave up on life. Now look! God is giving us both another chance at happiness."

Marci smiled her hundred-watt smile and said, "Let's get something to eat, I'm starved."

Jake laughed out loud and said, "You're something else, did you know that?"

"Be nice, that's what Andy always told Barney."

"That was because he liked him," Jake said.

"You're impossible, Jake McLeod."

He laughed again as he reached over, grabbed her hand, and

gave it an affectionate squeeze.

Marci kept her eyes on the road, but driving was not all that was on her mind. *I wonder if Jake would come to my house tonight if I asked? Boy, I've got it bad.*

"Marci, would you like to have dinner with me again tonight?"

"Let me check my social calendar and see if I'm free. I'll get back to you," she said. A few seconds passed and then she said, "Yep, it looks like I'm free. I had to cancel a previous engagement, but I think you may be worth it."

Jake laughed again. "Where would you like to eat tonight?"

"Would you like to come to my house? I'd fix you a sandwich."

"That would be nice. I'd love to see where the great female detective, Marci Meredith, lives."

The Galaxy Supermarket had closed and Jake's Jeep Cherokee looked forlorn sitting under the lone security light, like it was the only child that hadn't been picked up after a baseball game.

"Follow me," Marci said. "I don't live very far from here."

Jake said, "Okay, just lead the way." He hopped out of the Crown Vic and climbed aboard his Jeep. Marci turned right onto the venerable Old Mountain Road. Its often curvy route led through beautiful farmland and then eventually to the rolling hills of the Brushy Mountains. They had only gone a short distance when Marci turned on her right signal light and pulled the Vic onto a road that led into a housing development. A sign reading Lippard Springs greeted Jake at the entrance of the small subdivision. Marci made a few turns before pulling the cruiser into the driveway of an attractive, gray vinyl-sided house with dark green shutters.

They got out of their respective vehicles and she said with a smile, "Welcome to my humble abode."

"It's very nice," Jake said as he followed her onto the porch and waited as she unlocked the front door. The weather stripping made a popping sound as it relinquished its seal in the cold night air.

Marci flipped a switch and the comfortable den was flooded with a warm glow that came from two lamps setting on each side of an overstuffed sofa. "Nice. Comfortable. The way a room should be," Jake said. He was taken aback by the picture over the sofa. It was one of his early prints of a forgotten barn, living out its last days on an Iredell County hillside. The print had been sold out for years. "When did you get that?" Jake asked dumbfounded.

"I've had it for years. I got it at a yard sale for two dollars."

"A yard sale?"

Marci started laughing hysterically, "I'm just kidding. I wanted to see how you'd react."

"Well, did I react the way you thought I would, you devil, you?"

"Yes! Exactly!" She fell onto the sofa, laughing.

Jake fell onto the sofa beside her and playfully wrapped her in his arms. "Don't you ever do that again, you almost gave me a heart attack. Do you know what that print is worth now on the secondary market?"

"No I don't and don't really care. I like the print and wouldn't sell it anyway. I'm sorry about the joke, I just couldn't help it," she said still laughing. Then suddenly, she turned to Jake and said, "Kiss me, please."

Jake obliged. She definitely had not forgotten how Jake thought. They kissed each other tenderly as if they meant for each kiss to never be forgotten. And then, they just held each other for a while. Marci laid her head on his shoulder. Her breathing slowed and soon the lovely Marci Meredith was sound asleep. After a while, Jake eased himself from her warm embrace, being careful not to wake her, and gently laid her down on the sofa. He found her bedroom, where another of his prints was hanging over her bed, and found a blanket. She was still sleeping when he covered her up and kissed her on the forehead.

Jake washed up in her bathroom, enjoying the fragrance of Marci on everything he touched. The sight of his haggard face in her mirror jolted him back to reality and he went in search of food.

Marci's kitchen was small, but neat and clean. There was a breakfast nook featuring tall windows that reached from ceiling to floor. The blinds were open, but he could see no farther than the edge of the darkness. The wallpaper, covered with dainty flowers, gave the kitchen and breakfast area a homey, comfortable feeling.

He made himself at home, opened the refrigerator and found it well stocked. Jake found some deli-sliced ham and turkey and began preparing their dinner. His search of the pantry rewarded him with a can of Progresso Chicken & Wild Rice Soup. The aroma of the simmering soup soon wafted through the house as he prepared their sandwiches.

Jake turned to see Marci standing in the kitchen doorway wrapped in the blanket he had gotten her.

"I'm sorry, I didn't realize how tired I was," Marci said as she rubbed the sleep from her eyes. "I was laughing one minute and the next thing I knew, I was waking up under a blanket. You were nowhere in sight. I was afraid you had gone home without even saying goodbye."

"I would never have done that," Jake assured her.

"Well, I hope not."

He looked at her beautiful face, smiled and said "I actually enjoyed holding you, even while you snored and made noises like a pig."

"What? I did not," Marci shrieked. "Did I?"

"No, you didn't. I'm just getting back at you for the yard sale thing."

"Thank God. I'd die if I knew you'd heard me snoring."

"It wouldn't change the way I feel about you. You just laid your head against my shoulder and that was that."

"How long was I out?"

"Only an hour or so."

"An hour, or so! I can't believe that," she said looking at the kitchen clock. "And look at you, fixing my dinner. How sweet."

Marci came up behind Jake and put her arms around his waist. "Thanks for the blanket, too."

Jake turned and wiped his hands on a kitchen towel. He took her face in his hands and kissed her. "Now, let's eat dinner, I'm starved."

Jake poured soup into bowls and placed the sandwiches on plates. "Thanks for inviting me here for supper," he said.

"It's my pleasure, but I didn't mean for you to have to prepare it yourself," she said as she placed spoons in each of the steaming bowls of soup.

"I didn't mind at all," Jake said. "Let's eat while the soup's hot."

"What would you like to drink?" Marci asked. "I have tea, Diet Coke, or water."

"Iced tea would be great."

"Then tea it is," Marci said.

He pulled out a chair for Marci and bowed gallantly. "Please be seated, my dear."

Marci laughed as she took her seat. "Thank you sir."

Jake sat across from her and smiled broadly. "Bon Appétit," he said and picked up his spoon. He could not take his eyes off Marci.

"Jake, you're the first man who's been in this house since Mark's funeral," she said, choked with emotion.

He reached across the small table and took hold of her hand. "I'm honored to be here with you and among Mark's memories. I'll never do anything to tarnish them."

Tears leaked down her cheek as she looked up at him and said quietly, "Thank you."

They ate the rest of their meal, interspersed with idle chatter and questions of the whereabouts of the three missing women.

When they had finished eating, they took their dishes to the sink and Jake said reluctantly, "It's awfully late. I probably should be going."

Marci looked at the clock on her microwave. It read 1:45 A.M. "I wish you would stay," she said softly.

"I will another time, I promise. That is if I am invited back."

"Jake McLeod, you are some kind of nice man and I love you for it." She turned and faced him, wrapped her arms around him, and pulled him close. "Kiss me really good and I'll let you go this time, but I'm not making any promises about the next time."

Jake willingly obeyed and kissed her thoroughly. Finally, he withdrew from their embrace and she stood at her front door watching him back out of the drive and head toward home.

Jake's mind was filled with Marci as he listened to Nat King Cole's *The Very Thought of You* emanating softly from his CD player.

Nat and Jake drove slowly home. Nat sang; Jake listened. He was still thinking of Marci Meredith when he pulled onto Ferncliff Drive. It was almost 2:30 AM. He parked in the garage just as Nat finished singing *Unforgettable*. The house was dark and lonely. Jake was lonely, too. He had left her house less than an hour ago and was already desperate for her company. Marci Meredith was truly unforgettable. Maybe Kitt had been right. "Someday, the right woman will come along," she had told Jake. Maybe the right woman has finally come along.

He fell across his bed, clothes and all, and slept like a dead man.

The bedside phone brought him back to life.

"Hello," Jake managed groggily.

"Time to rise and shine, Big Boy. Up and at 'em. It's after five o'clock."

"Who is this?" Jake asked, sleepily.

"Who do you think it is? It's Marci. You gonna sleep all day or do you want to go with me to Wilkes County?"

"Why, yes, I want to go. I'll meet you at the Galaxy parking lot in forty-five minutes."

CHAPTER 44

THE DAWN greeted Yancey Saturday morning with heavy clouds the color of steel. *I hope it don't rain on me today. It'll slow me down and I don't need that. It's just a matter of time before they find them bodies and I've got to put a lot of miles between me and the law.*

Yancey stretched the stiffness from his cold muscles, rubbed his hands together for warmth, picked up his rifle, and headed northwest. He continued to keep away from the highway as much as possible until he came to Traphill Road, near the small community of Hays. *I gotta have something else to eat besides them damn apples.*

Yancey saw a small, white frame house with no car in the driveway. *I betcha they got some good food in there. I'll just take a look in the window to see if anybody's home.* He thought better about looking in the window and tentatively walked around to the rear of the house. He made sure that he hadn't been seen and then rapped loudly on the back door. Hearing no sound from within, he sliced his way through the thin wire screen on the door with his hunting knife and stepped into the comfortable back porch. A small table, loaded with apples, sat to the right of the kitchen door. *Damn, more apples,* he thought. *I gotta have some real food.*

The top half of the kitchen door featured a large window. Yancey took the butt of his 30-30 and smashed the glass into the kitchen, reached in and unlocked the door. He stepped through the door and looked at the neat country kitchen, complete with a 1950s dinette table featuring a red and gray Formica top. Six red and gray, vinyl-covered, chrome chairs surrounded the table. There was no clutter. Dishes, leftover from a recent meal, drained in a rack at the sink. The dishes reminded him even more, how hungry he was.

Yancey swiftly went to the cabinets along the wall and rifled through them, finding enough canned goods that would hopefully last him for a while. He knew they would be heavy, but the need for sustenance overruled his practicality He stashed a dozen cans of vegetables and an unopened pound of Maxwell House coffee into his sack. Next, he ambled across the kitchen to the Kenmore refrigerator where he found a plastic milk jug, half-full of fresh milk. Yancey turned it up and drank the rest of it and then flung the empty jug into the enamel sink before turning his attention back to the open refrigerator. He found less than a dozen eggs, an open package of bacon, a few slices of bologna, and some sliced cheese; which he hastily stowed in his sack.

Yancey then found some much needed kitchen matches in a drawer beside the sink. A drawer at the bottom of the electric range provided him with a Teflon-coated frying pan. *This'll help out a lot. I gotta get out of here 'fore somebody comes home.* He gathered his rifle, flung his sack over his shoulder, and left through the same door that he had just entered less than ten minutes earlier.

Feeling much better about his circumstances, he headed for the dense woods to build a fire and cook a hot meal for himself from his newfound treasures. Less than two miles farther into the hills; Yancey set his sack down and took a deep breath. After a minute, he cleared a spot on the forest floor and built a small fire with the help of the purloined matches. The smell of the frying bologna was too much for Yancey. He reached into the skillet, snatched up the simmering meat with his bare fingers, and wolfed down every piece, barely chewing them.

That ain't enough! I'm 'bout to starve! The huge man's hunger had not been sated, so he retrieved the bacon and eggs from the sack. Yancey then fried the slices of bacon, scrambled all the eggs, and consumed every bite with relish, making feral sounds with each swallow. "Damn," Yancey said aloud, "I forgot to get a coffee pot." He wiped his mouth with the dirty sleeve of his jacket and decided that a coffee pot would have been too cumbersome, anyway. Nonetheless, he opted to hang on to the coffee; he could use it when he got to his cabin.

After the much needed repast, Yancey lay down among the leaves and took a quick nap. He awoke refreshed after only thirty minutes and then continued northwest following his instincts toward the higher eastern slopes of the Blue Ridge Mountains.

He was playing it safe. Yancey may not have been too smart in the ways of the world, but he was a man at home in the ways of the woods. Stone Mountain State Park was several miles off to the northeast and he was careful to stay out of sight as much as possible. He didn't want a hiker to report his presence to the Wilkes County Sheriff's Department.

Yancey's plan was to cross the heavily traveled Highway 18 after dusk and make it to the uninhabited Game Lands for the night.

He didn't know how many days it would take him to get back to the place of his birth—the tiny cabin on Bowlin Creek. There were not many roads there, just miles and miles of beautiful, untouched woods where Yancey could hide forever.

When I get to the cabin, I can sneak into Glendale Springs and steal enough food to get me started and then take it from there. I'm a man of few needs. Just a few more days and I'll be safe.

CHAPTER 45

RIDING SHOTGUN with Detective Meredith was getting to be a habit for Jake. He didn't know if it was allowed, but he felt sure Marci did everything "by the book". Marci was radiant in her Iredell County Sheriff Department's blazer and tan slacks, a Glock-40 strapped to her belt. It was almost impossible for Jake to keep his eyes off her, so he quit trying.

"We're going to find them today, I can feel it," Marci said with conviction as she turned and caught Jake staring at her. She smiled and added, "Good morning, Handsome."

"Good morning, I hope you slept well."

"I really did, thanks to someone who's sitting close to me right now."

"My pleasure. It was a nice evening, wasn't it?"

"It was and I hope you slept well too."

"I did. It was the best sleep I've had in some time. Thanks."

"You're welcome," Marci said.

Marci and Jake talked while they drove up I-77, but tried their best to stay focused on the job ahead of them.

She found the narrow lane and pulled onto the shoulder of Staley Road. James and Ed pulled in right behind Marci's cruiser as she was turning off the engine. "Good morning," they said as they got out of James' Navigator.

"Good morning," Marci and Jake said.

James said, "I called Carson Wells and told him where to meet us."

"Thanks, I know he appreciated that," Marci said.

"He should be here soon," James said.

"I hope so," she agreed. "I really hope so."

"Did you two get much sleep?" James asked.

"The evening passed by so fast, it was after two o'clock by the time I got to bed," Jake said.

"How about you Marci?" James said smiling.

"Actually, I slept like a rock. What time was it when you left my house, Jake?" Marci said.

"What?" Jake said, clearing his throat. "It was pretty early, wasn't it?"

"No, it was real late. Don't you remember?"

James and Ed both laughed at Jake's embarrassment.

"It's all very innocent." Jake said. "I went to Marci's house; we ate a sandwich and talked until it was late. That's all there was to it."

"It's fun to see you squirm, Jake. We don't mean any harm."

"Well, you might embarrass Marci; kidding around like that."

Marci looked at Jake and winked. "Did you get all your clothes before you left last night, dear?"

"Stop it. You're as bad as they are, Marci Meredith."

Marci laughed, "I know. I'm sorry."

"Well, tell them the truth before they bust a gut."

"Okay, you guys. Jake came to my house and it was like he said. We ate a sandwich, had some soup, and talked. End of story."

An approaching vehicle interrupted their revelry.

Carson Wells pulled up in a shiny, black BMW. Introductions were made all around and Marci answered some questions Carson had about the women's disappearance.

"We'll get started as soon as Deputy West and the bloodhounds arrive," she told him.

"I just appreciate you letting me come along. I've been really worried about Debbie."

"Glad you could join us," Marci said. "I feel sure we'll find them today."

"Deputy West and Bert Conroy are coming now," James said pointing down the road.

The chief deputy greeted everyone and introduced himself and Bert to Carson. Bert sent out a stream of brown tobacco juice and said "Howdy."

A caravan consisting of three sheriff's cars, James' Navigator, and Bert Conroy's dog-laden truck struck out just as the sun rose to meet them on that cold October morning. The search team drove up the narrow, graveled lane and parked. Bert once again unfolded himself from the cab of his truck and went to unlatch the tailgate. Everyone was standing around the truck; waiting for the unloading of the dogs. Bert let go with another stream of tobacco juice, but this one fell short of its mark and landed on a young deputy's spit-shined, county-issued shoes. "Oops," Bert apologized.

"That's okay," the deputy said.

"Alright," Phil West began, "we're gonna try to pick up their scent again from here."

The deputy, who had been the target of Bert's erroneous stream of tobacco juice, picked up some dried leaves and wiped off his shoes the best he could.

The dogs did not disappoint. Barking wildly, they headed up the narrow lane dragging Bert behind.

After a while, the search team arrived at the place where Carmen's body had been found the day before. "Hey y'all; look over here," Phil West called out to them. He was examining the ground several yards from the makeshift gravesite. "It looks like the women tried to leave us a trail. I guess it was too dark for us to even notice yesterday evening, but there're some limbs crossed on the road and rocks placed in a row. And look here! They left the road and headed deeper into the woods."

The dogs began barking even more excitedly as they continued. Bert, holding on to the leashes of the bloodhounds, looked back at the rest of the group and hollered, "Y'all better hurry if you're gonna keep up with these dogs."

The team picked up the pace as they made their way through the woods, following the dogs and the marked trail. "Gail was in the girl scouts when she was young," James reminded them. "I'll bet marking the trail was her idea."

CHAPTER 46

"WHAT DAY is it?" Debbie asked. "I've lost all track of time."
Gail furrowed her brow and said, "We stayed in the barn
Wednesday night and then we slept with no fire Thursday
night."

"And," Joanie broke in, "last night was Friday and we had a fire,
so by God, this must be Saturday."

"I am so hungry," Gail said.

"Listen!" Joanie ordered. "Are those dogs I hear?"

"Maybe it's some hunters," Debbie said. "If it is, they may help
us get out of here."

"It might be hunters," Joanie said with tears in her eyes.

"I think we should turn around and head back toward the
sound of those barking dogs. They may be our way out," Gail said.
"The sooner they find us, the sooner we'll get home."

"Sounds like a winner," Joanie agreed. "Let's get on with it."

The beleaguered women changed their direction and headed
toward the sound of the barking dogs. Debbie suddenly stopped
walking and put her finger to her lips to silence the other women.
"Listen. I think they're over this way. It's hard to tell where the sound

is coming from. It's constantly bouncing off these hills and hollows; just a minute ago, I thought I heard the dogs coming from over there," she said pointing toward the east.

"Wait a minute! Maybe it's a search party instead of hunters and those dogs are tracking us!" Gail said.

"If it is a search party, those dogs have probably been going round and round in circles just like we have," Joanie said laughing. "Them dogs are probably so drunk they don't even know where they are."

"But, they'll find us eventually, won't they?" Debbie asked.

"Sure," Joanie said with confidence. "Why don't we just rest here on our butts and quit movin'. Let them to come to us. It sounds like they are getting nearer, anyway."

Debbie and Gail agreed.

"I'm goin' down here to the bushes for just a minute, y'all watch out for bears," Joanie teased.

"Bears!"

Debbie and Gail kept a sharp eye while Joanie was out of sight behind some bushes a few yards off the path.

"Well, how many did ya see while I went to pee?" Joanie asked coming through the bushes. Then she started to laugh.

"Were you just putting us on?"

"Heck, yeah. I just thought we needed a good laugh after all we've been through."

Debbie asked, "You mean there aren't really any bears?"

Joanie could barely stand from laughing at Gail's and Debbie's gullibility. Soon, they were all laughing hysterically. They fell to the ground, clutching their stomachs. Gales of laughter filled the surrounding hills and reverberated through the hollows. Liberation from their three days of hell was near and their joy could not be contained.

CHAPTER 47

"HUSH, DOGS!" Bert ordered. "Hush!"

"What is it?" James asked.

"I'm not sure, but it sounds like a bunch of women laughing their fool heads off."

"It can't be our women. Not after what they've been through," James said.

"I don't know, but we're going in the direction of the laughter," Phil West said. "Come on."

The Chief Deputy's radio came to life as they headed toward the sound of the laughter. He answered into the mike, was silent briefly, and then said, "What? Repeat that." He listened intently for another moment, longer than the first one, and said, "Okay."

"What's up Phil?" Marci asked.

"The department just had a report of a break-in north of Traphill Road. All the burglar took was food, matches, and get this, a frying pan. Sounds like somebody on the run to me. What do you think?"

"Do you think it could be 'Bigfoot'?" Jake asked.

"Yes I do. We have some deputies on their way to check it out.

They'll get back to us with an update. We're not to far from the Yadkin River and the burglary site is just a few miles north of the town of Roaring River."

"Sounds like our man," Marci repeated. "It sounds like 'Bigfoot' is running scared."

"I agree," Chief Deputy West said.

Gail, Debbie, and Joanie lay among the leaves exhausted from their fits of laughter. "I'm not movin'," Debbie said. "They're just going to have to find me right here on this spot. I'm too tired to go any farther."

"Okay. We'll wait here, but I don't hear the dogs anymore," Joanie said. "Maybe we need to make some noise and let them know we're here."

The three tired, bedraggled women stood up and began shouting at the top of their lungs. "Help! Help! Somebody help! We're over here! We're over here!"

Before Bert could get his dogs on the trail again, the sound of women's voices reverberated across the wooded hills.

"Did you hear that shouting?" Jake asked Marci.

"I think I did, listen again everybody. Quiet!"

Everyone drew quiet, even the dogs, and the faint sound of women's voices could be heard in the distance.

"There it is," Marci said. "I hear them again, it is women shouting! It's coming from the west, but it's hard to tell how far away they are because the sound echoes through these hills."

"Alright people, let's head for the hollering. Let's move it," Phil West ordered his deputies and the assembled crowd. "Let's go while they are still making some noise."

The bloodhounds picked up the women's scent again and began their wild barking. Marci, Jake, James, Ed, and Carson were trying to keep up, but the younger deputies had raced ahead.

"Hey, I hear barking again and it sounds like the dogs are gettin' closer. Hot damn!" Joanie said with uncontrolled exuberance. "They're comin', they're comin'. Keep hollerin' girls; keep hollerin'."

The three women strained their already strained voices, their pleas echoed through the hills and hollows, bringing their deliverance closer and closer.

"I'm gonna kiss everybody I see, as soon as I lay my hands on 'em," Joanie said.

"They're over there. I hear 'em good now," shouted one of the young deputies. "It sounds like they're just across the hollar."

"Listen to them dogs," shouted Joanie. "They're comin' to get us."

The three, soon to be rescued women, jumped up and down, shouting, crying, and holding on to each other. As their jubilation grew, they yelled even louder. "We're here! We're over here!"

"There they are," shouted a blond headed deputy who was almost too young to shave. "There they are! I found them. Hurry up y'all!"

James and Ed ran ahead to join the deputy. "Where? Where are they?" James demanded, as Carson Wells caught up with them.

"Over there on the other side of that hill, yonder," pointed the deputy.

"That's them! They're here! It's a search party!" cried Joanie.

"Look, James is with them and there's Ed, too," Gail said almost crying. "Can you believe it?"

Debbie wondered if Kevin had come along, but hoped he hadn't. When she saw Carson Wells she began crying with relief. "Look! Look who's over there with them. It's Carson. He came, too!"

James stood where he was for a second, frozen in time. He watched Gail scramble down the steep embankment. When she fell headlong through brush and dried leaves, he dashed down the opposite embankment to help her. James was at her side almost before she finished tumbling. He fell next to her, crying, grabbed her in his arms, and brushed the leaves from her tangled hair.

"Are you alright, darling? Are you okay? I've been so worried. God, I love you." James paused to catch his breath.

She lay there looking up at James as his tears fell across her dirt-stained face. "I knew you would come."

"Oh, Gail, I thought I'd lost you. I have been scared to death."

"We've all been scared to death. So much has happened. Carmen was murdered."

"I know. We found her body."

"There's so much to tell you, but first let's get the other girls down the hill."

"Oh, my God, it's Ed. It's Ed," Joanie screamed. She raced down the hill as fast as she could without repeating Gail's folly.

Ed met her at the creek. He gazed into Joanie's eyes and saw for the first time in years, the old Joanie he'd fallen in love with many years ago. "Thank God you're alright," was all Ed could say as he choked back tears.

Joanie flung herself into his arms and wrapped an embrace around him that almost strangled the life out of the poor man. They fell to the ground laughing and crying together. "I'm not ever goin' anywhere again, if you'll have me back, Ed Mitchell," Joanie cried as they lay tangled in the leaves.

Ed looked into Joanie's eyes, "Of course, I'll have you back, are you crazy? I never gave up on you Joanie. I never quit lovin' you."

"I never quit lovin' you either. I didn't know what the hell I wanted, but I do now and, by God, you're it," Joanie said as she covered Ed's face with kisses.

"I love you now more than ever before Joanie."

"If that's the case, let's get married again as soon as we get home. We can invite the whole damn town."

"Sure, anything you want, just don't ever leave me again."

"Honey, I'm yours for keeps."

Joanie and Ed held each other tightly and neither could stop their tears.

Debbie carefully made her way down the steep embankment. Carson met her at the bottom of the hill. "Thank you so much for coming Carson. Your being here means a lot to me," Debbie said as their eyes met. "Where's Kevin?" she asked as she looked through the faces of the other rescuers.

"He's not with us," Carson said. "I need to tell you something, Debbie." He took Debbie's hand and led her to an old hickory stump and helped her sit down.

"What is it?" she asked looking up at Carson.

He swallowed hard and began. "Kevin was killed in an automobile accident Thursday morning," Carson said with sympathy.

"What!" said Debbie, unable to believe what she'd heard.

"I'm sorry to be the one to tell you this. The County Sheriff will be able to give you all the details," he continued. Debbie stood up and leaned into Carson for comfort and he tenderly wrapped his arms around her.

Jake waited on the opposite hillside, his arm around Marci.

When Gail saw him, she waved wildly and began climbing the hill to meet him. When they reached each other, Gail threw herself into Jake's arms and hugged him gratefully. "James told me what you have done for him through all this; how you stood beside him and everything. I just can't thank you enough, Jake."

"Here's who you need to thank," Jake said. "Let me introduce you to Detective Marci Meredith of the Iredell County Sheriff's Department. We wouldn't have found you if it hadn't been for her. I've been right at her side for most of the last three days, and I don't think I'm ever going to leave."

Marci and Jake smiled at each other.

"Oh, Jake, it's so good to see you smile again," Gail said with dusty tears running down her grime-covered cheeks. "Thank you, too, Marci," Gail said as she extended her hand, but thought differently, and wrapped her arms around Marci in a grateful hug and whispered in her ear, "and thank you for giving a wonderful man his life back."

Marci tearfully whispered back to Gail, "He's done the same for me, and you're right, he is a wonderful man."

Phil West took Debbie Seacrest aside and related the events to her that had taken place over the last few days. He told her there was the possibility that Carmen and Kevin were involved in their kidnapping.

Debbie shocked the deputy by saying candidly, "I think you might be right."

After the women drank their fill from the bottles of water the deputies provided, the group made their way back to the parked vehicles and drove down the narrow lane to the charred skeleton of Yancey's barn. Phil West motioned for everyone to gather in one area where he could address them all. "I want to thank everyone for the help you gave the Wilkes County Sheriff's Department over the last several days. Special thanks to Marci Meredith from Iredell County and to Bert Conroy and his faithful dogs."

While the group was still assembled, Gail asked if she could say something. "Joanie, Gail, and I want all of you to know how grateful we are that you worked so diligently to find us. We can't thank you enough. Would you bow with us for just a moment and let us thank God for our deliverance?" James and Gail each offered a brief prayer and then hugs and tears once again went round the gathering.

Afterwards, Chief Deputy West took Marci aside and gave her an update on the break-in they had talked about earlier. "A rather large man was seen running near the site, carrying a rifle.

From all indications, he's heading toward the headwaters of the Roaring River. He could be our man. The women believe he murdered the Romano woman. They say he's a 'moonshiner' by the name of Yancey. They don't know a last name. The department is running his name and description through records right now."

"I appreciate you keeping me informed," Marci told him.

"Sure thing, Detective," he said.

CHAPTER 48

"DID YOU ladies really burn that man's barn down, Gail?" James asked later.

"We surely did and we'd do it again," she said.

"I think we all have learned a lot about ourselves these last few days, don't you?" James asked.

"Definitely," Gail said as she wrapped her arms around James. "Let's go home."

"But what about your car?" James asked. "I have your extra car key."

"Give it to Marci. She said the deputies would see that the car was returned to us. Right now I just want to be with you. We have some things to catch up on. We've been too busy making money. Now we need to concentrate more on living."

James grinned at the prospect. "Do you think you may need some help getting cleaned up? I could get in the shower with you and soap you up."

"That's exactly what I need," Gail said smiling.

Carson offered to drive Debbie home.

"My car is in Statesville, but Carmen took my keys and my purse. Right now, all I want to do is go home. I'll worry about my car later," she told him. She thanked him as he opened the door for her.

He couldn't help but notice a silent tear as it ran down her cheek. "I'm so sorry, Debbie. You've been through an awful lot."

"Oh, it's not that, Carson."

"Then, what is it?"

The tears became more plentiful as Debbie explained, "No one has ever opened a car door for me." Debbie finally broke down and sobbed.

Carson walked around the car and slid into the driver's seat. He reached over and took Debbie's hand in his. "Everything that happens from now on is going to help you forget what you've been through."

Debbie looked at Carson. "Thank you for being so nice to me all the time I've worked for you and thank you especially for being here today. You can't imagine what that means to me."

Marci and Jake watched as Ed opened the door of his pickup for Joanie. They couldn't help but laugh when they overheard her telling Ed how she had escaped from Carmen and Yancey. As Ed drove the truck across the downed gate and on to the road that brought the women to the barn four days before, Joanie was sitting up next to him just like they were a couple of teenagers on their first date.

"That Joanie's something else," Marci said.

"She is that for sure," Jake agreed.

"Do you think they'll stop in Statesville to pick up Joanie's car? Marci asked.

"Not a chance," Jake said, "she's only got one thing on her mind and it isn't jump starting a car."

Marci and Jake walked toward the cruiser. "Okay partner, I guess this is our last ride together as the famous crime-fighting duo of Meredith and McLeod," Marci said.

"What's wrong with McLeod and Meredith?" Jake countered. "Can't we still be a dynamic duo from time to time?"

"I may get in trouble for letting you ride with me these last few days, but I made an exception this time, due to your age and the circumstances."

"What was that about my age! There you go again. Wait until I get you home, young lady," Jake kidded.

"I can't wait. Let's go get started on whatever it is we're going to do."

The Crown Vic's engine roared to life and Marci headed the cruiser toward Troutman and Jake's old Jeep Cherokee.

The trip back to Troutman sped by too fast. When Marci pulled into the Galaxy parking lot, she looked at Jake and said in her best Mae West impersonation, "If you ain't doin' anything tonight, handsome, why don't ya come up and see me?"

Jake surprised her by saying, "No."

"No! Why? Did I really snore and sound like a pig?"

"No; nothing like that. I want to have you over to my house for dinner. How about that?" Jake asked. "Would you like for me to come and pick you up for our date?" he asked.

"No, I'll drive. Give me your address?"

Jake gave her directions to his house on Ferncliff Drive. When he got out of the cruiser, he walked around to the driver's door. "Lower the window," he said. When she did, Jake leaned through the open window and kissed her. "Maybe that'll hold you until tonight."

"Whew! What time? I can come now if you like," Marci said breathlessly.

"Let's make it six o'clock." Jake said.

"That works for me."

Jake drove to Mooresville listening to Nat King Cole sing, *The Very Thought of You* again. He was happier than he'd been in years.

CHAPTER 49

MARCI WHEELED into Jake's driveway at 5:45. She was in her Iredell County Sheriff's car with the flashers going and the siren blaring. *So much for a quiet evening at home,* Jake thought. Marci Meredith made an entrance; that was for certain.

"You're something else, did you know that?" he said when he greeted her at the door.

"I know, you told me that already and tonight I'm all yours," she said as she stood on Jake's front porch. Marci wore a soft, cream-colored, cowl-neck sweater over stylish, pleated slacks of almost the same color, just a little darker. Her flaming red hair, softly curling around her exquisite face, made him stop and stare.

"You look absolutely beautiful, Marci. Please come in."

"I would, but you're standing in the doorway."

"Oh, sorry. You just look so beautiful that I was momentarily dumbfounded."

"Why, thank you," Marci said, brushing against Jake as she entered the foyer leaving a hint of perfume lingering in the air.

"What's the matter? Are you alright?" Marci asked Jake who was still standing in the foyer.

"No, I am not alright. I feel like I have been hit by a Mack truck, if you want to know the truth."

"My gosh, what happened?"

"You! You're what happened."

Marci looked embarrassed and said, "Oh, I'm sorry about the siren and flasher thing. I thought you'd get a kick out of it. I didn't mean to upset you. I'll leave now if you want me to," Marci said.

"Come here you crazy woman," Jake said as he grabbed her hand and pulled her into his arms. He kissed her once and then again.

"I kiss even better when I'm not standing," Marci said.

"I'm sorry. Where are my manners?" Jake said. "Come in and sit down. I'll fix us something to drink."

"I'd better help. You don't look too steady on your feet," Marci replied.

"I was very steady on my feet, until you got here."

She followed him into the den.

"Marci, I don't know exactly how to say this, but I will anyway."

"What have I done now?" Marci asked.

"You haven't done anything wrong. It's just that…that you're an extremely attractive woman."

"Why thank you. What's wrong with that?"

"Not a thing is wrong with that. You're young, vivacious, energetic, and one of the most wonderful women I have ever known. What I'm trying to say is this, what in the world do you see in an old man like me?"

Marci took Jake by the hand, led him to the sofa and said, "Jake, you need to lie down. I think the last three days have taken their toll on your brain."

Jake lay down on the sofa as Marci requested. She stuffed a soft pillow under his head and leaned down and softly pressed her lips to his. "Is that any better, Jake?" she whispered.

"What about dinner?" Jake asked when he caught his breath.

"I think dinner will just have to wait." Marci slid onto the sofa beside Jake, wrapped her arms around his neck, and pressed her warm body next to his and said, "something else has come up."

Jake nuzzled his face against her, intoxicated by the smell of perfume on her sweater. She ran her fingers through his hair and eagerly pulled him closer.

Dinner waited. When they finally pulled themselves apart, Jake looked into Marci's eyes and exclaimed, "Wow."

With her breath coming in shallow gasps, Marci said, "You can say that again."

"Maybe we should take a break and eat now," Jake suggested.

"I'm just getting warmed up, but that's probably a good idea. We might need to keep up our strength." She added before Jake could reply, "I think that was awfully nice. It was almost like having dessert before dinner, wasn't it?"

"Didn't it remind you of being a teenager again, making out in you parent's living room?"

"It did and I think that made it even better." Marci trailed her fingers along his thigh.

"You devil, you," Jake said as she got up.

"Hang in there sport, the night's not over yet," Marci promised. "Let's see what we're having for dinner." She then helped Jake up and accompanied him to the kitchen. Marci was impressed with the neat, roomy kitchen.

Jake opened the oven door and they both peered inside at the bubbling dish. "Lasagna," Jake said, "I hope you'll like it."

"It looks wonderful. I'll eat just about anything that won't eat me," Marci said laughing, "except liver."

Jake opened a bottle of Shelton Vineyards' Madison Lee Red. They took the wine to the breakfast table. It was set for two—complete with linen napkins, silverware, and candles. Jake poured a glass of wine for each of them and lit the candles."Here's to us," he said.

"This is so nice, Jake. Here's to us."

He was falling in love and there was absolutely no turning back. The buzzer on the range sounded, signaling that the lasagna was done.

It was difficult for both of them to concentrate on eating.

"The lasagna is wonderful," Marci said smiling over her fork. "Don't tell me you can cook, too."

"I manage when I have to. Most of the time I eat out," he told her.

Long after they had finished eating, Jake and Marci lingered at the table. They talked about everything that interested them and found they had a lot in common—they both liked art, bluegrass music, reading, and hiking.

Jake refilled their glasses with the last of the wine and they talked on into the evening. Marci looked at her watch. "It's getting late; I think I'd better be going."

"I remember you saying to me one time, I wish you would stay," Jake reminded her.

"Do you want me to stay?"

"What do you think?"

"Well, you'd better ask me now, before I have a chance to change my mind," Marci said with a smile.

"Please stay with me," Jake asked with sincerity.

"I'd like that very much," she said as she gave him a quick kiss. "Do you mind if I use your bathroom?"

"Use the one in the master bedroom, it's more private and a little nicer," Jake said.

Jake cleared the table and was wiping off the counter when he heard Marci calling from the bedroom. "Jake, can you come here and help me, please?"

He opened the door to his bedroom and was taken by surprise to see the lovely Marci Meredith lying in his king-sized bed with the comforter pulled up to her chin. Her clothes were heaped on the floor beside the bed—except for her bra, which she gently let fall from her fingers to the floor. "You did ask me to stay, didn't you?"

"Yes, I did, but I didn't mean for you to—"

"Are you coming to bed," she asked with a wicked grin on her face, "or are you going to stand there and argue?"

Jake quickly undressed and climbed beneath the covers beside her. Marci wrapped her arms around him, placed her hand behind his head, and pulled him close. Jake could feel the heat radiating from her body as she said, "We don't have to do anything you don't want to do, Jake, but right now, just hold me."

He snuggled up closer and kissed her gently. He pulled back and stared into her emerald eyes and said without a doubt in his mind, "Marci Meredith, I love you."

"Oh, Jake," Marci answered, "I love you too." She kissed him hungrily and then gingerly guided his face between her ample breasts. "Just stay there a while," she whispered, running her fingers through his graying hair, "and make yourself at home."

Jake felt more at home than he had in two years.

"Don't you stop now or I'll have to arrest you," Marci said breathlessly.

"Don't worry your head about that," Jake answered with muffled voice.

"You truly are an artist, Jake McLeod," Marci whispered.

They spent the night together doing their best to make up for two lonely years of being without a loving partner. They took their time at first, exploring each other's body; their hands never stopped moving and caressing.

The couple made love tentatively at first, all the while, reminding each other how much they cared. Later, after making love again, Marci snuggled up to Jake and began snoring softly. He held her in his arms and laughed quietly to himself. *I'll never tell her that she really does snore.*

When it was almost daylight, Marci woke Jake, looked at him him sleepily with her magical green eyes, and asked, "Do you really think we could be in love Jake? We've only known each other for three days."

"I think I loved you the very first time I saw you," Jake answered. "If it wasn't love, I don't know what it was, but whatever it was, it was there. Does that make sense?" he asked.

"Every damn bit of it," she said smiling. Marci kissed him and then got out of bed. "I really have to go now."

"I know, but I don't want you to go. I want you to stay forever."

Jake lay in bed until he heard the water running. He got up and went into the bathroom and opened the glass door to the large, walk-in shower where Marci was lathering soap over her body. "Would you mind soaping me up?" she asked, just as casually as if she had been expecting him.

"I'd be delighted, Ms. Meredith," he said as he began slowly and methodically running the soapy washcloth over her. Marci turned around and he washed her back. Jake tenderly rubbed soap over her back until it was completely covered with a thick lather and then slowly slid his hands down to her buttocks. A moan escaped Marci's lips and she moved her hips in concert with the motions of his hands. Jake then reached around her body and rubbed the cloth gently between her spreading thighs. "Ummm," Marci whispered. "That feels so good."

Marci eagerly kissed him as the warm water rained down on their glistening bodies. She took the washcloth from Jake, applied more soap, and then rubbed it over Jake's chest. He let out a gasp as she lowered the cloth to his stomach and then down between his legs. Jake moaned and pulled her into him and kissed her long and hard.

Later, they had a cup of coffee at the breakfast table. "I really should be going," Marci said sadly as she reached across the table to hold Jake's hand.

"I know," Jake said. She gathered her purse and he walked her to the Crown Vic and opened her door.

"It really has been a lovely evening and a fantastic morning," Marci said as she looped her arms around his neck and kissed him again with the fervor as was her custom. "We'll just take it one day and night at a time and see what happens."

"Okay," Jake agreed. "Let's just play it by ear."

"By ear, mouth, hands, or any other body parts we might need," she said.

"Marci Meredith, you're something else, did you know that?"

"Yeah, I think you've told me that a few times already."

"You are something else and I love you," Jake said as he kissed her once more.

"I love you, too," she replied as she climbed into her car. Marci closed the car door very quietly, as not to wake the neighbors, pulled out of Jake's driveway, and then turned on the siren and flashers. Lights came on all over the neighborhood—so much for keeping secrets with Marci Meredith.

Jake had no idea how in the world he was going to keep up with the wild and wonderful Marci Meredith. *I guess I'll just have to hold on for a wild ride,* he said to himself as he watched her drive away.

CHAPTER 50

Yancey was tired and hungry and would have to stop and rest soon. Another day spent in the wooded hills of Wilkes County had brought him closer to his final destination of little Bowlin Creek—the place of his birth.

Alma and Cletus Darwood had eked out a meager living along the banks of the little creek during The Great Depression by farming their tiny hillside farm and selling the illegal whiskey that young Cletus made in his still. Cletus got a temporary job helping clear land for the Blue Ridge Parkway in the 1930s. The extra money helped put food on their table, but Cletus was fired for failing to show up at work regularly. After that, he still stopped by the job site to sell his moonshine to the other workers when the site boss wasn't looking.

Alma Darwood was up in years when she finally gave birth to a squalling, twelve pound-eleven ounce boy on a cold October morning in 1955—Yancey Darwood had arrived. He was a big boy from the beginning and was a tremendous help to them as he grew older.

Cletus kept his still hidden at the rear of his property where he turned out a few gallons of moonshine every month. Without the cash that the illegal whiskey brought in, the Darwoods would never have made it. Yancey learned how to make moonshine from his father at an early age. He carried firewood, sacks of sugar, bags of yeast, malt, cornmeal, or any other ingredient that was needed. Cletus's age made it difficult for him to carry the heavy supplies and firewood, so Yancey's brawn was a big help. Darwood taught Yancey how to mix the ingredients, move them into the still, and to observe the mash carefully as it fermented.

At one time, moonshine was one of Wilkes County's chief sources of income for farmers. It's been said that "every man in Wilkes County made moonshine except the preachers and they made the barrels."

Revenuers eventually found the Darwood's still in the 1970s and destroyed it with no compunction whatsoever. The government agents brought axes and chopped away until the still was just a memory. They turned over barrel after barrel of the treasured liquid while Cletus and his young son watched it pour onto the ground. Yancey never forgot the look on his father's face. The still was not the only thing destroyed that day. The Darwood family was never the same.

Yancey's mother died not long after. Cletus died just six months later leaving the young boy alone. With both parents dead, Yancey had to learn to fend for himself.

He drifted down the mountain toward Miller's Creek, beyond Wilkesboro, and finally ended up miles east from there on a graveled road, south of the Yadkin River.

It was there that Yancey happened upon a kindhearted widower who had been living alone for years. He could no longer manage the farm by himself and couldn't afford to pay someone to help him.

Yancey was kindly taken in by the old man and soon his strong, young back was put to use, helping with the farm work. His loyalty to the farmer was greatly appreciated, thus the old man willed the farm to Yancey before he passed away.

Yancey never did like all the manual labor it took to run a farm and soon reverted back to doing what he knew best—making moonshine. He made a good living, making and selling the illegal whiskey. That was, until Carmen Romano entered his life.

He could still see her in his mind...There she was, lost, her car pulled over onto the side of Highway 421, trying to read a road map. "Can I hep' you?" Yancey had said as he peered into the driver's side window at Carmen. He'd never seen such a beautiful woman.

"Yes, you can," Carmen said as she looked up into the eyes of this giant of a man. "I'm lost."

"Where you wanta go?"

"To Roaring River."

"Heck, let me ride with you and I'll show you," Yancey said.

"Just tell me how to get there and I can find it."

"You'll get lost, sure as the world," Yancey said.

Hesitantly, Carmen flipped the unlock button and let Yancey get in the car. They drove silently for a while, sizing each other up until Yancey said, "Turn right up here on Red White and Blue Road and we'll follow it until we cross the Yadkin River. There's not much when you git there," he said, "but I'll be glad to show you."

"Okay," Carmen agreed as she tentatively turned her Lexus onto the road that Yancey had advised her to take. "Did you grow up around here?" she asked.

"Nah, I grew up near Glendale Springs."

"Did you go to school there?"

"I didn't go to school hardly at all. I never was too good at book stuff."

"I'll bet you're smarter than you give yourself credit for," Carmen replied.

"Nah, I ain't. People say I'm a bit slow."

"I can't believe it, a big, good-looking man like you."

They continued talking while Carmen sized him up to see if he would meet her needs, in more ways than one. "How would you like to make a little money?" she asked.

"Doin' what?"

"Let me ask you something first," she said. "Do you have a place of your own?"

"Yeah, I gotta place. I gotta a barn and a house, too."

"Well, you must do pretty good to have all that. What do you do, by the way?"

"I can't tell you that."

"Why not?" Carmen pressed.

"I just can't. I'm not suppose to be doin' it."

"Why not?" Carmen continued pressing.

"It's agin' the law."

"I can't imagine what a nice man like you would be doing that's against the law."

"I make moonshine."

"Is that all?"

"That's enough, ain't it? You won't tell nobody, will you?"

"No. I won't tell anybody, I promise. Now, do you want to make some extra money?"

"Doin' what?"

"You said you have a barn and a house. Where is your place?"

Yancey told her, "It's hard to find."

"That sounds just like what I need," Carmen said happily.

They never did make it to Roaring River. They went to Yancey's place and his life was never the same again.

Yancey's thoughts returned to his present situation as he continued on his quest. *I'm glad I killed her. She messed up my life forever. I'm goin' where nobody will ever bother me agin'. Just a few more days and I'll be home. In the meantime, I gotta get me somethin' else to eat.*

He neared Highway 18 at dusk, but decided to wait until dark to make his crossing. He waited amid a stand of white pines that offered cover while he took a quick nap as the gloaming settled along the rural highway.

He awoke refreshed, but hungry. He drew closer to the road where he saw a small store, closed for the evening. There was no car in sight. It seemed to Yancey that the store was just begging to be broken into. He went around to the back of the building where a large cedar tree stood between a small window and the view from the road. Being tall had its advantages. Yancey reached up and smashed the window with the butt of his rifle and hoisted himself inside.

He found cases of Pepsi and Mountain Dew stacked along the walls, almost to the ceiling. He rummaged through the store at his leisure, grabbing bags of his favorite thing, Cheetos. He then took several cans of Vienna sausages, pork and beans, and sardines and stuffed them in his sack. The cooler rewarded Yancey with a quart of milk, most of which he drank while gathering more supplies. He picked up a pound of bologna, a package of sliced ham along with a loaf of bread, and a box of kitchen matches and slid them into his sack. Yancey looked around the store's interior one more time to see if he had forgotten anything, then made his way to the window. He made sure no one was coming and then eased the sack to the ground before he climbed through the window. He gathered up his pilfered supplies and once again headed in a northwesterly direction.

The rest of his trip to the cabin on Bowlin Creek was all uphill.

CHAPTER 51

MOORESVILLE WAS abuzz with news of the women's ordeal—their kidnapping and subsequent safe return, Carmen Romano's murder, plus the death of Kevin Seacrest. "How could this happen in our sleepy little town?" was the talk at all the local eateries.

When Ed and Joanie returned from Wilkes County, they went to Ed's home and were not seen for three days. When they finally emerged, the look on their faces said it all—satisfied.

News traveled fast in Mooresville and everyone was elated that Joanie and Ed were back together. Joanie let it be known that they were getting remarried, and in a church this time. Central United Methodist Church on North Academy Street was chosen to accommodate the crowd.

"I told you I was going to invite the whole damn town, didn't I?" Joanie shared with Gail and Debbie one morning, as she was making a flower arrangement for a customer.

"Yes, you did, but we thought you were kidding," Debbie said.

"I ain't kiddin' about this marriage. I'm dead serious. I've been such a fool and there ain't no way that Ed Mitchell is gonna have to wonder where his little Joanie is at night ever again. I'm gonna to be snuggled up to him so close when I go to sleep, we'll be just like two spoons in the silverware drawer."

"I am so happy for you," Gail said.

"Me, too," said Debbie.

"Are things getting back to normal at the law office?" Joanie asked Debbie.

"Yes and no."

"Whatcha mean, yes and no?"

"Well, when I get to work in the mornings, there're fresh flowers on my desk. And now, Carson takes me to lunch or has it brought in. Why couldn't I have married someone like him the first time?"

"God has a plan for you, Debbie. I truly believe that you will find happiness," Gail said.

"It's only been a few weeks since Kevin died and sometimes I feel guilty that I'm enjoying my life."

"What?" Joanie said. "Guilty for what? That scumbag treated you like dirt. He was havin' an affair with Carmen, he beat the crap out of you, and last but not least, he was willin' to have you killed so he could run off with that hussy, and you tell me you're feelin' guilty. Damn, I'll never understand the way you Yankees think."

Gail interjected, "Debbie just needs some time to sort things out. She just wants to take things slow for a while, right Debbie?"

"Something like that."

"Have you fallen in love with Carson?" asked Joanie.

"I've probably been falling in love with him ever since I went to work in his office. He is such a gentleman and I really think he loves me, too. I just don't want to rush things."

"I don't blame you, Debbie," Gail said. "You two make a very nice couple and I think the entire town is excited, seeing their number one bachelor escorting such a lovely young lady."

"I hope so."

"Hellfire and damnation! It ain't nobody else's business what you do. You and Carson deserve to be happy." Joanie said.

"I just don't want anybody to think badly of us, that's all."

"Listen to me," Joanie said, pointing a finger at Debbie. "Everybody in this town knows what a son-of-a-bitch Kevin was. They saw the bruises on you. Makeup can only cover so much, you know. Get on with your life. Screw old Carson's brains out and marry him before somebody else snatches him up."

"Joanie!" Debbie said.

"Well, all I'm sayin' is, you'd better not let this one get away."

"I don't plan on it, but it will be on our time schedule. As a matter of fact, he's taking me to dinner tonight."

"That's wonderful," Gail said. "I think you two will be very happy. Listen to your heart. You'll know what's right."

"I know."

"What do you think of Marci Meredith?" asked Gail, changing the subject. "James thinks Jake is really serious about her."

"Oh, I think she's the best thing that's happened to Jake McLeod since Kitt passed away. I was beginning to worry about him," said Joanie.

"We all were," Gail concurred.

"I think she's really a neat person. Did you hear what she did over at his house one night?" Debbie offered.

"Do you mean about the siren and the flashing lights? I think that was a hoot. That girl's got a sense of humor, that's for sure," Joanie added.

Gail asked, "What do you ladies think of inviting Marci to join our Wednesday night group?"

"Hell," Joanie said, "That's a great idea. She'll be a lot of fun."

CHAPTER 52

THE MOUNTAIN laurel grew thicker and thicker as Yancey weaved his way steadily up the steep slopes of western Wilkes County. The laurel was so dense in places that it often blocked out the sun even in midday and made his trek extremely difficult. The constant uphill climb took its physical and mental toll on Yancey, but he kept putting one foot in front of the other. Despite stumbling and falling into numerous small streams, he was never deterred from his mission.

The only pair of overalls he now possessed was ragged and filthy. Earlier, he fled through a patch of saw briars while being chased by a pack of wild dogs. Only after he shot what he thought was the lead dog, did they give up their chase and run away.

Miles and miles of rugged terrain were behind him now, only a few more hills and hollows were between him and the lonely little cabin on Bowlin Creek. Exhausted, Yancey Darwood finally crossed the middle fork of Reddie's River and climbed the last hill before his final destination. He had never been so tired in all his life.

Familiar woods now surrounded the bedraggled Yancey and he was filled with hope. He trudged on until he saw the forlorn cabin in which he had been born. The little stream still trickled a few yards in front of the dilapidated porch and wound its way among the laurel thicket that had overtaken the property. Yancey sat down on the bank of the stream and looked at the cabin with a devotion he could not describe. It was as if he were a mighty salmon returning to the place of his birth to die. He sat there for a long time, taking in his surroundings and listening to the stream gurgling at his feet.

Home. By God, I did it. I'm home, Yancey thought. He got slowly to his feet and walked the short distance to the cabin. He stepped up on the big rock step and then onto the porch. Memories flooded his mind. *Daddy put that rock there for me when I was too little to climb up on the porch by myself.*

Yancey tentatively pushed the door open and peered inside. A homemade table lay overturned in the middle of the room. Three handmade chairs were tossed about as if a hurricane had flung them to-and-fro. A bucket, a few plates and cups, and some kitchen utensils lay beneath the table. A faded blue and white mattress lay on the floor near a small bed that was pushed against the wall. *This'll do. This'll do just fine.*

He turned the table upright and set the chairs around it. Yancey picked up the dishes, set them on the table, and sat down on one of the chairs. *Home, I'm home.*

The food he'd taken from the little store was long gone and gnawing hunger pains brought his mind back to reality. He picked up his rifle and left through the only door. Squirrels were plentiful here and soon Yancey had one stuffed in the pocket of his overalls as he headed back to his cabin. He gathered fallen limbs for firewood and placed them in the fireplace. He struck one of his stolen matches and soon had a nice fire going. Yancey cooked the squirrel over the fire and the aroma of roasting meat soon filled the cabin.

He found a battered, tin coffeepot and was glad he had carried the pilfered pound of coffee with him all those miles. He scrounged around the cabin until he found a piece of discarded cloth. Yancey cut

215

off a small rectangular piece with his knife, spooned some coffee onto the remnant, folded it up, and then tied the top of it with some thread he found under the bed. Yancey filled the pot with water from the little stream, dropped the small handmade sack of coffee into the pot, and soon the smell of freshly brewed coffee brought him immense pleasure. *Yes, I'm gonna be alright*, he thought to himself.

The warm fire and his full stomach made Yancey drowsy. Realizing just how weary he was, he pulled the worn mattress onto the bed, fell on it, and drifted off into a deep sleep.

CHAPTER 53

WINTER HAD come and gone and Marci, now a member of the Wednesday Night Club, enjoyed meeting her new friends each week at The Crimson Cape. She and Jake had become an "item" and were almost inseparable since those eventful days in October.

Spring was in the air along the Blue Ridge Parkway. Jake and Marci left early one Thursday morning for Alleghany County hoping to see the rhododendron in bloom. Soon the beauty of the rolling hills captured their attention as they drove along the curvy road that led to the crest of the Blue Ridge Mountains. There was a decided difference in the flora after they crossed the Continental Divide at Roaring Gap. Evergreen trees and rhododendron became more plentiful with each mile.

When they turned onto the Blue Ridge Parkway and headed south, clusters of rhododendron blossoms in varying shades of pink greeted them. Rustic, split-rail fencing lined the parkway. "It takes a lot of work to maintain those fences," Jake said, admiring their craftsmanship.

"I'd never thought about that," Marci said, "I just appreciate the charm they add to the Parkway."

Ten miles later, Jake pulled into the parking area for Brinegar's cabin. They walked hand-in-hand down the winding path to the weathered, nineteenth century log home. Marci climbed onto the back porch and leaned over the handmade, wood railing. "Take my picture, this is so pretty," she said. Jake snapped a few shots as she showed off for the camera.

Marci peered into the back window of the cabin. "Look inside, the old loom is still there," she said, her nose pressed against the glass. "I betcha Mrs. Brinegar used to sit at that loom and make rugs for the cold floor."

"You're probably right." Jake agreed. "The cabin is the only structure on the entire Blue Ridge Parkway that has never been moved. It looks just as it did when it was built in 1885," Jake told Marci on the way back to the car.

He pulled his Cherokee out of the parking area and headed south while Marci chatted away. The big sweeping curve past Low Notch Gap was lined with split-rail fencing that was festooned with blooming rhododendron. The curve seemed to angle upward toward the sky that was filled with white, popcorn clouds.

Jake turned left in front of the rock store and adjoining restaurant at the top of the hill. He rounded a curve and then turned right onto the road that led to the picnic area of Doughton Park. He drove all the way to the parking area at the end of the road, near the trail to Bluff Mountain.

Jake and Marci climbed out of the Jeep, sat on the floorboard, and put on their walking shoes. He was retrieving the quilt out of the back of the Jeep when Marci ran around to where he was standing, threw her arms around him, and said, "Isn't this exciting? I've never seen so many rhododendron."

"Yes, it is exciting," Jake said as he kissed her. "I've *always* loved Doughton Park and even looked forward to coming here when I was a child."

After Jake helped Marci through the stile in the split-rail fence, she looped her arm in his as they hiked up to the top of the hill. At the crest, they were afforded a panoramic view of the mountains in every direction as far as they could see.

"It's so beautiful up here," Marci said. "We are going to lie down on the quilt under the tree, aren't we?" she asked teasingly.

"Why yeah! Why do you think I brought you up here?"

"To take advantage of me, I hope" Marci said, flashing her beautiful smile.

The breeze was cool, so they opted to go down the hill a little ways to get out of the wind before they spread their quilt. The sun warmed their backs as they hiked to a secluded spot in lee of the northwest wind.

"I love you, Jake McLeod," Marci said tenderly as he unfolded the old quilt. "I never want to be without you. Not ever!"

They lay there side by side in the warm sun, eyes closed. Jake was thinking of the question he wanted to ask Marci. When he could stand it no longer, he leaned on one elbow so he could look directly into her eyes. "Will you marry me, Marci Meredith? I am no longer a complete person unless you're with me."

Tears inched down her cheeks as she answered, "Oh, Jake, you devil, you. I would have married you months ago if only you would have asked me."

"I take that as a yes," Jake said.

"That's a definite yes! I'll marry you and put you out of your misery."

"You have just made me the happiest man on earth, Marci."

"Well, you've just made me the happiest woman on earth, so I guess we're even." She wrapped her arms around his neck, pulled him to her, and kissed him as if she would never have another chance. "Oh, Jake, I'm so happy."

"Me too," he replied as he kissed her again and again.

"Jake, you know I'm not going to be able to stop if we keep this up, don't you?"

"I kind of figured as much."

"Well, you know what's going to happen if you don't stop kissing me like you're kissing me, don't you?"

"I can hope," Jake said.

"I think we need to consummate our engagement," Marci said.

"Marci, I think you consummate a marriage."

"Well, whatever. Do you want to make love to me on this mountain hillside or not, Jake McLeod?"

"What do you think?" Jake said as he helped her stand and quickly gather the quilt. "Lead the way, darlin'."

Marci grabbed his hand and led the way down the hill through the tall pasture grass and pointed to a secluded spot behind a stand of white pine trees. "Perfect," she said, taking off her jacket.

Jake watched as she quickly pulled her shirt over her head, exposing her white bra in the sunlight.

"What're you lookin' at, Jake McLeod?"

"At the most beautiful woman God ever created, that's what."

"I love it when you talk like that. Now come over here and unhook my bra," she prompted as she knelt on the quilt.

Jake knelt in front of Marci and kissed her. He felt her shudder in his arms as her voluptuous breasts met the chilled mountain air. Her breath came in short gasps as he slowly and deliberately kissed his way down her naked body. Marci tenderly ran her fingers through his hair and held him close. Jake could hear her breathing become more labored. He concentrated on one nipple at a time, drawing it tenderly into the warmth of his mouth, releasing it to the chilled air, and then going to the other one. Jake played no favorites.

Breathing hard, Marci drew back, lifted his head in her hands, and brought Jake's lips to hers. Marci unbuttoned his shirt, helped him out of it and threw it on the ground. She took the rest of his clothes and tossed them, to join hers, in the pile on the grass.

They lay together on the quilt, oblivious to anything but the feel of each other's body. The chill in the air was exhilarating and it heightened the awareness of each other's caresses. They made love on that sunny hillside in Doughton Park and, according to Marci Meredith, consummated their engagement.

"That was fantastic!" Marci said. "Let's get engaged again tomorrow so we can consummate our engagement again."

"Marci Meredith, you're something else, did you know that?"

"So I've heard. What do you want to do now? Are you ready for an encore?"

"Not quite yet," Jake answered weakly, "I'm not as young as I used to be."

"I won't let you forget," Marci said.

"Let's head home and start making plans before you change your mind," Jake said.

"Not a chance on that happening, my man."

"Won't the girls be surprised when they find out I proposed to you?"

"Jake, everybody in Mooresville knew you were going to ask me sooner or later. I couldn't have stood it much longer," Marci said, "I was going to ask you to marry me, if I had to."

Jake laughed and said again, "Marci, you're something else, did you know that?"

"Oh, shut up and kiss me," Marci said.

He did, being the obedient, newly betrothed man that he was.

They dressed in the warm sun, pausing occasionally to kiss, gathered the quilt, climbed the hill, and then strolled leisurely to Jake's Jeep. As he stowed the quilt in back of the Jeep, Jake said, "Let's stop at the Northwest Trading Post in Glendale Springs and get some goodies to take home. I love the fried apple pies and fudge they have. I also want to tell the ladies about our engagement."

"Works for me," Marci said.

CHAPTER 54

J AKE PULLED into the parking lot at the Northwest Trading Post and Marci bounded from the Jeep like a puppy that had been let outside for the first time in days.

The Trading Post was a quaint gift shop that sold arts and crafts, homemade jams, baked goods, and a variety of merchandise indigenous to the area. The Post had sold Jake's artwork for years and he'd become friends with the ladies who worked there.

Annie was slicing a slab of homemade fudge for a customer as Jake and Marci walked through the door. She carefully wrapped the fudge in some paper, bagged it, and then rang up the sale. "Hey y'all, see you got your girl with you today, Jake."

"Yeah, I do. But one of these days pretty soon, she's going to be more than my girl. She has seen the light and has agreed to marry me," Jake said.

"Praise the Lord," Annie said as Peggy walked up. "It's about time."

"What's about time, Annie?"

"Jake's finally gotten around to asking Marci to marry him."

Peggy said with a twinkle in her eye, "We all knew you'd get around to asking her someday."

"It looks like just about everybody knew except me," Jake said.

Annie laughed, "That's true!" She turned and called to the other two ladies who were working behind the jewelry counter. "Hey Karen, you and Marie come here. We've got some exciting news!"

"What news?" Marie asked as she and Karen greeted Jake and Marci.

"These two are getting hitched!" Annie said.

"I could tell a long time ago they were meant for each other. I've been praying they wouldn't wait too long. Jake's no spring chicken you know," Marie said.

Everybody laughed and congratulated them with hugs.

Karen asked, grinning, "What took you so long, Jake, were you enjoying bachelorhood too much?"

"No, it wasn't that at all. To tell you the truth, I was afraid she'd say no, so I kept postponing the question."

Marci laughed out loud, "You've got to be kidding, and I thought you were so smart."

Karen, Peggy, and Marie wished Jake and Marci well and left them with Annie, who had changed from her lighthearted demeanor to one of seriousness.

"Not wanting to change the subject, but are you still with the sheriff's department, Marci?"

"Yes. Anything wrong?"

"Well, let me ask you something. I don't know if we should be really concerned or not, but somebody's been stealing food from us. We haven't caught him in the act yet, but we're pretty sure we know who's doing it."

"Have you contacted the Ashe County Sheriff's Department?"

"No, we haven't. I don't know if it's worth it or not. So far, the only things missing are just some ham biscuits, fried apple pies, packages of cheese straws, baked goods, and things like that. The man looks so hungry; we've just kind of let it go."

"What does this man look like?" asked Marci, the detective in her taking over.

"He's kind of scary looking," Annie said.

"Describe him to me."

"Well, he's probably over six and a half feet tall and he's real hairy. His clothes are always dirty and he seems to have only one pair of overalls."

The hair rose on the back of Marci's neck, "Did you say over six and a half feet tall?"

"I sure did," Annie verified Marci's question.

"Do you have any idea where he lives?"

"No, not really. I've seen him come up from the pasture over yonder," Annie said, pointing east and across the Parkway. "He usually crosses that fence on the other side of the road. That road will eventually take you all the way to Miller's Creek. He may live down there in the woods somewhere. I know everybody who lives in the houses along the paved part."

"So you don't think it's one of those folks?" Marci asked.

"No, I don't think so. I've never seen this man before. Last October, we started noticing a little food missing. It wasn't much to begin with, but it's gotten worse since we re-opened this spring."

"Have you ever seen him carrying a gun of any type?"

"One time I thought I saw him carrying a rifle, but he's never brought it in here. He leaned it against that tree over there by the fence."

"I'll look into it and let you know what we find out."

"Thanks, Marci. I really appreciate it."

Jake looked over at Marci and nodded toward the door. "Well, it's always good to see you ladies," he said as he paid for the pies and fudge that he just couldn't resist. "We've got to get started down the mountain."

"It's good to see that you two have finally made the decision to tie the knot. Be sure to let us know when the big event will be." Annie and the other ladies wished them well as they were going out the door.

"We surely will," Jake said.

As soon as they were outside, Jake said, "Let's take a little ride down the road and see if we see Yancey or what-ever-his-name-is walking through the woods."

"I think we'd better notify Phil West or the Ashe County Sheriff's Department," Marci countered. "The Wilkes County line is not far down that road. Let's call Phil, let him know what we just found out, and see what he says," Marci said.

"Okay, Kemosabe," Jake answered. "You're the boss."

Neither Jake's nor Marci's cell phone had a signal on that section of the Parkway. "Damn," Marci said as she closed hers. "Let's go over to the gift shop behind Holy Trinity Church. They'll have a phone we can use and while we're there, we can ask if they've had anything stolen lately, too."

Holy Trinity Episcopal Church had become rather famous in the past few years. Ben Long of Statesville, a noted artist, painted a large fresco of The Last Supper on the wall behind the pulpit of the church. Since then, bus loads of tourists have visited the tiny chapel to see the magnificent work of art. A well-stocked gift shop stood a few yards up the hill behind the church's parking lot.

Marci showed her badge to the bearded, young man behind the counter and asked if she could use his phone to call in an emergency. "Sure," he said, "help yourself."

Before she picked up the phone, Marci asked the man, "Have you had anything stolen in the past several weeks?"

"Matter of fact, we have. It's just food. Nothing else is ever missing. It's the strangest thing. Usually people steal CDs and stuff like that."

"Has anyone else around here been broken into lately or had anything stolen?"

"Yeah, somebody broke into the Parkway Grill a couple of

times."

"Where is the grill?" Marci asked.

"It's right down the road, on Highway 16," the man answered.

"I think I'd better make that call now," Marci said. After telling the deputy on duty why she needed to speak with Phil West, the deputy promptly patched her through.

"Phil," Marci said, "I need to let you know what's going on up here in Glendale Springs."

"Well, that's not my jurisdiction, but I'm listening."

"Do you remember the big, hairy man who was involved in the kidnapping of those three women a few months back?"

"Sure, went by the name of Yancey."

"That's the one," Marci said. "A man fitting his description has been seen in the Glendale Springs area. It's believed that he may be the one who's responsible for stealing food from the local businesses."

"Listen," West said, "I'm up that way now checking on a disturbance on Highway 16 at the edge of Wilkes County. There are some other deputies handling the situation here now, so I can be there in just a few minutes."

"Great! We'll wait for you in the parking lot at the Northwest Trading Post."

CHAPTER 55

"Now, WE can see him when he drives up," Jake said, as they pulled into the parking lot.

"Maybe we can snuggle a little bit while we wait," Marci suggested.

"I think we'd better straighten up and act right," Jake said.

Jake saw a Crown Victoria pull into a parking space across the lot. "There he is now," Jake said looking through the driver's side window. "Behave yourself."

"Damn it." Marci pouted.

"You're the one who called him, remember?"

"Yeah, yeah, I remember. Let's have a little powwow with the chief."

Chief Deputy Phil West opened the door on the Crown Vic, swung his six-foot frame out of his car, and walked over to the Jeep.

"Long-time-no-see," he said smiling as he looked through Jake's window. "Are you two still hanging around together?"

"Yeah, I can't get rid of him," Marci said. "As a matter of fact, Phil, he just asked me to marry him."

"Well, whadaya know? I've wondered what he's been waitin' for.

What did you tell him, Marci? You gonna wait til something better comes along?"

"No, I felt sorry for him, so I said I'd marry him, but he'd have to make it quick because of his age."

Phil West laughed and said, "Congratulations. When's the big day?"

"He asked me less than an hour ago," Marci said, "but I thought we should wait a couple of days anyway, what do you think?"

"Knowing you, Marci, I'd say that's just about right," West said. "I know you two will be happy and again, congratulations."

"Thanks, Phil," they said together.

"Well, I know you didn't call me up here to talk about getting hitched, so tell me about this big guy suspected of stealing food around here," West said. "He sounds an awful lot like our man, Yancey."

"That's the reason we called," Marci said, more serious now. "We think it might be him. He's been seen crossing the Parkway over there," Marci said, pointing through the Jeep's window to the spot Annie had shown them. "Isn't the Wilkes County Line somewhere down that road?"

"That's right. It begins about where the pavement ends. Maybe I need to drive down there and take a look-see," West said.

"Do you mind if we ride along with you?" Marci asked. "I'd really like to find out if this 'foodnapper' is the same man who was hooked up with Carmen Romano."

"I'd be glad to have you. Since you're not in uniform though, you should wear a jacket with the Wilkes County Sheriff's Department logo on it."

"If you insist," Marci said.

"We don't want any complications," West told her. "Jake, since you're not here in any official capacity; you'll just have to observe. You okay with that?"

"Sure," Jake agreed, "I'll stay out of your way."

"Fine, let's do it then," West said as they climbed into his cruiser. Jake got in the back seat and Marci rode in front alongside the Chief Deputy.

West steered the Crown Vic down the curvy road and stopped where the pavement ended in front of a small, well-kept home covered with white vinyl siding. Dark blue shutters adorned each window and flowers sprouted from well-tended beds. A lone woman of indeterminable age was sitting on the front porch dipping snuff from a can of Tube Rose.

Deputy West walked up to the porch and asked her a few questions. He returned with a satisfied smile on his face.

"Bingo!" he said as he climbed into the cruiser. "The old woman says she's seen him several times walking up the road carrying a rifle." West paused briefly and added, "She also said that he is one big, hairy man and he scares her to death."

"Annie at the Trading Post thinks he's a little scary, too," Marci said, validating the woman's observation. Jake let her and the Chief Deputy do all the talking since he was just along for the ride.

West said, "I asked her when she first noticed him being in the area. She didn't know exactly, but she said she hadn't heard shooting in the woods around here for years until last October. Since then, she's heard it regularly."

"Where are the woods she's talking about?" asked Marci.

"The woods she referred to are a mile or so further down the road," West said. "If y'all want to do this now, let me know. We don't know for sure he's our man, but I would like to ask him a few questions while we're here."

Marci was quick to say, "Let's go talk to him and see what he has to say for himself. He might just be a hungry thief, but on the other hand, he might be 'Bigfoot'."

"Do you have your vest with you, Marci, and are you packing?"

"I don't have my vest, but I'm always packing."

They had gone only a mile down the graveled road, when Jake called out, "Look through the woods on our right. That looks like a path going down the side of the hill."

Chief West pulled the Crown Vic over to the edge of the road. "Let's take a look."

Marci and West drew their Glock-40s and had them ready as they made their way slowly down the wooded path. After going less than a quarter of a mile into the dense woods, he warned, "Shhh, look up there. See that old dilapidated cabin? The path leads straight to it."

"There's smoke coming out of the chimney," Marci observed.

They inched closer for a better look. West said, "We'd better identify ourselves. There's no tellin' who's inside or what they might do. Jake, you'd better stay back."

"Okay. I'll just wait here," Jake said as he ducked out of sight behind a large laurel bush. "You two be careful."

West and Marci inched ahead to what he thought was a safe distance and took cover behind a large hickory tree. "Hello, in the cabin," shouted the deputy. "This is the Wilkes County Sheriff's Department."

After a long pause with no response, Marci said, "Maybe they didn't hear you. Try again."

"This is the Wilkes County Sheriff's Department," he shouted a little louder. "We just want to ask you a few questions." Still no response.

"What do you think, Marci?"

"It's your call," she answered.

"Let's go take a look."

He and Marci stepped out from behind the tree and walked down the path. Suddenly shots rang out from the doorway of the cabin. Marci was thrown backward as if she were a Raggedy Anne doll being tossed aside by an angry child. Jake watched in horror as Marci's body slid limply to the ground. Blood poured from her chest.

"Marci!" Jake screamed, "Marci!"

The deputy hit the ground in a cloud of dust as bullets peppered the ground around him. He crawled toward Marci and found cover several yards from where she lay.

"Is she alright?" Jake pleaded.

"I can't tell yet, let me check."

It seemed as if the world had stopped before Jake heard the deputy call out, "She's breathing Jake, but she's bleeding pretty bad. We gotta get some help immediately."

"What do you want me to do?" Jake asked.

"I'm going to radio for help. There's a shotgun in the cruiser—go get it. Here, you'll need keys," West said, as he tossed them to Jake. They landed a few feet out of his reach. "Damn. I'm sorry, Jake."

Dropping to the ground, Jake crawled to within several feet of the keys and began reaching for them when shots exploded again from the cabin sending stinging dirt and gravel into his face.

"Damn!" Jake wiped his face with his hands.

"Are you alright?" West called out.

"I'm okay."

"Do you think you can you reach the keys now?"

"Hold on," Jake said. He picked up a fallen limb and stretched it over the keys and tried to drag them toward him. Shots rang out again and gravel flew in every direction in front of the limb. West began firing at the cabin as Jake tried again and this time the keys came with the limb. Jake cried with relief as he retrieved them. "I've got 'em now. How's she doing?"

"She's hanging in there, but hurry. I'll try to keep the bastard in the cabin pinned down. Go!"

The cruiser was still parked at the end of the lane. The shotgun was just like the one in Marci's cruiser. He ran back to retrieve the gun and found it locked in its rack. He fumbled through the keys until he found the right one. After several tries he unlocked the rack, grabbed the shotgun, found a few extra shells in the console, and ran back.

The deputy was still at the foot of a laurel bush.

"Are you okay, Phil?" Jake asked.

"Yeah, I'm alright. Did you get the shotgun?"

"Yeah, how's Marci?"

"She hasn't moved."

"I'm going to check on her," Jake said.

"No, don't even try it," West warned. "I got a glimpse of the shooter. I think he's our man."

"I don't care."

"Alright, but you watch out for that son-of-a-bitch. He'll shoot you if he sees you. He's a desperate bastard and a good shot, too, so be careful," the deputy warned.

Jake crawled through low-hanging laurel limbs, clutching the loaded shotgun in his right hand. He took a circuitous route that eventually led him to Marci's side.

"Marci, can you hear me?" Jake whispered, not wanting to give away his position. "Marci, Marci." She never answered. Jake tried again, "Marci. I'm right here. Help's on the way. I love you. Don't you leave me now," Jake begged. Her right hand moved ever so slightly as if she was reaching for him. He grabbed her bloody hand and told her again, "I love you, Marci. Hang on, please." She weakly squeezed his hand and then her fingers went limp. Jake reached in his rear pocket, took out his handkerchief, and placed it over the wound.

Anger suddenly raged within Jake McLeod like he had never experienced before. He rose from where he was hiding. "That's it, dammit! I'm not gonna lose the woman I love to some worthless son-of-a-bitch who won't even come out and fight," Jake yelled as he came out onto the path.

"Get down, Jake!" West yelled. "We don't want anybody else to get shot."

I'm going after the bastard. We've got to do something or she's going to die," Jake said, his voice choked with emotion.

"Get down!"

Two shots rapidly came from the cabin barely missing Jake as he dove for cover.

"I've got an idea," West said.

"Alright, let's hear it."

"Give me a chance to crawl through this laurel thicket and get up behind the cabin," West said. "The cabin butts right up against that hill. I think I can climb onto the edge of the roof from the hill and put my coat over the chimney. We'll smoke the son-of-a-bitch out."

"All right then, be careful and don't let him hear you climbing on the roof."

"I won't, but you stay down Jake, I mean it."

"Go on, I'll watch the door," Jake said.

The deputy slowly crawled through the thicket, making his way to the hill behind the cabin and then carefully climbed on to the roof. He waved when he got into position and Jake aimed the shotgun at the cabin door. West took off his jacket and draped it over the top of the smoke-filled chimney.

Spasmodic coughing was soon heard from within the cabin. Unable to breathe with choking smoke filling the cabin, a huge man came barreling onto the porch. Jake crawled over and positioned his body between Marci and the gunman to protect her. The man began firing his rifle wildly as he stumbled off the porch and headed toward Jake and Marci. He wiped the smoke-induced tears from his eyes, brought the rifle to his shoulder and aimed directly at Jake.

Jake did not hesitate. He fired both barrels of the shotgun. The load hit the huge man in the chest, knocking him back four or five feet. Then there was deadly silence.

"Are you alright, Jake?" Deputy West hollered.

After a prolonged silence, Jake said, "I'm okay. I think I killed him. He was standing there with his rifle pointed directly at me and getting ready to pull the trigger. I didn't have a choice!"

West hurriedly climbed down from the roof and ran toward Jake.

"He would have killed us both; you should have seen the look on his face."

"You did what you had to do," the deputy said as he walked over to the body of the huge man.

Then they heard the sirens of the approaching emergency vehicles. "Oh, God," Jake said, "I just hope they're not too late."

The EMTs asked Jake to step back and give them room.

"How bad is it?" Jake asked.

"We're stabilizing her now. It's not far to Ashe Memorial Hospital. We'll have her there in ten minutes. You can ride with us if you like."

"Thanks. Is she gonna be alright?"

"She's lost a lot of blood. We've started two large-bore IV lines to try to her stabilize her. We also inserted an endotracheal tube into her lung to help her breathing. They'll know more at the Trauma Unit."

Jake followed the stretcher to the awaiting ambulance. The ambulance doors were open and the EMTs slid the stretcher in quickly. Jake sat beside Marci and never let go of her hand all the way to Jefferson.

CHAPTER 56

A
T THE HOSPITAL, emergency staff whisked Marci away on a gurney. Jake was directed to a reception desk where a nurse spoke to him from behind a sliding pane of glass. She shoved some papers in front of him and told him to fill them out. Jake filled in each blank as best he could and then handed the clipboard to the nurse. He paced back and forth in the waiting room briefly before collapsing into an upholstered chair. Jake silently prayed because there was nothing else he could do.

Sometime later Chief Deputy West joined him and placed his hands on Jake's shoulders. "You did good back there, Jake."

Jake mumbled, "Thanks."

He had almost forgotten, in his concern for Marci, that he had just killed a man. The events of the day came flooding back to him: he had proposed to the woman he loved; she had accepted his proposal; they had made love on a sunny hillside in beautiful Doughton Park; Marci had been gunned down, critically wounded and may not live through surgery; someone had tried to kill him; and he had taken a person's life, all in one day.

West took the chair beside Jake and they both sat quietly. After a while West said, "We'll have to talk about the shooting, you know. It was a clean one, but I still have to fill out a report."

"Thanks Phil, for all you've done," Jake said, "and for getting that man out of his cabin. Marci wouldn't have had a chance if she'd had to wait any longer for help. What you did took a lot of guts."

West patted Jake on the shoulder as he rose and started toward the door. "I'm going to check on the investigation…hang in there, Jake."

After Deputy West left, Jake thought he'd better let his friends know what had happened. He dialed James Caldwell's number. Gail answered. "Gail, this is Jake."

"You don't sound like yourself. What's wrong?"

"Marci's been shot."

"Shot? Where are you, Jake? What happened?"

Jake related the days events as best he could.

Gail said, "We'll be there in less than two hours."

CHAPTER 57

GAIL CALLED Joanie with the news and asked her to call Debbie. She hung up the phone and quickly threw some clothes in a bag. Gail joined James in their Navigator and they were soon headed toward I-77.

"Marci just has to be okay. I don't know how Jake could bear another devastating loss," Gail said.

"I know," James agreed. "Just pray for her. That's all we can do."

Gail closed her eyes and said a prayer for them. *God, please bless Marci and Jake and bring them safely through this ordeal. Thank You Lord. Amen.* She opened her eyes after the prayer, looked through the window at the passing scenery, and felt confident in her faith that God was watching over them.

The interstate was not very crowded, so James set his cruise control near eighty and headed north. When they passed I-40, the speed limit was seventy miles per hour, so James bumped it up a little over eighty.

"You know this is the same road Jake and I traveled when we were searching for you?"

"I know," Gail said.

"A lot has happened since then, hasn't it?"

"It certainly has," Gail said. "Little did we know how much good would come from that terrifying ordeal. Now we all appreciate each day more than ever and no longer take our lives for granted."

Gail laid her head back and thought about all that had happened over the past few months. *Jake and Marci found each other and will probably get married some day. I don't know why he doesn't go ahead and propose. She said she was going to ask him if he didn't hurry up and pop the question. Marci is so funny. She's the perfect woman for Jake.*

Gail smiled as she thought of Joanie and Ed's wedding. The big event had been held at Central United Methodist Church only a few weeks after their harrowing experience. Joanie was right—the whole damn town came, just like she said they would. She sold her townhouse and moved back in with Ed. Now, they're talking about selling the flower shop, taking it easy, and enjoying their lives together. I don't know how they could be happier.

While James concentrated on his driving, Gail's thoughts turned to Debbie. Being married to a man like Kevin Seacrest had stripped her of all self-confidence, but because of the kidnapping, she had found love and acceptance with Carson Wells.

Gail looked over at James as he steered their Navigator westward and thought fondly, *I love James more than ever. I can't imagine my life without him. He has worked so hard to help us establish a battered women's shelter in Mooresville. I have learned so much volunteering there twice a month with Debbie. If it had not been for those days we spent in the woods together, I would never have understood the deplorable situations that so many women face each day.*

"What are you thinking about?" James asked.

"Oh, just how things have turned out for us all," Gail confessed. "How much farther?"

"We've making really good time. Probably thirty minutes," James said as he turned north on Highway 16 and raced through Miller's Creek and up the mountain.

CHAPTER 58

GAIL AND JAMES found Jake in the waiting room. "God, it's good to see you two here," Jake said as he fell into Gail's arms. "We're here for you as long as you need us, Jake," James said. "How's she doing?"

"I don't know. I haven't heard a thing."

"It's been two hours, what are they doing?" James asked.

"They told me they had to rush her to surgery and that's all I really know."

"I called Joanie before we left," Gail told Jake, "so half the town probably knows by now. How are you doing?"

"I'm scared. I'm just praying that she'll be alright."

"She will be, Jake," Gail said.

"I asked Marci to marry me this afternoon. She said yes. Can you believe it?"

"How could she have said anything but yes? The whole town knew you two were going to get married. Didn't anyone tell you, Jake?" Gail said.

"We're lookin' for Jake Mcleod." Jake looked up when he heard Joanie Mitchell's unmistakable voice. "Oh, never mind, there he is,"

Joanie said excitedly as she hurried down the hall toward him with Ed, Carson Wells and Debbie Seacrest following close behind.

"You didn't think we were going to let you sit through all this by yourself, did you?" Joanie said. "I want to know what the hell's goin' on up here," Joanie demanded. "Tell me exactly what happened."

After hearing all the facts, a somber mood fell over the group of friends in the little waiting room.

"Go on and tell them the rest," Gail said, breaking the silence.

"Tell them what?" Joanie asked.

"They probably already know anyway," Jake said.

"Will somebody please tell me what in the hell y'all are talking about?" pleaded Joanie.

"I asked Marci to marry me today and she said yes."

"What took you so damn long? She's been ready and waitin' on you for months. I was beginning to wonder if you had brain damage or was just plain blind."

"Well," Debbie said, "I have some news, too. Carson and I are getting married next month."

"Well, shut my mouth and call me a dirty name," Joanie said, laughing and brushing away fresh tears.

Everyone congratulated Debbie and Carson while she proudly showed her ring to everyone.

As the conversation quieted down, James said, "I think I'll go find some coffee. Can I bring you all some?"

"Wait, I'll go with you," Ed offered.

"Before you go, let's all join hands and pray," Gail said.

They all joined hands while Gail prayed for Marci. She then thanked God for saving Marci and for each person in the circle and their special friendship. They all joined her and softly said, "Amen."

"Thanks, Gail," Jake said. He admired her faith and was amazed that she had thanked God in advance for Marci's recovery. After the men left, Gail and Joanie sat beside Jake and talked quietly while Debbie and Carson sat on the other side of the room and held hands.

Jake considered Gail and James his dearest friends, but he could not understand how their faith remained so strong. He had prayed and prayed when he'd found out Kitt had cancer, but became so disillusioned when she died just a few months later. Now Gail was praying for Marci. *God, help my unbelief.*

CHAPTER 59

JAMES AND ED returned with coffee, and still they waited. The clock on the waiting room wall read 7:36 when a tired surgeon, still dressed in green scrubs, approached the anxiously awaiting throng. "Which one of you is Mr. McLeod?"

Jake weakly rose from the chair where he had spent the entire afternoon and evening and asked, "How is she?"

"I'm Dr. Brent Samuels," the man in green scrubs said as he extended his hand. "I performed the surgery on Ms. Meredith." Jake shook his hand and realized it was probably that very same hand that had operated on his beloved Marci.

"Is she going to be alright?" Jake asked.

"The bullet passed through the top of her right lung. She's lost a lot of blood. The EMTs saved her life by inserting the endotracheal tube and re-inflating her lung."

"Is she going to make it, Doc?"

The doctor continued, "We could find no major vascular damage, so things look pretty good there. I think she'll be fine. She seems to be a strong, young woman. She'll have to stay here for a few days before she can be moved, so just be patient."

A collective sigh came from everyone in the room after hearing the prognosis. Jake was preparing to thank Dr. Samuels when the doctor added, "You'll be glad to know, the baby's going to be fine, too."

"Baby?" Jake gasped and collapsed into one of the nearby chairs.

"Baby?" everyone said at once.

Joanie squealed with delight. "Why in the hell didn't you tell us Marci was pregnant?"

"I…. uh…I…..I didn't know," Jake stammered.

"You mean, Marci hadn't said anything about it?" Joanie asked.

"No, that's the first I've heard of it. I'm as surprised as you all are!"

Jake rose from his chair again and asked the good doctor, "Are you sure she's pregnant, Dr. Samuels?"

"I'd stake my reputation on it," he said smiling.

"When can I see her?" Jake asked.

"She's in recovery right now, maybe in another hour. I think she'll be fine. Just give her time. She has had extensive surgery and will be a little slow convalescing."

Jake thanked the doctor again and watched him as he turned and walked down the hall.

"My Marci, my beautiful Marci. Thank you dear God," Jake cried as he fell into Gail's arms. "A baby," he said, "a baby."

Gail took his hand in hers. "Let's thank God for saving Marci," she said, "and thank him for the new life that He has entrusted in your care." They all held hands as Gail offered a prayer of thanksgiving.

"Y'all want somethin' to eat, I'm starved," Joanie said. "Why don't we grab a quick bite? Jake needs to stay here so he can get in and see Marci and ask her a few questions. He'll probably want to be alone when he does, don't you think?"

Gail joined in, "I think that's a good idea. Can we bring you a sandwich, Jake?" she offered.

"Yes, thanks. That would be really nice. Would you bring me a Diet Coke, too?"

"Will do," James said. "Marci should be out of recovery by the time we get back." He added, "Congratulations again."

"Thanks, everyone, for coming to be with me and especially for your prayers. I can't begin to tell you how much it means to me. I'm kind of overwhelmed right now. I think I'm going to have to sit down again," Jake said as he collapsed in his chair.

They all laughed and waved goodbye, but James waited until everyone else was headed down the hall before he turned toward Jake, smiled, and said, "You still got it old man." He then hurried to catch up with the others.

CHAPTER 60

JAKE WAS alone when a rather large nurse, wearing a badge that identified her as Edith Dillard, a printed smock covered with penguins, and solid black pants, approached him and said, "Mr. McLeod, they have just moved Ms. Meredith from recovery to Intensive Care. You can see her for ten minutes."

Jake rose numbly and followed the penguin-smocked nurse down the hall and through a set of automatic doors to ICU.

Marci looked like a battered angel. Her beautiful red hair formed a halo on the pillow. Jake looked at the IV-drip that hung on a pole beside her. An oxygen apparatus was attached to her nose, but she was breathing on her own. Jake was grateful she was not on a respirator. Marci's eyes were closed and Jake stood there for a moment daring to watch her breathe.

After being convinced that she was breathing okay, he quietly pulled a chair close to her bedside and took her hand in his. He sat there and talked to her for his allotted ten minutes. Jake told her how much he loved her and how happy he was about the baby. Marci gave no indication that she had heard a word Jake said, but he was grateful just to be with her. The nurse came in to let him know that his time was up and that he could come back in two hours and see her again. Jake kissed Marci on the forehead and returned to his chair. Two hours went by. Jake looked out the window at the imposing Mount Jefferson. A feeling of helplessness was trying to worm its way into Jake's psyche, but he tried to be patient and remain hopeful.

The nurse returned and allowed Jake another ten minute visit with Marci. He followed her quietly, studying her penguin-covered smock and thinking, *she even walks like a penguin.*

Jake entered Marci's room again, sat beside her bed and held her limp hand in his. Little had changed in Marci's appearance since his last visit. Jake talked quietly to her as he looked at her lying in the hospital bed, wondering why this was happening to them. He was remembering the overwhelming sorrow he had already experienced once in his life when he heard a feeble groan coming from Marci's parched lips. Jake leaned over her. "I'm here, Marci. Can you hear me?"

"Time's up Mr. McLeod," Nurse Dillard said as she entered Marci's room.

"Can't I stay just a little while longer?" Jake begged. "I think she's trying to talk."

"Right now, she's struggling to regain consciousness. Give her a little more time. Maybe on your next visit," the nurse assured him.

Jake thought the next two hours would never pass, but the nurse finally came to get him and led him to Marci's room. Jake leaned over and kissed Marci tenderly on the forehead.

"Marci," Jake said quietly as he held her hand, "I love you. You're not going to get out of marrying me, you know? "

"Who's trying to get out of anything?" Marci said weakly.

"Marci, you're awake! Thank God," Jake cried.

"What happened?"

"You're in the hospital. You and Phil went to question the man who was possibly Carmen's accomplice in the kidnapping and you were shot."

"I don't remember anything. I remember going up a path, but that's all."

"Maybe it's best that you don't remember everything."

"I do seem to recall that somebody asked me to marry him, but I'm not too sure whether I said yes or no."

"You definitely said yes."

"Who asked me to marry him?" Marci asked with a weak smile.

"You know very well who did."

"I'm going to be alright, aren't I?" Marci questioned as she opened her tired eyes a little wider and tried to focus on Jake.

"Yes, you and the baby are both going to be fine."

"What did you say?"

"I said you and the baby are both going to be fine."

"Baby! What baby?"

"Marci, didn't you know you're pregnant?" Jake asked.

"Pregnant!"

"Yes, pregnant!"

Nurse Dillard entered the room. "Mr. McLeod your time is up."

"Please let him stay just a little longer," Marci begged.

"Are you okay?" the nurse asked when she saw Marci was crying.

"She just found out she's going to be a mother," Jake explained.

Nurse Dillard smiled as she left the room. "Five more minutes, Mr. McLeod. She really needs her rest."

Jake leaned over the bed and kissed Marci. "You're something else, did you know that?"

"And you're something else, too, Jake McLeod," Marci said smiling.

"Right now we have to get you well, so we can get married."

"Right now, how about something to drink?"

"God, I love you," Jake said.

"It's really okay to just call me Marci."

Jake burst out laughing. "Guess what? Gail, Joanie, and Debbie are in the waiting room."

"Really?" Marci asked.

"Yes, and James, Ed, and Carson are here with them, too. A lot of folks care about you and have been praying for you to get better. It looks like all our prayers have been answered," Jake said.

"Thank them for me."

"I will," Jake promised.

The nurse came bustling through the door with a styrofoam container of ice-water and shooed Jake out of the room.

"She's going to be fine," Jake said as he greeted his friends with a mile-wide grin on his face. "This time she was able to talk me. She even joked with me just like the old Marci."

"Did she know she was pregnant?" asked Gail.

"No, she didn't! Can you believe it? She was as surprised as everyone else."

Everyone hugged Jake as he told them everything Marci had said. He thanked them all for coming, but encouraged them to go home and get some rest. "We'll be fine now," he told them. "We'll be just fine."

"We packed some clothes before we left home and we're getting a room for the night at the Best Western," Gail said. "We're not leaving you alone just yet. We'll see you in the morning."

"You're the best friends anyone could ever hope for, thank you again," Jake said. As Gail hugged him goodnight, Jake whispered in her ear, "Thank you so much, Gail. Now I believe."

CHAPTER 61

THE NURSE wore a smock covered with purple flowers on the second day and one with green ivy on the third. She let Jake stay with Marci a little longer at each visit until he was up to thirty minutes each time.

On the third day, Marci was moved out of ICU and into a regular room. When they were finally alone, Marci took Jake's hand in hers and asked, "Can we get married now?"

"What? You're still in the hospital!"

"I want to be Marci McLeod and I don't want to wait. I love you, dammit! Why do we have to wait?"

"We have to wait until you're well enough, and don't call me 'dammit'."

She laughed, "Oh, it hurts when I laugh, dammit."

"Remember what I told you, don't call me 'dammit'," Jake said jokingly.

"Okay, but I really do want to get married before I start showing," she said. "I don't want people to think that we were doing something we weren't supposed to be doing, before we were supposed to be doing it."

Jake couldn't help but laugh. "Marci, the entire population of Mooresville and Troutman already knows about it, for God's sakes. You're something else, did you know that?"

"Since you tell me that all the time," Marci said, "I really must be."

"You are, and I love every bit of you," Jake said.

She laughed again and said, "I guess you're right about everybody knowing. We haven't been very discreet, have we?"

"No, we haven't. I want to be with you all the time and I guess I should have asked you to marry me months ago, but I thought people would think we hadn't known each other long enough," Jake explained.

"Marci said, "I don't believe in long engagements and we've already been engaged for days. Just look at that view from my window," she said pointing to Mt. Jefferson. Let's get married in the mountains and let's do it soon."

"Okay, how soon?"

"How about next Sunday?"

"Next Sunday!"

"Well, what are you standing here for? You've got a lot to do!"

"Yes ma'am," Jake said as he leaned over and kissed her lightly on the lips. "But, I'm not going anywhere until I know that you're okay. I'm staying here through the weekend."

"I'll be fine," Marci said. "Kiss me harder this time, I'm not going to break." Jake obliged. "Now get outta here and let me get some rest, I'm gonna need it. And, Jake..."

"Yes?"

"I love you," Marci said as he turned toward the door.

"I love you, too," Jake replied. "Try to get some rest, you are going to need it."

CHAPTER 62

JAKE DROVE home Monday morning to get some fresh clothes and buy a new suit from his friend, Johnny Smith, at John Franklin, Ltd. Johnny specialized in fine menswear and helped Jake select a dark, pin-striped suit, a matching shirt and tie, and a new pair of shoes.

He stopped by to see Joanie at her flower shop. When he told her about the wedding, Joanie squealed, "Hot dog! A wedding in the mountains. Where you gonna have this shindig, Jake?"

"I've been thinking about Doughton Park. That's where I proposed," Jake said.

"Sounds perfect to me," Joanie agreed.

"Have you decided on a date?" Joanie asked. "Gail and Debbie and I would like to help."

"She wants to get married Sunday."

"This Sunday?"

Jake nodded.

Joanie said, "You leave the details to us women. You don't need to worry about a thing." Joanie was on the phone as soon as Jake closed the door to her shop.

Jake went home, hurriedly showered, and packed what he would need for the next few days. He decided to put in a call to Marci's pastor, Reverend Chandler, before heading back to the hospital. Marci had been a member of First Baptist Church in Troutman for many years and Reverend Chandler readily agreed to perform the ceremony.

"Marci must be doing much better since my visit with her on Saturday if she's wants to get married this coming Sunday," Reverend Chandler said.

"You know Marci," Jake laughed. "She's not one to wait around if it's something she wants to do."

"Yes, I know her well," the pastor said.

"I'm sorry we're asking with such short notice, but we're really anxious to begin our lives together," Jake said.

"Would you permit me to announce this wonderful news to my congregation at our Wednesday night prayer meeting?" Reverend Chandler asked.

"I think that would be wonderful," Jake replied.

Dr. Samuels agreed that Marci could leave the hospital to drive to Sparta and get their marriage license Wednesday morning.

There was a slight chill in the mountain air as Jake and Marci left Jefferson and headed north on the Blue Ridge Parkway. "It's so good to be out of the hospital," Marci said. "Don't be in a hurry, Jake. I want to enjoy my time out of that place."

Jake pulled the Jeep into one of the overlooks along the Parkway so Marci could get out and breathe in the fresh mountain air. "This is just what I needed," she said as she inhaled deeply, but then began coughing.

"Are you okay?" Jake asked.

"I'll be alright. The cold air just shocked me a little bit, that's all. Let's go to Doughton Park since it's on the way," Marci said.

"You sure?"

"Sure, I'm sure. I wouldn't have said I was sure if I wasn't sure I was sure."

"You're something else, Marci Meredith, did you know that?"

"Quit stalling and take me to Doughton Park."

"Okay Ma'am, you're the boss."

Jake pulled into the Doughton Park picnic area and Marci made an attempt to get out of the Jeep as soon as it stopped. "Where do you think you're going young lady?" Jake asked.

"I'm going to hike up to our tree at the top of the hill," Marci said defiantly. "I feel much better now. I just needed some fresh air. Come on," she said.

"There's no way," Jake said. We're going to get the marriage license and I'm taking you back as soon as I can."

"Okay, Dr. McLeod. Let's go get the license," she pouted.

After filling out the papers for the marriage license, Jake took Highway 221 back to Jefferson.

Dr. Samuels came by Marci's room at 4:30 that afternoon and listened to her labored breathing through his stethoscope. He looked at both of them as he said, "I shouldn't have let her go to Sparta today. She's still very weak."

"Is she going to be okay for the wedding on Sunday?" Jake asked.

"We'll just have to take it day by day. Then, we'll see," Dr. Samuels said.

The doctor left them alone in the room and Jake went to her bedside. "We'll see; my ass!" Marci said. "We're getting married on Sunday."

"Be nice," Jake said.

"I am nice," Marci said pouting.

"I'll go now and let you get some rest," Jake said.

Always the one to get in the last word, March responded, "Give me a big kiss and let me take a nap, I'm really tired."

CHAPTER 63

SUNDAY FINALLY arrived and Dr. Samuels signed Marci out of the hospital. Just as Joanie had promised, the ladies had taken care of everything. They met Marci at the hospital and helped her dress. The ladies believed in tradition—the groom was not allowed to see the bride until the ceremony, so James, Ed, Carson, and Jake went ahead to make sure everything was in order at Doughton Park.

Reverend Chandler, met them there. "Thank you so much for being a part of our special day," Jake told him.

"I wouldn't have missed it for the world," the Reverend said smiling.

The ceremony was to be held under the lone maple tree that stood beside the picnic table in the circle drive of the Bluff Mountain Trailhead parking lot. Sunday had dawned with a crystal clear sky of Carolina blue. Perfect!

At precisely ten minutes before eleven, James drove down the gently curving road to the Bluff Mountain parking lot with Jake and Reverend Chandler aboard his newly-washed Navigator. Jake was wearing the new, dark suit, white shirt, and burgundy tie he'd just bought on Monday. Everything seemed to be going as expected until they rounded the curve and pulled into the Bluff Mountain Trailhead parking lot.

The hillside was filled with a throng of well-wishers. Jake scanned the crowd recognizing countless members of Troutman Baptist Church. Standing nearby was Sid Bellman, smiling broadly, along with dozens of Marci's fellow officers from the Iredell County Sheriff's Department. Phil West and a supporting group of Wilkes County deputies stood alongside their Iredell County counterparts.

When Jake saw Annie and the ladies from the Northwest Trading Post, he blew them a kiss. To their right stood Dr. Samuels, along with the unforgettable Nurse Dillard and other members of the hospital staff. He even saw Myles and Pal Ireland from The Cook Shack. His friend, Johnny Smith, smiled as he gave Jake a reassuring "thumbs up". All Jake could do was wave to the crowd as he fought to gain control of his emotions. He never dreamed they had so many friends.

Everyone grew quiet when the strands of *Wagner's Bridal Chorus* reverberated from speakers that were set up in the back of a Ford 150 pickup. All eyes looked toward the last curve of the winding road for a glimpse of the bride and her entourage.

Leading the way was Joanie Mitchell, driving a bright red 1966 Corvette convertible, with a smiling Debbie Seacrest seated beside her. A second Corvette followed closely behind with Marci sitting atop the back seat much like a beauty queen at the local Christmas parade. Gail Caldwell, Marci's matron of honor was at the wheel of the vintage, red and white 1960 classic.

Joanie always loved doing the unexpected and she could tell by the look on Jake's face that she had once again pulled it off. Ed was a member of a classic car club and Joanie had cajoled two of his friends into loaning her their classic Corvettes for the special occasion.

Marci was dressed in a white Italian silk two-piece suit and held a simple bouquet of pink rhododendron in her lap. When she saw the multitude of guests who had come to share in their happiness, she too, could not believe how blessed they were.

The Corvettes made the circle around the parking area and pulled next to the picnic table under the maple tree and stopped. Marci and Jake gazed at each other, overwhelmed by the magnitude of the moment. She motioned for him to join her. Jake climbed in and sat beside the radiant, but teary, Marci Meredith as Gail drove them to the trailhead sign and came gently to a stop.

Jake and Marci sat side by side in the wonderful sunshine and joined hands. Joanie, Gail, and Debbie took their places on the left side of the Corvette while James, Jake's best man, stood on the right.

"Dearly beloved, we are gathered here in this beautiful place of God's own making, to join this man and this woman in Holy Matrimony," Reverend Chandler began. The crowd moved in closer to share in the ceremony as Jake and Marci exchanged vows.

Before Jake knew it, Reverend Chandler said, "You may kiss the bride." He kissed her tenderly, oblivious to the fact momentarily that they were not alone.

"I love you Marci," Jake said as he looked into her eyes.

Marci saw Jake's tears and whispered, "I love you, too."

They embraced and then turned to face the wedding guests as Reverend Chandler said, "May I present Mr. and Mrs. Jake McLeod." Jake and Marci waved to the crowd who eagerly surrounded them with congratulatory wishes, handshakes, and hugs. The newlyweds patiently greeted each and every well-wisher before they finally had a few minutes alone.

"Marci, I am so proud of you and I love you more today than I did yesterday, if that's possible," Jake said as he looked into her eyes.

"I feel the same way about you, Tiger," she growled. "I can't wait to get you home and in that big, king-size bed of yours, but we gotta play nice in front of all these people right now."

Jake laughed. "What a prize I have in you Marci Meredith."

"Hey, watch it Buster. My name is Marci McLeod now and

don't you forget it. If you're nice, I'll tell you a surprise."

"What?" Jake asked, not knowing if he could take any more surprises.

"Dr. Samuels has released me from the hospital. I get to go home with you and have a 'proper' wedding night. What do you think about that, Mr. McLeod?"

"That's wonderful, Mrs. McLeod, absolutely and positively wonderful."

The men from Troutman Baptist Church began unloading tables from a large truck and setting them up. The ladies of the church quickly covered the tables with white linen tablecloths and brought out picnic baskets overflowing with fried chicken, ham, deviled eggs, potato salad, and, of course, homemade pies and cakes.

Reverend Chandler had said on many occasions that God provides and He surely did that day. He brought Jake a wonderful, loving wife with a terrific sense of humor who helped him back to life again—the very woman who was carrying the child who would bring more sunshine into both of their lives. God brought Marci a loving, compassionate mate to share her hopes and dreams. He brought their friends and colleagues to share in their happiness. He provided a beautiful Carolina blue sky for the ceremony and reception. Truly, God's bounty was overwhelming.

Life was surely good!

EPILOGUE

NOT LONG after the wedding, Marci and Jake settled into a daily routine. Marci was back at work…still on desk duty, but glad to be back. She sold her house near Troutman and moved all her things into Jake's house on Ferncliff Drive.

Marci woke Jake early one morning, rolled over on her side, and looked at him with her beautiful green eyes and asked, "What are we going to name the baby, Jake?"

"I have a name in mind for a girl," Jake said.

"Well, I have one for a boy," Marci said. "Let's hear yours first."

"Oh no, I'm not going there. You go first," Jake teased.

"Okay," Marci began, "Do you remember how we talked about never forgetting Kitt and Mark?"

"I certainly do, how could I forget?"

"Well, I just thought we could name him Kendall, in honor of Kitt, if it's a boy."

Tears welled up in Jake's eyes. He could hardly speak. "You're something else, did you know that?"

"Yes, you've told me that a thousand times now. Well, what do you think?"

"I think you are the sweetest, kindest, and most beautiful woman in the whole wide world and I am the luckiest man that has ever lived. Kendall McLeod, that sounds perfect. Thank you, Marci."

"You're welcome," she said as she kissed the tears from his cheeks. "Now, tell me the name you've chosen."

"Like I said, I've been giving it a lot of thought."

"Well, let's hear it," Marci said growing impatient.

"If it's a little girl, I thought we could name her Meredith, in honor of Mark."

Marci laid her head on his chest. "Oh, Jake, I absolutely love it and I love you more than you can ever imagine."

"I guess you know what this means now, don't you?"

"What?" she said as she dried her tears on his undershirt.

"That means we'll have to have a boy and a girl."

"Guess we better stay in practice then," Marci said as she pulled off her gown and rolled over on top of him.

"Marci McLeod! You're something else, did you know that?"

"So, I've heard."

ACKNOWLEDGEMENTS

Writing my first novel proved not only to be an interesting undertaking, but a challenging one as well. Little did I know what lay ahead for me after typing the first few words.

I owe a special thanks to the Iredell County Sheriff's Department for clarifications on certain procedures. I hope I got them right.

Thanks to Beth Garrett who offered encouragement at the very beginning and helped select the perfect names for some of the characters.

I want to thank all the people who read my manuscript and offered advice: Beth Garrett, Jackie Gerrard, Michele Bolling, Janice Swann, Susan Williams, Noreen Vag, John Vest, Carol Corey, Rhonda Pitts, Nancy Wakeley, and Laurie Lund.

Thanks to Myles and Pal Ireland of the Cook Shack in Union Grove, North Carolina for allowing me to use their establishment and their names for this book.

I would like to thank the staff of the Northwest Trading Post on the Blue Ridge Parkway for the use of their names that added authenticity.

To Dr. Peter Enyeart and Carl Pitts who shared their medical knowledge, thanks.

This work of fiction would not have been possible without the guidance and help of Leslie Rindoks of Lorimer Press. Thanks for your ideas and inspiration.

I want to especially thank my wife Vickie for staying up late at night, reading and editing my third book. Without her patience, advice, understanding, sagacity, and attention to detail, this book would never turned out as well as it has. God bless and thanks, Vickie.

"Cotton" Ketchie published his first book, *Memories of a Country Boy*, in 2006. This memoir was soon followed by *A Country Boy's Education* in 2007. Both books provide an amusing glimpse into the life of a country boy growing up in North Carolina in the 1950s.

Ketchie is also a nationally known watercolorist and was selected as the featured artist for the 2004 North Carolina Governor's Conference on Tourism. His works, which celebrate the beauty of the country, can be found in collections throughout Europe, Asia, the United States, and Canada. In 2001, he received the coveted Order of the Long Leaf Pine for working to preserve the legacy of his state and his community.

"Cotton" and his wife Vickie invite you to visit Landmark Galleries in downtown Mooresville, NC, where his original watercolors, limited edition prints, and photography are on display.